"I must ask that you conduct yourself as a gentleman."

He leaned closer, his mouth inches from her ear. "I'm trying, lass, but it takes some doing."

Her breath whooshed out of her lungs, and she stared up at him, caught in the mesmerizing strength of that blue-eyed gaze. The power of him captured her, distracted her . . .

"You must leave," she managed to say.

"Soon enough." He closed his eyes, breathing in softly. "You smell like heaven."

"You should not say such things." Her heart pounded in her breast. She should run. Scream. Anything to escape . . .

His breath brushed her ear. "Be glad I've a strong will, my bonny one, else I'd be kissing you already."

"A kiss should be given, not taken." She swallowed hard, striving for dignity.

He chuckled, and the vibration of it shivered along her spine. "Indeed, lass, it wAnd gladly, too."

Did he imply he could coax a wi her lips? The audacity!

The truth?

She glanced up, saw the surety in tional thought slowly spiraled away pressed the point, she had no dou willingly offer her lips to his kiss.

Dangerous, dangerous man.

Other **AVON ROMANCES**

Debra Mullins

The Night Before The Wedding

AVON
An Imprint of HarperCollinsPublishers

AVON BOOKS
An Imprint of HarperCollins*Publishers*
10 East 53rd Street
New York, New York 10022-5299

First Avon Books paperback printing: February 2008

*To Susan Meier,
for wise advice and
keeping me on track*

The Night Before The Wedding

Chapter 1

A broken vow when peace was sworn,
The price shall be a daughter born
Of Farlan blood to wed our chief—
Each generation, no relief.

Mist rolled along the ground and clung to the stones of the castle like wraiths in the light of the half moon. Fires burned in the central courtyard, drums pounded, and pipes wailed as two clans gathered in silent distrust. One clan chief knelt on the ground, his head bent beneath the threat of a gleaming sword.

A frail old woman raised her hands to the skies, one hand clutching a dagger. The wind whipped up with a vengeance, sending the woman's garments flapping about her slender limbs. Her silvery hair danced and tangled like a living thing, though she never moved, never blinked. In a voice

1

vibrating with the power of the Ancient Ones, she chanted.

> *The dagger is her mark of grief,*
> *The girl who's born to wed our chief.*
> *By eighteen years, the girl shall wed*
> *Else madness comes and sees her dead.*

Someone cried out. A young woman fell to her knees on the damp ground, gripping her upper arm as her red hair snapped madly around her. Her kindred rushed to her, and when they pried her hand away, they beheld an angry red mark on her skin, in the shape of a dagger.

The old woman didn't notice. She kept keening her words up to the skies, to the moon and the heavens and the powers that lived all around them.

> *Should MacBraedon break this pact*
> *His clan shall suffer for this act.*
> *Only the dagger will bring him sons;*
> *Should he wed another, there will be none.*
> *When lightning flashes and stones run red,*
> *When MacBraedon wakes Farlan from the dead,*
> *Only in this darkest hour*
> *Shall my words then lose their power.*

Lightning crackled, singeing the earth nearby. Without even flinching, the old one thrust the dagger point-first into the ground at her feet, burying it to the hilt. The earth shuddered and thunder boomed, and with a harsh gasp, she crumpled to the ground like a discarded toy to lie panting, completely spent, her eyes still wide and dark with power as she gazed at the heavens.

Her clansmen rushed to her and lifted her fragile form from the ground. The mists swirled and danced, laughing in their silent way, and the world shimmered with magic.

Then he was there, stepping through the foggy tendrils as the scene with the old witch faded away, his shoulders broad and his muscled body bare but for the plaid that wound around him. His sun-kissed brown hair reached nearly to his shoulders, ragged yet masculine, emphasizing the strong bones of a warrior's face. Blue eyes appeared to look right at her, searing through all pretense to her very soul.

"Catherine," he said, reaching for her. "You are mine."

Catherine Depford jerked awake to find herself standing beside her empty bed, her palm extended as if to accept the clasp of another. With a cry, she covered her face with her hands.

Again. It had happened again.

This was the third time since her eighteenth birthday only a week ago. She dreamed of Scotland, over and over again, even though she had never been there.

Her body burned with unfamiliar hungers, puzzling and shameful. It was the man in the dream; he brought forth these shocking feelings. Just his presence, just knowing he was reaching for her. That he wanted *her*.

Even though the dream had faded, even in the cool anticipation of dawn, her body still throbbed.

Chilled, she moved closer to the low fire smoldering in the grate, limbs trembling with fatigue. And fear. But she dared not seek her bed again. If she slept, she might dream.

She sank down to her knees before the soft red glow of the hearth, folding her arms around her for security as much as for warmth. She had hoped and prayed that the Farlan curse would spare her. That her mother's words that horrible day had been false. But the evidence spoke to the contrary.

Dreams of a place she had never been—always the same dream, always the same man. Voices whispering to her on the wind, words and chanting no one else could hear. All those times she had found herself standing outside her father's London town house, staring to the north, with no memory of how she'd gotten there.

No, she had not been spared.

She closed her eyes, clenching her fingers around her upper arms, rocking gently to soothe her shattered nerves. Even now she could remember her mother, standing poised by the open window, the remnants of her bonds dangling from her wrists. Red hair—as blazing as Catherine's own—tangled and curled around her shoulders in unkempt disarray. Her blue eyes were wild, her smile broad and beautiful and terrifyingly wrong.

Her mother. Mad Glynis.

"You will see," Glynis had warned, shaking a finger at her six-year-old daughter as the servants burst into the room, frantic to recapture their escaped mistress. "You will see, daughter mine, on your eighteenth birthing day, when the curse of the Farlans falls upon you! You will see the hell I was forced to bear!"

"Mrs. Depford," called one of the servants, racing for her. "Please wait!"

"Eighteen," she hissed, eyes glittering. "The curse will come!"

Then she turned and leaped from the window onto the cobblestone street below.

Catherine remembered screaming, over and over again. And the softness of Mellie's bosom as the

5

maid scooped the shocked child she had been into soothing arms, hiding her face so she could not see the window anymore. The smell of lemon that clung to Mellie, comforting and pure.

She opened her eyes now, looking around her room, seeking to dispel the memory. Her heart pounded, her fingers clenched so tightly around her arms that she could barely feel them anymore. Whispers lingered just beyond human hearing, drifting through her mind like phantoms.

A broken vow when peace was sworn . . .

She took a shuddering breath. She had no doubts. She had not been spared. The Farlan curse had indeed taken her.

Madness was her fate.

Thunder boomed, and lightning split the night sky, briefly illuminating the barren lands surrounding the castle. Rain slapped against ancient stone, hissing in harmony with the wailing wind. Rocks formed strange shadows as lightning flashed again to reveal trees bending beneath the onslaught of the elements, naked branches shivering.

Gabriel MacBraedon stood at the open window, heedless of the chilly rain that splattered his face and clothing. This was his domain, this corner of Scotland—every dry well, every fallow field, every ragged cottage that graced the landscape. Though the sky belched torrents of rain, not a drop would linger in any well or burn. By morning, it would all vanish like mist beneath a summer sun, except for the barrels set out by the people to collect the precious water. And at that, some of those barrels would develop a mysterious crack or hole, and the liquid so carefully gathered would drain away into an unforgiving earth. Once again there would be barely enough to keep the clans alive. And he could do naught but stand here and watch it all happen.

Day after day, his people struggled to eke some living from the stubborn land. Their crops withered and died; their cows would give no milk. Their lambs were born with two heads and did not last the week.

Cursed. The MacBraedons were cursed, and their neighboring clan, the Farlans, with them. As clan chief, he had done everything in his power to fight the unseen enemy. He had implemented farming techniques learned at university in Edinburgh, all to no avail. His attempts to trade with other clans had met with some success, but still his people starved.

There was only one way to appease the curse, to bring prosperity back to the land. Every instinct within him demanded that he act, but instead he was forced to wait, for weeks now, while others did the searching he would rather have done himself.

"A rider!" His nineteen-year-old brother, Patrick, burst into the great hall. "Gabriel, a rider comes, like the devil himself!"

"Who is it?" Gabriel turned away from the window.

"I canna tell; 'tis too dark. You must come!"

He dared not hope. Too many times he had raced outside to meet a rider, only to be disappointed. Patience was not his strongest virtue, but it was one a leader had to learn for the good of his people.

"I will wait here."

Patrick goggled at him. "I canna believe you dinna want to see who's come."

"Bring him to the hall as soon as he arrives." Gabriel went over to the hearth and picked up a piece of wood—a chair leg by the looks of it—and laid it carefully on the struggling flames. "He'll be glad of the fire to ease the wet."

"Aye, and in need of food as well. I'll see if there's aught in the kitchen."

"You're a good lad, Patrick."

His brother scowled at being called a lad but turned toward the door. Before he could step through, though, the mysterious rider staggered into the hall, assisted by Angus and Andrew, Gabriel's personal guard. As alike as two peas, the twins assisted the ragged, exhausted man to an empty chair.

The man swept his soaked hat from his head, letting it fall with a wet slap to the floor. Then he lifted his eyes to Gabriel's.

"Fergus." Hope leaped into his throat, and Gabriel crouched down before his bedraggled kinsman. "Angus, whisky! And where's that stew?"

His clansmen scrambled to do his bidding. Young Patrick raced from the room, calling for food. Angus came forward with the whisky, and Fergus reached out a shaking hand to accept the drink. Gabriel steadied the glass for Fergus as he gingerly sipped at the fiery brew.

"Och." Licking his lips, Fergus pushed away the glass, leaving Gabriel to set it aside. "'Tis nectar, God's truth."

"Someone will fetch some supper for you. 'Tis a fierce night to be riding."

"Aye, but I wanted to get back to you right away." Color was returning to the man's cheeks, chasing away the pallor of cold and wet. His dark eyes gleamed with excitement. "We've found her, Gabriel. We've found your bride."

Gabriel's knees buckled, and he grasped the arm of the chair for balance. Finally. After nearly three months . . . "In England?" he choked. "You are certain?"

"Aye, in England." The man sucked in a breath. Already his cheeks were reddening from the warmth of the fire. "It took a while to get a place in the household, but there isna any doubt. She's your bride."

"What the devil?" Brodie Alexander, his brother-in-law, entered the room, a steaming plate of stew in his hands. "Did he say England?"

"He did." Gabriel rose to his feet.

"You canna mean to go there."

"I do." Despite his elation, Gabriel allowed no emotion to show on his face. "Our people have done well, and finally I can claim what is mine. We ride for England tonight."

Brodie set the plate down in front of Fergus, who immediately began to eat. "'Tis a fierce storm out there. Can we leave in the morning?"

"Enough time has been wasted." Gabriel glanced away to the window, where the storm still raged. "I must go claim my bride. Now. Tonight."

"But—"

"Brodie." Gabriel cut him off with a look. "She's the salvation of our people."

"She's a Sassenach!"

"She's a Farlan."

"I dinna know which is worse."

Gabriel sighed and closed his eyes for only a moment. "We leave tonight, Brodie. And hopefully, in a very short time, I will be riding through the gates again as a married man."

"Fine then. Just dinna fall in love with her."

As Brodie stalked out of the hall, Gabriel glanced down at his ring, its plain black stone an unchanging reminder of the past. "Have no fear of that," he murmured. Clenching his fist, he turned away and began planning for the future.

Chapter 2

One Week Later

Lady Dorburton's ball to show off the new decor of her London town house was expected to be the biggest crush of the season. Catherine agreed with this assessment as she and her dearest friend, Miss Beth Waters, followed Beth's mother through the jostling bodies as that lady surged forward to greet one of her cronies.

Mrs. Waters immediately engaged in deep conversation with the other matrons seated along the wall, leaving Catherine and Beth to linger a few steps away, listening to the orchestra tune their instruments.

Or rather, Catherine listened. Beth chattered on, vibrating like an excited puppy, much as she had done the second Catherine had stepped into the Waters carriage earlier that evening. Catherine really didn't mind; the nonstop prattle helped to keep her own shadows at bay.

"And then Mama said that Miss Featherton had nothing to recommend her except for that piece of land, which was the only reason he offered for her," Beth said with a giggle, "and that Lord Dirby would regret marrying her instead of you as soon as the papers were signed."

Despite the fatigue of yet another restless night, Catherine couldn't help but smile at such a vote of loyalty. "Really, Beth, I am far from devastated that Lord Dirby decided to offer for Miss Featherton."

"But he is the son of a duke! And everyone said he was enchanted with you!"

"But he offered for another. There is no use talking about what could have been."

"Did you not want to be a duchess?" Puzzlement filled Beth's dark eyes.

"I am more interested in a man's character than his title."

"In what way?" Beth tilted her head, dark curls tumbling in careful disarray.

"I want a husband who will care for me and not my fortune. One I can trust." *One who will not lock me away in Bedlam so he can squander my dowry.*

Beth nodded. "Perhaps you will find a duke

who will care for you, and then you can still be a duchess."

Catherine laughed. Leave it to Beth to see the brighter side of things.

"How lovely that you can still laugh," purred a female voice. Catherine looked up to see Miss Penelope Lillibridge and her friends, the Misses Rose and Lily Pendleton, smirking at her. "If I had been cast aside by a duke's son, I would be hard-pressed to show myself in public anymore."

Catherine arched her brows at the blond beauty. The girl's sweet smile and creamy complexion gave her an angelic look, but the gleam of malice in her acclaimed blue eyes betrayed her true nature. "I was hardly cast aside, Penelope. Lord Dirby simply chose Miss Featherton to be his bride."

"But surely you expected him to offer for you," Rose trilled, her thin, foxy face aglow with anticipation. Though Rose and Lily had no good looks to recommend them (which was no doubt why the very vain Penelope allowed them to befriend her), they were the daughters of an admiral and quite well-connected socially.

"It was a possibility, but not something which disturbed me unduly."

"Lord Dirby will regret wedding Miss Featherton," Beth inserted, narrowing her eyes at the other debutantes.

"Perhaps," Penelope conceded, her rosebud mouth curving slightly. "But I hardly think he will regret the fact that his heirs will have their mother's impeccable bloodlines, as opposed to the common heritage of a merchant's daughter."

Beth gasped as the Misses Pendleton tittered behind their fans. Catherine simply held Penelope's gaze, watching while anticipation slowly faded to confusion.

"At least," Catherine said calmly, "I shall not be sold in marriage to pay my father's gaming debts."

Rose and Lily squealed in dismay, and Penelope's cheeks flushed deep red. Eyes glittering, the blond beauty turned and swept away, one hard glance spurring the Misses Pendleton to scurry after her.

Lily lingered a half second behind. "I see now why they call you Catherine the Cold," she hissed, then hurried after the others.

"The cheek!" Beth pursed her lips, slapping her fan against the palm of her hand. "Penelope is simply jealous because you are more popular than she is, merchant's daughter or not. And your fortune is bigger."

Catherine just laughed. "You are the most loyal of friends, Beth, but Penelope does not bother me in the slightest."

"Catherine the Cold," Beth sniffed. "Hardly. It

was awful of Viscount Nordham to begin calling you that just because you rejected his suit."

Catherine wrinkled her nose. "That man believes all women fall in love with him. He has no constancy, no moral fiber." She lowered her voice. "I hear he goes through mistresses as quickly as normal men go through neck cloths."

"Cat!" Beth flushed and looked around them to see if they had been overheard. "It is not ladylike to speak of *those kinds of people*!"

Catherine shuddered. "Then let us end the discussion by saying he is the last man on earth I would wed. He loves himself far more than he could ever love a wife."

"Agreed." Beth glanced around in response to her mother's call. "Oh dear, Mama wants me to come and greet Mr. Harrison."

"I had best stay here then."

Beth rolled her eyes. "Indeed. The poor man always turns beet red and makes sounds like a donkey whenever you are in his presence. I believe he finds you daunting!"

"And I would not want to interfere with your mama's matchmaking efforts in that direction."

Her mock-serious tone spurred a burst of laughter from Beth. "You are too wicked! Mr. Harrison is barely twenty and hardly hanging out for a wife."

As Beth turned to go, Catherine laid a hand

on her arm. "Beth, do try not to break the young man's heart."

Her friend giggled again and then headed for her mother. Alone for a few precious moments, Catherine turned her attention to the dance floor, where the first set was starting to form.

The strain of maintaining some semblance of normality was beginning to wear on her. How much more peaceful it would have been to stay at home with a book, rather than come here to be on display for the Polite World. But her purpose was to find a husband, and she would not find the man she sought between the pages of Mrs. Edgeworth's latest novel.

Lord Kentwood appeared to be the most promising prospect of late. He was wealthy in his own right, which eased her mind about him wedding a woman for her fortune. More importantly, he had a kindness in his eyes that touched her. He took care of his elderly mother without giving the impression of still being on leading strings. In fact, he held her in such high regard that it was considered a sign of serious intentions should he introduce a young lady to his mama.

He managed his estates with the same easy competence he applied to everything else. He frequently supported policies in the House of Lords that benefited the needy, rather than pursuing

grandiose ideas to further his own consequence.
While not a dramatically handsome man, one
could not consider him an ogre by any stretch of
the imagination.

The main reason she was not terribly perturbed
about Lord Dirby's defection—something she
had not even confided in Beth—was that Lord
Kentwood had been paying her singular attention
of late. She had hopes that he might soon approach
her papa with an offer.

Was he in attendance? He had indicated to her
that he might be present at this function, most no-
tably because she had told him she would be there.
She let her gaze drift idly over the familiar faces
that crammed the room, searching for his dark
head. Then the breath froze in her lungs.

On the other side of the dance floor stood the
man from her dream.

Their eyes met in a moment of painful connection. Her heart somersaulted in her breast, then
kicked into a gallop as he started walking around
the dance floor toward her.

He moved like water, fluid and graceful. His
black evening clothes only emphasized his warrior's body—broad shoulders, lean waist, strong
arms and legs. The memory of her dream flashed
into her mind. This man, naked but for the plaid
wrapped around him.

She choked back panic. Was he real? No one spoke to him or appeared to notice him at all. Was this her imagination? The madness taking over? If he asked her to dance, would she be dancing with no one to the eyes of the *ton*?

Oh, how Penelope would enjoy that spectacle!

Lord Hollerton appeared before her, blocking her view of the Scotsman. "May I have this dance, Miss Depford?"

Habit forced the polite smile to her lips. "You may, Lord Hollerton." Grateful for his timely arrival, she laid her hand on his arm—a flesh-and-blood arm, thank goodness—and allowed him to lead her out to the dance floor. As she took her place in the set, she glanced over at the Scotsman. He stood at the edge of the floor, arms folded and a frown on his face.

Did anyone even see him but her?

What would she do if he came to talk to her? If he wasn't real, she would be observed talking to no one. A chill rippled along her skin. That must not happen. She must not be alone for a moment, not permit herself to drift into her fantasy. If that meant dancing with every man in the place, even until her slippers wore out, so be it.

She refused to give the gossips any fodder about Mad Glynis's daughter.

The orchestra launched into song, and with a

brilliant, practiced smile on her face, Catherine stepped into the dance.

He watched her from across the room, mesmerized by her movements, fascinated by her every expression. Her hair burned flame-bright in precariously piled curls, glowing like rubies beneath the light of the chandeliers. Errant tendrils slipped from their bonds, brushing her cheeks, her ears, her neck.

The flesh there looked so very soft.

He prowled along the edge of the dance floor as she settled into the set with her partner. Her laughter rippled to him over the strains of the orchestra and the low rumble of conversation. She smiled at her dance partner, her cheeks lightly flushed. Her blue-gray eyes never left her escort as she danced. She stepped and whirled, her white muslin dress sweeping along with every motion, her discreet pearl necklace shifting over creamy flesh.

It was all he could do not to stride into the middle of the set and shove away the other male who dared touch her.

He curled his hands into fists, one finger at a time. Patience, not emotion, would win this battle.

He began to walk again, skimming the edge of the dance floor. The other guests moved out of his way, vague traces of alarm and curiosity on their faces. His evening clothes were the best money could buy—elegantly cut and fitted to his large form with the utmost perfection. He might not know these people, but on the outside, even with his long hair tied back in a queue, he looked like one of them. An English gentleman.

On the inside, he was still Gabriel MacBraedon, chief of his clan, and a warrior.

But this was not a battle, at least not one that could be fought with swords or cannons. He had one purpose for coming to London, one purpose for accepting Lady Dorburton's invitation to this ball.

Catherine Depford.

His information had reported that she was beautiful, but her vibrant coloring and flawless ivory skin had stunned him from the first glance. She was tall for a woman, with a fine, rich form. Not one of these wee, sickly English lasses, with their vapid conversation and whinnying giggles. When *she* laughed, his flesh tightened in sheer lust.

He didn't think he had ever reacted so strongly to a woman before. Not even Jean.

What do you expect? This one is your destined bride.

He scowled, resenting the attraction. It seemed almost insulting, as if he would not do his duty unless led there by desire. But hadn't he already proven himself? Hadn't he already walked away from a true and loving woman to meet his destiny?

He pushed aside the painful memory. Since he had no say in choosing his bride, he was glad she was comely. Truly. And she was also the wealthiest heiress in London. Her fortune would go far in soothing the harm her family had done to his.

The curse must be appeased.

A pox on the curse! It chafed him that something so intangible could forge his destiny. He himself had done nothing wrong to warrant such oppression. The curse was centuries old, visited upon his many-times-great-grandfather.

But for twenty years his clan had suffered starvation and poverty, a direct result of the actions of the woman who'd thought she could escape the curse.

And he was to marry that woman's daughter.

He had come to terms with his fate. Resigned himself, though he longed to choose his own path and his own life. But now that he'd seen *her* . . .

Sweet Christ, now that he'd seen her, he wanted her with a hunger that clawed inside him like an uncontrollable beast.

Aye, she was the only wife for him.

He paced along the perimeter like a wolf scenting his mate, his blood burning in his veins. He'd attempted to meet her formally, but as he had approached her, she had taken one look at him and retreated, her eyes wide with shock. Then she had proceeded to dance with every man in attendance, which kept her effectively out of his reach.

For now.

But she could not flee forever.

Where was he?

Keeping her smile firmly in place, Catherine glanced about the ballroom, searching for the tall Scotsman with the sharp blue eyes of a predator.

He was hunting her.

Her skin prickled with awareness, as if every bit of flesh, blood, and bone had risen from slumber to reach for what he offered. Her heart raced, just knowing he was near. She tried to focus on the steps of the quadrille, but the thundering of her pulse distracted her from the music.

She glanced at her newest partner. His lips moved silently, and she realized he was focused on counting out the dance steps.

Good. Better that he be distracted. She certainly was.

Panic rose like a scream in her mind, and she quieted it with intense concentration. It wasn't easy, not with her own body betraying her with its violent reaction to the presence of *that man*. The room had become suffocatingly warm. Or was it her own temperature that had risen?

She licked her dry lips, more uncomfortable by the moment as her corset suddenly felt too tight. Her breasts ached, the exposed tops ridiculously sensitive to the brush of air against them. Her fingers trembled as she placed her hand on her partner's arm for the promenade.

Dear God, how could it be happening? Right here, in the middle of all these people? That curious awakening of her body that had before only haunted her in the secrecy of the night . . . The scorching dreams of a Scottish warrior who claimed her for his own. How could these shameless yearnings take control of her very flesh here and now, rousing outside the safety of slumber?

She turned at the end of the line of couples— only to come face-to-face with *him*. He stood just at the edge of the crowd, his face taut, those penetrating blue eyes burning into hers.

Immediately, humiliatingly, her body responded. Her private parts bloomed with heat and wet. Warmth flooded her cheeks, and she turned back around to her place to finish the set.

Heaven help her, how could it be? How could a man she had met only in her dreams be standing mere feet away from her? Staring at her as if he knew her? Making her feel like this, outside the privacy of her bedchamber?

Was he even real?

But deep inside she knew the truth.

Oh yes, she *knew*. She had expected it her entire life, had both waited for it and dreaded it. Had tried to deny it. In a way, it was a relief to know that it had finally started. The waiting was over.

The madness had truly found her.

Desperate to betray nothing, she surrendered her hand to her next partner.

The lass toyed with him.

Gabriel struggled against the impulse to rip *his* woman from the arms of yet another pale Englishman. Did she not realize she was his? How could she not recognize the connection between them?

But of course she didna know who he was. And she couldna know about the curse, not when the knowledge of its existence was the most closely guarded secret of the clan. He inhaled slowly, calming his clamoring emotions. Catherine Depford had been raised an Englishwoman, outside the clan. The only way to win her was by English rules.

The notion sat like curdled milk in his belly.

Winning the woman would not be as simple as tossing her on his horse and galloping like the wind back to the Highlands. Not if he meant to keep her. He had no doubt her wealthy father would be after him like a hound on a hare should he choose that route.

No, there were steps to be followed in wooing this bride, though his instincts demanded he claim her in the most basic, physical way possible—and in front of the whole of society if need be. But he prided himself on his intelligence and logic, so he forced himself to suppress the immediate needs of his body and think like the warrior he was.

She had challenged him. He had seen it in the way she looked at him, as if she knew what he wanted of her. The awareness in her eyes spoke to him, even as she had so skillfully eluded him. Did she sense his passion? Did she feel the same?

If she thought her evasive tactics would discourage him, she was far from the truth. On the contrary, her deliberate avoidance only whetted his hunter's appetite. He would wait for the right opportunity, then he would savor sweet victory when he won the game.

He retreated to a corner of the room, and waited.

The set ended, and Catherine's fourth partner escorted her back to her chaperone, a widow named Mrs. Waters, who chatted with a crony. Gabriel knew that the woman's daughter, Miss Elizabeth

Waters, was Catherine's closest friend. As the two young women put their heads together in conversation, he started toward the group, determined to ask her to dance before another man could.

His hostess and distant cousin, Lady Dorburton, halted him by stepping into his path. "Cousin, you are frightening my guests with your scowling."

He raised a brow at the diminutive blond. "My apologies, Lady Dorburton."

"Keep your charms for the more susceptible," she scoffed. "And do try to behave in a way that befits an earl, not a Highland barbarian."

He stiffened. "I am hardly a barbarian, madam."

"Thank heavens you have an earldom, even if it is Scottish." She waved a dismissive hand. "Now, do not look like that. You know I did not mean to insult you."

"Earl of Arneth is just a name bestowed on my family by the English king. Chief of the MacBraedons is who I am." He leaned closer to her. "See to it you dinna forget your own roots among the Highland *barbarians*, Lady Dorburton."

She sucked in a breath, her eyes widening as her cheeks reddened. "And you kindly keep a civil— and *discreet*—tongue in your head, Lord Arneth, or I will no longer sponsor you to the *ton*."

"I think we understand each other," Gabriel said.

"Indeed." With a sniff, Lady Dorburton marched away.

Gabriel immediately forgot about the encounter and looked back at Catherine. She was gone.

Scanning the room, he located his prey near the garden doors. As he watched, she glanced furtively about, then darted outside. Muttering a curse that earned him a startled glance from a passing servant, he set off after her.

Her hunter had vanished.

The instant she had lost sight of him, the joy of reprieve became tempered with a hint of disappointment. Something inside her had relished the chase, even as agitation and alarm churned in her stomach.

If that was not evidence of madness, nothing was.

Catherine slipped down a shadowed garden path, relishing the moments alone to calm her jangling nerves. So far she had managed to keep herself busy dancing, had managed to hide her struggle for sanity from everyone else, but the reality of her situation had worn her composure thin.

Was the Scotsman real? She had considered asking Mrs. Waters to introduce him to her, to prove that he was a flesh-and-bone human being.

But fear of the impossible—that only Catherine could see him—prevented her.

And even if he was a real person, what would she say to him? *Why do I dream of you? How do you make me feel this way with just a look?* The rules of society provided no answer for her dilemma.

She clenched her trembling hands as she hurried down the garden path. What would people say if Catherine Depford, the toast of London, were to lose control of her dignity in public? If her fear overwhelmed her upbringing, and she surrendered to the chaos of her mind?

Like mother, like daughter. That's what they would say. What else could be expected from the child of Mad Glynis?

A pang of dismay pierced her heart. Her impeccable poise and natural charm had held off the gossips this long. But now her control teetered on the brink of unraveling, and all because of that . . . that *Scotsman*.

The mere thought of him triggered an avalanche of heat and confusion that physically stopped her in her tracks and left her gasping for air. She stumbled off the path into a small clearing and braced herself with a hand against a cool marble garden statue, struggling for control.

Thank heavens Lord Kentwood had elected not to attend this evening.

The madness had been trying to creep upon her for more than a fortnight now, but so far she had won the battle. It would not always be that way. But for today . . .

She shuddered and shoved the stirrings of apprehension into submission. She was safe. Tonight she was safe. At least until she dreamed again.

She closed her eyes, willing her heart to stop racing, regaining command one breath at a time. She could do this, *would* do this. Softly she whispered to herself—her father's name, her birth date, her new maid's name, the name of her horse. Indubitable facts in the face of uncertainty. The recitation eased the sensation of her world spinning out of control. Everything was all right. Normal. Nothing had changed.

She opened her eyes, took a steadying breath, then turned back toward the path.

He stood there, her Scotsman, with his arms folded and his lips curved in amused victory as he blocked the pathway.

"Well then, lass," he said in that low, rolling brogue she had heard only in dreams. "I believe this dance is mine."

Chapter 3

"**Y**ou cannot be real," she gasped.

He grinned like a rogue. "As real as any woman could want."

"Who are you?" She gathered her dignity around her and took on her most haughty mien. "And why do you follow me?"

"I am Lord Arneth." Unfolding his arms, he took a step closer, crowding her back against the statue. "And you, Miss Depford, are a troublesome lass to be sure."

His blue eyes blazed at her from that familiar face, his features a harshly handsome combination of angled cheekbones, a cleft chin, and a wide mouth. And a tiny scar at the corner of that mouth. A scar she had known would be there.

"Troublesome?" She trembled inside, yet she cast him a practiced look of displeasure. "I do not even know you, Lord Arneth, so I cannot see your reason for calling me such a thing."

He stepped closer, and the air seemed to freeze in her lungs beneath his intent regard. "Aye, I think you can."

Warmth flooded her body. His clean scent teased her, awakening her every sense with fierce vengeance. Such vivid imaginings! She wanted to touch his face, to trace the faint shadow of his jaw, to tangle her fingers in his hair. Could she touch him, or would her hand pass through thin air?

"You've led me a merry chase, lass. All I wanted was an introduction."

"And now you've had one." She exhaled slowly, clinging to her infamous control. "Please step aside."

"And leave you to flee from me again? Nay, I think not."

"Lord Arneth, please—"

"Please. Aye, now there's a pretty word coming from your lips." He hissed out a breath. "And me a gentleman. 'Tis a fair coil. Madness, to be sure."

She stiffened at the word. "Madness?"

"Indeed." He took a step back. "I forget myself when I look at you. 'Tis a sort of madness."

He smiled with considerable charm, and her knees nearly melted from beneath her. She stood straighter, willing her dissolving body parts to cooperate. "You have been watching me most boldly this evening."

His gaze slid down along the length of her and back up to her face, his expression frank and admiring. "You're a beautiful woman, lass. Can you blame a man for staring?"

"You are very forward." Heat bloomed in private places all over again.

"I'm chief of my clan, Miss Depford, and accustomed to getting what I want." The warmth of his quick smile eased the sting of arrogance in his words. "I didna mean to frighten you."

"I am not frightened," she lied, "but perhaps you do not realize that here in England, it is most improper for us to be speaking together alone." Her insides quivered with the instinctive desire to throw herself into his arms, imagined or not. "It is best if you return to the ballroom, Lord Arneth."

"Improper or nae, I find I canna leave you so easily, Miss Depford. I've heard tell of your beauty and have come a long way to see it for myself."

A thrill streaked through her. Stunned her. "I am flattered," she whispered. "But I must ask that you conduct yourself as a gentleman."

He leaned closer, his mouth inches from her ear. "I'm trying, lass, but it takes some doing."

Her breath whooshed out of her lungs, and she stared up at him, caught in the mesmerizing strength of his gaze. The power of him captured her, distracting her from rebuilding her will, which his soft words had so easily decimated.

"You must leave," she managed to say.

"Soon enough." He closed his eyes, breathing in softly. "You smell like heaven."

"You should not say such things." Her heart pounded in her breast. She should run. Scream. Anything to escape this dangerous, tantalizing intimacy.

His breath brushed her ear. "Be glad I've a strong will, my bonny one, else I'd be kissing you already."

"A kiss should be given, not taken." She swallowed hard, striving for dignity.

He chuckled, and the vibration of it shivered along her spine. "Indeed, lass, it would be given. And gladly, too."

Did he imply he could coax a willing kiss from her lips? The audacity!

The truth?

She glanced up, saw the surety in his eyes. Rational thought slowly spiraled away. Oh yes, if he pressed the point, she had no doubt she would willingly offer her lips to his kiss.

Dangerous, dangerous man.

"I am flattered," she whispered, "but I really must return to the ballroom."

His soft voice curled around her like an embrace. "I willna hurt you, lass."

"Your stare is very direct," she said. "I find it unnerving."

"'Tis not my stare that touches you, but the fire between us." His eyes nearly glowed with heat. "We're a fine match, you and I."

A tingle of excitement rippled down her spine at the thought of being his match. She didn't like it, not one bit. How could she be feeling this way about someone she had only just met? Especially when her interests lay elsewhere?

She had never before tolerated such boldness from any man. But then, he was not real.

"There are rules for courting a lady," she said sharply. "And endangering her reputation is not one of them."

He chuckled. "Now, lass, dinna play your woman's games with me. My intentions are honorable. I came here to England to fetch a bride."

"A bride." She reached behind her and clung to the cool stone of the statue.

A breath hissed from between his teeth at her retreat. "Indeed. And I've decided that you are the one I want."

His bride! Such a thought! But the idea wrapped itself around her faltering willpower and would not let go. How tempting was this path to lunacy! She almost wanted to see where it led.

Almost.

"Good evening to you, Lord Arneth." She tried to dart around him, but he blocked her path again. Her stomach clenched, and the silence of the night weighed on her with its ominous solitude. "Please let me go," she whispered.

"We can go back together."

"No! We cannot enter together; it is not done!"

"Then promise to dance with me. A proper dance, in full view of everyone." He reached out to touch her face, but she pulled back to avoid the contact. His hand dropped to his side.

This was illusion. Madness. She had to escape, to return to the company of people who could save her from herself.

"A proper dance," she lied, trying to appease him. "In the ballroom."

"I will come for you. Now go, before I canna let you."

A voice echoed from beyond the hedges, calling her name. She jerked. "Beth is searching for me."

"I'll not be the one to shame you," he said, stepping back. "Remember my dance."

Beth called again, and the Scotsman slipped into the shrubbery and disappeared from sight.

"Here, Beth!" Catherine called, her gaze on the place where he had blended with the shadows.

"Catherine, my heavens." Worry robbing her of her usual good spirits, Beth stepped off the path to join Catherine near the statue. "You must come back to the ballroom with me this moment. Mama has noticed your absence and is about to turn the house upside down to find you. She worries you have fallen into the clutches of a Nefarious Villain. I have convinced her that you are more likely indisposed."

"Beth, surely you did not say such a thing?"

Beth shrugged. "Indelicate or not, that is the only reason why Mama has not yet raised the alarm."

Both girls turned back toward the house. Catherine could not resist glancing back. Her Scotsman was gone.

If he had ever been there.

"What were you doing out here?" Beth lowered her voice in fond conspiracy as the two of them made their way back toward the ballroom. "Were you meeting a suitor?"

Catherine stopped in mid-step. She had never confided her secret to anyone, not even her father. Beth was her dearest friend, and above all, loyal. Still . . . "No, I just wanted a moment alone."

"Are you well?" Beth laid a hand on her arm.

"No, actually, I would like to go home." She

managed a weak smile. "My head throbs near to bursting."

"Oh, dear Cat!" Beth gave her a quick squeeze. "Come, I will ask Mama to call for the carriage immediately."

As they strolled back toward the light and music, Catherine gave a brief thought to the Scotsman's request that she dance with him. She dared not do any such thing. After all, had she seen him speak with anyone else? Dance with anyone? Perhaps both the man and her reaction to him were creations of her worsening mental faculties. Had she conjured him from her dreams?

If he was merely her imagination, then she would be dancing with no one in front of the world.

And if by some miracle he *was* a flesh-and-blood man, then her body's reckless reaction to him would be enough to disgrace her in front of everyone.

The breeze came up, and with it, a familiar hushed chanting, the eerie words only she could hear. *The price shall be a daughter born* . . .

Head down and near to tears, she stepped up her pace, eager to leave the ball and find some peace in the privacy of her bedchamber.

Gabriel burst through the elegant front door of his rented town house and into a darkened entry hall that did nothing to ease his foul mood. One stubby candle burned stingily in a nearby sconce, providing just enough light to keep him from bumping into the furnishings.

Curse the wench, but she had eluded him again! Left him fumbling with humiliation like a young boy rejected by his first woman. He had eagerly sought her in the ballroom, only to discover her gone.

Was it some family tradition that Farlan women ran from the husbands destiny had chosen for them?

He snatched off his hat and threw it on the table, then scowled at the elderly man who belatedly came forward to collect his belongings.

"Why the devil is it so dark in here, Donald?"

"We're preserving the candles, what do you suppose?" Grumbling beneath his breath with ill-concealed impatience, Donald picked up Gabriel's fashionable hat, brushed it off, then replaced it carefully on the table.

Gabriel handed over his elegant walking stick. "Have a care with your tone. You're supposed to be a proper London butler."

Donald paused, his fingers tightening around the walking stick. "Dinna be mistaking me for one o' your servants, Gabriel MacBraedon. You ken well enough why I'm here."

"Indeed. And you ken well enough why we dinna have enough coin for candles. It took all the gold of both clans to pay for one month's rental on this house."

Donald curled his lip, then gestured down the hall. "Your men are there in the library, *my lord*."

Gabriel winced as the sarcasm hit the mark. Donald was as much a victim of their situation as any of them. He clapped the old man on the shoulder, the thin bones beneath his hand reminding him of the urgency of their mutual task. "I met her, Donald."

Donald sucked in a breath, hope glimmering in his eyes. "And?"

"A bonny lass with hair like flame and the spirit of her ancestors."

Tears sprang into the elderly man's eyes, embarrassing both of them.

"I intend to call on her tomorrow," Gabriel continued, turning away from the old man and clearing the lump from his throat. "Just like any normal English gentleman."

"Pah!" Donald's voice was only slightly gruffer than usual as he scooped up both hat and walking stick and turned away. "'Tis a sorry state of affairs for a clan chief."

"You ken she doesna know about the curse, Donald. She was raised in England by—"

"I know the tale." With a hard glance, Donald shuffled off into the shadows of the house.

Swiping a hand over his face, Gabriel shook his head and walked down the long hallway toward the library. So much history and pain. How much easier it would be to simply carry the lass off to the Highlands.

Leave it to English civility to complicate things.

A shadowy figure emerged from the doorway of the library. "I see you have returned and are abusing the help."

Gabriel smiled despite his heavy heart. "He abused us by insisting on coming along, Brodie."

His brother-in-law grinned and swept a hand toward the doorway in welcome. "I'm certain he sees it differently."

With Brodie on his heels, Gabriel entered the library, the only public room that contained furniture not draped in white coverings. Before the low fire, three men sat playing cards.

"Gabriel!" Slapping his cards facedown on the table, his brother, Patrick, jumped to his feet. "Did you meet your bride, then?"

"Aye." Gabriel came over to the table and gave the two men still seated a questioning look.

"The lad just wanted to learn to play," Angus told him, getting to his feet.

"Aye," agreed his twin brother, Andrew, also standing. "We didna see the harm in it."

Gabriel studied the identical faces. "My brother is here as a punishment, not a reward."

"Dinna be angry with them, Gabriel," Patrick said, stepping forward, his blue eyes earnest. "There was nothing to do here while you were gone."

Gabriel cast him a sharp look. "Had you not taken it upon yourself to reive our neighbor's cattle, dear brother, you'd not have that problem."

Patrick stiffened. "Our people are hungry."

"So they are. But now you've cost the clan money they canna afford to pay in reparation. And you've cast the honor of our family into doubt. Consider yourself lucky to have me as your jailer. Hugh Ross wanted your head."

"The Rosses can well spare the cattle," Patrick snapped. "Someone had to do something while we waited for you to find your precious bride!"

Gabriel took the hit without flinching. "'Twas an ill-conceived plan, Patrick."

"I am not sorry for what I did."

Gabriel shook his head and glanced at Brodie. His brother-in-law merely gave a little shrug, but Gabriel needed nothing more to know his friend's feelings on the matter. "Angus, Andrew, my thanks for keeping the lad out o' mischief."

"Mischief!" Patrick exclaimed.

"'Tis late, Patrick," Gabriel said, ignoring the outburst. "To bed with you."

The young man narrowed his eyes. "But—"

"No argument."

"I'm not a child!"

"You're acting like one."

Patrick clamped his mouth shut, collected his meager coin from the table, then stormed from the room. A nod from Gabriel had Angus and Andrew scooping up their own winnings and following the young man.

"He's a handful, that one," Brodie murmured, dropping into one of the chairs near the fireplace.

"Aye, and worse with it since he's become a man." Gabriel followed suit, stretching out his gleaming Hessians before him.

"'Tis a natural thing for a lad to seek his place in the clan," said Brodie, "especially as brother to the chief."

"Indeed, but he's following too much after Lachlan. Would that he had taken more after my sweet mother."

Brodie gave a bark of laughter. "Your mum would clout a man over the head with the stewpot for arriving late to supper."

Gabriel grinned. "Indeed."

"And as for taking after your mother's husband, well, he's young yet. But he's still MacBraedon blood, for all that your father died when he was but a bairn. And he has you to guide him."

Gabriel stared into the flickering fire. "A fine guide I am. Educated in Edinburgh, chief of the clan, yet our people are starving and our lands are dying."

"But you're planning on changing that, aren't you? Going to take yourself a bride."

"Aye." Gabriel let his head fall back, staring at the shapes the firelight made on the ceiling.

"'Tis certain then?"

"I said it was, didn't I? There's little choice." Gabriel scowled. "Courtesy of the blasted curse that haunts my family."

"I know this wasna what you wanted, Gabriel. There was Jean . . ."

"I have a duty to the clan." Gabriel glanced at him, then away to the fire. "Jean is in the past."

"So you'll follow your destiny then and marry your Farlan bride." Brodie pulled his pipe from his pocket, followed by a pouch of precious tobacco. "You're a man of honor, Gabriel MacBraedon, and I wish you happy."

"Thank you." Gabriel shifted in his chair, dislodging the sense of entrapment that shrouded him whenever the curse was mentioned. "I met her tonight."

"Did you now?" Brodie measured tobacco carefully into his pipe, then tucked the pouch away. "Does she bear the mark?"

Gabriel barked a laugh. "Not where I could see it."

"Then how do we know for certain she is the one?"

"The lass does bathe, you know. The information from our wee birdie in the household is that Catherine Depford indeed bears the mark."

Brodie chuckled, then reached down to pull a slender twig from the fire to light his pipe. "Good enough. Is she bonny then?"

"It doesna matter if she's uglier than one of my sheep, Brodie. The curse demands I wed her, no matter what she looks like."

Brodie snorted. "It may well make a difference when you have to bed your bride."

"I'd snuff the candles if need be, but as it turns out, that will nae be necessary."

"She's comely, then."

"Aye."

"And wealthy with it."

"Her dowry could sink a ship."

"Indeed." Brodie sat back in his chair and puffed

on his pipe. "'Twill not be a hardship to wed the lass then."

"Not at all." Just the memory of her—the body of a siren with the face of an angel—had him hard in seconds. "She's mine."

Chapter 4

"I want you, lass." He stroked a hand down her throat, over her bosom, and gripped her waist, yanking her against his big body with both hands. "Kiss me."

Lost in sensation, she eagerly leaned up to meet his descending mouth, curling her arms around his neck with willing abandon. His mouth demanded everything, and she gave everything, straining for more of his touch. His kiss liquefied her insides, her heart and will and mind a bubbling cauldron of unceasing hunger.

He growled deep in his throat. Tearing his mouth free, he grabbed the back of her dress in both hands and tugged, easily ripping the two edges apart. Buttons scattered everywhere, and the garment slid down to cling to her hips. His hungry eyes devoured the sight of her nearly exposed breasts, pushed up by her corset as if in offering, her nipples hard and thrusting and barely hidden beneath the thin white chemise.

He tugged down the edge of the chemise and traced a finger along the dagger-shaped birthmark on the side of her left breast. "This is my mark upon you," he muttered, then bent to press his mouth to it.

A rap at the door jerked Catherine awake. She lay panting in her bed, her body burning with unfulfilled needs, as her maid called to her. The familiar surroundings of her own bedroom slowly sank into her consciousness. A dream. Just a dream.

Erotic. Inappropriate. And achingly real.

Her heart was still pounding, her fingers twisted in the coverlet as if tangled in a lover's hair. Longing made her tremble. She closed her eyes and turned her face into the pillows, frustration holding her fast in its relentless grip. Why in God's good name was she haunted by these heated dreams of a man who did not exist? What had she done to warrant such torment?

Except be born of a Farlan?

Oh, this was a curse, all right. A curse that taunted her with what she could not have. A man who quite possibly did not exist. Who made love to her only in the shadowy realm of her dreams.

She had always thought insanity meant incomprehensible ramblings. Not wicked fantasies. Not indecent imaginings that left her damp and shaking with the dawn.

This madness was . . . well, madness.

The bedroom door creaked open. "Miss Catherine? Your father is waiting for you in the breakfast room. He wishes to leave in one hour."

"Leave?" Catherine turned her gaze toward the door as Peg came into the room and went to pull open the draperies at the window.

"For Farlan House, miss."

Farlan House. The balloon launch.

She started to throw back the covers, then realized that her nipples thrust prominently against the thin cotton of her night rail, embarrassingly hardened from the dream. She jerked the blankets back up again.

Peg chuckled. "Now, now, Miss Catherine. We must not keep your father waiting." Her graying hair coiled neatly in a knot at the base of her neck, Peg was easily of an age to be her mother, and despite her ample, matronly figure, she nonetheless had the strength of a woman much younger. Peg pulled at the covers, but Catherine would not relinquish her hold. For a moment, the two women engaged in a bizarre tug-of-war, but Peg was victorious and threw back the blankets with a triumphant fling of her arm.

49

Then, without even noticing her charge's distressing condition, she turned and bustled over to the wardrobe.

Catherine blinked, then realized she had been given a reprieve. She hopped from the bed and ducked behind the screen where the chamber pot was hidden.

"Do not dally now," Peg called to her. "Mr. Depford is impatient this morning; you don't want to be walking to Farlan House."

Farlan House, a wedding gift from her father to her mother.

When she was a child, Papa had refused to tell her much about her mother, except to harangue about how Mama's wild Scottish blood had driven her to her death. But Catherine was a woman grown now, and the answer to all this had to be more than heritage or blood.

Somehow, she needed to find out more about her mother—and the mystery of the Farlan madness.

Dressed in her favorite blue-sprigged muslin for an afternoon out of doors, Catherine entered the breakfast room, feeling more herself after the familiar routine of her morning toilette. Sunshine spilled in through the windows, and her father's bald pate gleamed in the morning light. "Good morning, Papa."

George Depford glanced up from his newspaper. "Good morning, daughter."

She sat down at the table to her father's right and smiled her thanks at the footman who placed her morning chocolate before her. The question of her mother burned in her mind, and her father seemed the most likely place to start. However, she had learned early in life that blunt questions earned her nothing when it came to her father. Especially when he was engrossed in the *Times*. She would have to lead up to the subject subtly, perhaps by engaging in small talk to begin—

"How was Lady Dorburton's ball last night?" her father asked, briskly folding up his newspaper and setting it aside.

She blinked that it had been so easy.

"A complete crush, as expected." A footman set her favorite breakfast, eggs and ham, in front of her.

As she began to slice her ham, her father leaned forward, his dark eyes glinting with eagerness. "Tell me about the evening. Was Kentwood there?"

Ah. So that was it.

Amused at his ill-concealed enthusiasm, she deliberately took a bite of ham. Chewed. Swallowed. Only then did she answer, "No, he did not attend."

"Bah." With an exasperated wave of his hand, her father sat back in his chair. "It is frustrating enough that young Dirby announced his betrothal just as we thought he was coming up to scratch. And now Kentwood did not appear? That is indeed a disappointment." He reached for his steaming cup of coffee. "I so want you to become a countess, daughter."

With a sigh at this familiar refrain, she glanced down at her plate and sliced more ham. "I do not care if I am a countess, Papa."

"But *I* do!" He took a gulp of coffee and set the cup back on its saucer with a clatter. "I have more wealth than most of the *ton*, Catherine, but none of the bloodlines. I want that life for you."

She met his gaze. "My husband should be a kind man, Papa. One I can trust—titled or not."

He made a sound of impatience. "You deserve a life of comfort with a man who will take care of you properly."

"Perhaps our ideas are different on what that entails."

He caught her hand as she reached for her chocolate. His gaze held hers for a long moment. "Catherine, you know I want the best for you."

She squeezed his fingers, then tugged free to lift her cup. "I do know that. So to ease your mind, Papa, I shall tell you that I find Lord Kentwood most agreeable. Should he offer for me, we will both have what we want."

"I am most pleased to hear you say that." The knocker sounded at the front door, and he smiled like the cat who had eaten the cream.

She paused in lifting eggs to her mouth, arrested by his expression. "Papa? What have you done?"

"I have a surprise for you, my dear."

Stodgins, the butler, appeared in the doorway. "Mrs. Waters and Miss Waters, sir."

"Good morning!" Barely giving the butler time to move out of the way, Mrs. Waters sailed into the breakfast room with Beth right behind her. "Such a lovely day for an outing!"

Her father got to his feet. "Good morning! Do sit down. Will you take tea or coffee? Or perhaps chocolate?"

"I will take tea," Mrs. Waters announced, claiming the chair a footman pulled out for her to Papa's left.

"Chocolate, please," Beth said, sitting down beside Catherine. The footmen scurried to comply with their requests.

"Thank you so much, dear Mr. Depford, for inviting Beth and me to accompany you to your balloon launch," Mrs. Waters trilled.

Catherine's father gave a gruff nod and sat

down again. "A pleasure to have your company, madam."

"So you are both riding out to Farlan House with us? How lovely!" Catherine sent her father a questioning look. Was this the surprise? The Waters ladies frequently accompanied them on outings, though it was true she had not known they were attending this one.

"Oh yes!" Beth practically bounced in her chair. "I have never seen a balloon launch before. I imagine it is quite exciting."

"Mr. Depford has a great interest in such things, do you not, sir?" Mrs. Waters gave Catherine's father a warm smile.

He cleared his throat. "Indeed. Yes, I do."

Was Papa blushing? Surely not! Catherine glanced at Mrs. Waters in speculation. *That* lady was all sparkling eyes and rosy cheeks herself.

Was there a bit of a romance going on between them? Did that explain Papa's behavior?

The knocker sounded again.

Stodgins came to the doorway. "Lord Kentwood."

Aha. Catherine glanced at her father. He gave her an indulgent smile.

Lord Kentwood entered the room, a brown-eyed, brown-haired fellow with an affable smile. If not for his title, his very average looks might have caused him to be nearly forgettable, but the extensiveness of the Kentwood lands, coupled with the man's clever sense of humor, served to separate him from his peers.

He made his bow and greeted all parties.

"Good morning, Lord Kentwood." Her stomach fluttered with nerves at the sight of her chosen suitor in her very own breakfast room. "To what do we owe the pleasure of your company this morning?"

"Your father invited me to attend the balloon launch today."

"How wonderful!" Beth squealed with a clap of her hands.

"Yes," Catherine agreed, sending a grateful look to her sire. "How kind of you to join us."

"Do sit down," her father invited. "Coffee? Tea?"

"Coffee," Kentwood replied, sitting down beside Mrs. Waters. "Thank you."

"So lovely to see you again, Lord Kentwood," Mrs. Waters said.

"I had hoped to see you . . . all of you . . . at Lady Dorburton's ball last night, but I was detained elsewhere."

"How unfortunate," Mrs. Waters said.

"Lady Dorburton should be in attendance today," Catherine's father said.

The footman came with Lord Kentwood's

coffee, and Catherine asked, "How is your mama, Lord Kentwood?"

"She is well. Thank you for asking." Kentwood gave her his affable smile, and the moment stretched as his gaze lingered on her face. "Will you be at Lady Helverton's tomorrow evening, Miss Depford?"

"Regrettably, I shall not." His obvious admiration warmed her. "We are engaged at Vauxhall."

Disappointment flickered across his features; then his smile came back. "Perhaps I will see you there then." He glanced at her father. "I assume you have secured a supper box, Mr. Depford?"

"Indeed, and for the Waters ladies as well. Would you care to join us, Lord Kentwood?"

"Thank you, sir, that is most kind." Kentwood looked at Catherine. "Provided Miss Depford has no objection."

"Of course not," Catherine replied. "We—"

A broken vow when peace was sworn . . .

The whisper swept through the room, cutting off her thoughts and her words.

No, no, not now!

"We are to hear the orchestra that evening," Beth piped up, looking at Catherine with some concern.

The price shall be a daughter born . . .

The chant came louder, swelling in volume and insistence. Catherine glanced at the others. Did they not hear? Her father was frowning at her, but it wasn't anger in his eyes. It was fear.

What did he know?

"Yes, the orchestra," she said, somehow managing to smile. "Do join us, Lord Kentwood."

Her father's relieved nod did nothing to ease her shattered nerves. The voices continued to whisper to her through breakfast.

And in the carriage on the way to Farlan House, located just outside London.

And as she stood watching the fuss going on around the hot air balloon with Beth, Mrs. Waters, and Lord Kentwood, while her father and Mr. Brown, the operator of the balloon, got the device ready to launch.

She did all she could to ignore the strange chanting, to act normally, to carry on a conversation with her companions, but she could tell from the anxiety in Beth's eyes that she was not completely succeeding in hiding her preoccupation.

Still, she forged on, determined to let no one see her weakness, and praying that the Scottish Apparition would not make an appearance and ruin any chance she had with Lord Kentwood. The voices had never been this strong before, this insistent.

The Farlan madness was taking greater hold on her. How long would her sanity last?

Lord Kentwood bowed his head and murmured, "Are you well, Miss Depford? You look a bit pale."

"I am fine." She managed a laugh. "Redheads are notoriously fair, Lord Kentwood."

"So I have observed." His swift, approving glance over her form sent a tingle through her. Her cheeks heated, and she glanced down at her hands.

The price shall be a daughter born . . .

With effort, she forced the voices to the back of her mind and looked up to find him watching her. "Have you ever witnessed a spectacle such as this?" she asked.

That dark-eyed gaze never wavered from her face. "Not like this."

This time there was no mistaking his implication. "Lord Kentwood," she chided softly, shifting beneath his regard. "Mrs. Waters might think you are flirting with me."

His cheeks creased as he gave her that amiable grin. "Perhaps because I am."

"Oh." Blushing, she glanced away again.

Of Farlan blood to wed our chief—Each generation, no relief . . .

The voices clashed in a crescendo of sound.

She winced, then glanced over to see if he was watching. His attention had been claimed by the balloon.

Concentrating, she attempted to mentally banish the chanting. If it were at all possible, she would will the voices to stop. She must not scare Lord Kentwood away with any odd behavior. She would need a husband more than ever in the coming months when the madness took its toll, and Lord Kentwood appeared to be just the sort of kind-hearted, protective gentleman she sought. It was imperative she secure an offer from him as soon as possible.

While she was still lucid enough to accept.

"That contraption means to fly?"

Gabriel nodded, admiring the balloon with the avarice of a novice inventor. "It does indeed, Brodie."

His brother-in-law muttered a short prayer in Gaelic. "I dinna ken the need to float on the clouds like a bird. Better a man keep his feet firmly on the ground."

Gabriel ignored the comment, his entire attention on the activity around the balloon. Part of him wanted to be down there beside the apparatus, to talk to this Mr. Brown, who would be going up in the basket of the balloon. How did the mechanism work? What made the balloon fly? What did it feel like to soar above the earth?

But that wasn't why he was here.

A flash of sunlight off a fiery curl beneath the rim of a fashionable straw bonnet drew his attention. Aye, *she* was why he was here.

"Is that the one, then?" Brodie whispered, following his gaze. "Indeed, she's bonny to be sure."

Gabriel nodded, dazzled like a lad viewing his first naked woman. His body roared to life like a fueled forge, demanding he touch her. But then he saw her delicate fingers resting on the arm of the Englishman standing beside her. Fury ripped through him. She was *his*, by God!

She looked in his direction. When she caught sight of him, he watched her eyes widen in recognition, her lips form a sweet O of shock. He took a step forward, but Brodie grabbed hold of his arm.

"Let go of me." He yanked at Brodie's hold, but his brother-in-law used the weight of his whole body to hold him back.

"You canna rip the man's head off," Brodie advised in a low murmur. "There are rules to this sort of thing, you ken."

"He has no right to touch her."

"Gabriel." With effort, Gabriel managed to take his gaze off Catherine and look at his best friend. Brodie held his stare for a long moment. "You must control yourself or you will lose everything. 'Tis the curse, man."

"She's mine." Even Gabriel was surprised by the possession in his tone.

"Aye, she is. But she doesna know it yet."

"You're right." The tension melted from his body and the red haze cleared from his vision, though jealousy still throbbed like an open wound.

"Fetch your cousin," Brodie said, slowly loosening his hold. "Let her introduce you, formally and correctly."

"Good idea." With effort, Gabriel managed not to look back at the fair Catherine and instead turned his gaze to the throng to locate the petite Lady Dorburton. "There she is. Standing on the edge of the crowd."

"Fetch her then, and observe the proprieties," Brodie urged. "Only then can you claim your bride properly, at least according to English rules."

Needing no further encouragement, Gabriel began to make his way to Lady Dorburton.

Each generation, no relief . . .

Grateful that Lord Kentwood had chosen to go and examine the balloon more closely, Catherine wrestled with maintaining control. The voices had not relented, and she had indeed caught a glimpse of the man from her dream. The afternoon looked to become an utter disaster. She had visions of herself speaking to Scotsmen who did not exist or becoming dizzy from the constant chatter in her head, all under the interested eyes of Lord Kentwood.

She should have stayed abed.

"Catherine, dear, are you feeling quite the thing?" Mrs. Waters peered at her, concern on her kindly face.

"So many people." Catherine managed a smile, though the continuous chanting was making her temples throb. "It makes one feel nearly smothered."

Mrs. Waters nodded in sympathy. "Indeed, it was kind of your father to open up the grounds to everyone in the area, but it does make for a fearsome crowd."

"I think it is a lovely idea," Beth said. "Even the tenants can watch the balloon soar into the heavens!"

"Oh, Beth, you are such a generous heart," Mrs. Waters said with a chuckle.

"I simply believe—my goodness, but who is that?" Beth's voice lowered to an astonished whisper, compelling her mother to lean closer to hear her.

"Who is whom?" Mrs. Waters asked.

"The handsome man with Lady Dorburton. La, he is a tall fellow!"

Mrs. Waters immediately turned to locate the mysterious gentleman in the crowd. "My word!" she exclaimed. "I believe they are coming this way."

"Perhaps he seeks an introduction." Beth patted her dark curls, keeping her eyes lowered and her spine straight.

Catherine started to look, but Mrs. Waters laid a hand on her arm. "Do not appear overly eager, my dear," she murmured.

More than grateful for the reprieve, Catherine shut her eyes and focused on tuning out the persistent chanting. Lord Kentwood could return to her side at any moment, and she wanted to be in full control of her faculties.

"Good afternoon, Mrs. Waters," Lady Dorburton said, reaching their group.

"Good afternoon, Lady Dorburton," Mrs. Waters trilled. "I must say, your ball last night was spectacular! We all had a wonderful time."

"I am so glad. Please allow me to introduce my cousin Lord Arneth, who is newly arrived in London."

Arneth! Catherine whipped her head around, and her heart lurched into a gallop. There he stood, watching her with those penetrating blue eyes. Her dream Scotsman. Her own personal hallucination, who haunted her nights and her days.

The sensual lover who lived in the forbidden part of her mind, who touched her so scandalously in her dreams . . .

And as soon as their gazes met, the voices abruptly stopped.

The relief nearly drove her to her knees.

"Gabriel, this is Mrs. Waters and her daughter, Miss Waters. And this is Miss Depford, whose papa is hosting this fête."

Gabriel. He was a real flesh-and-blood man.

Which meant everything that had happened in the garden had been real as well. The conversation, the flirtation. The very obvious sexual heat.

Lord Kentwood had never engendered such dangerous, intimate emotions from her as the ones that melted her insides at this moment. He had never looked at her with unrestrained ardor in his eyes, making her feel that only the barest glimmer of civility was preventing him from carrying her off and having his way with her.

As Lord Arneth was regarding her now.

"'Tis a pleasure to meet you all." The Scotsman smiled at all of them, lingering half a second longer on Catherine. "And my thanks to you and your father, Miss Depford, for allowing me to accompany my cousin on this outing."

She answered through dry lips. "You are most welcome."

"And you, Lord Arneth." Mrs. Waters looked him over with the critical eye of a cautious mama. "Is this your first time in London?"

"No, Mrs. Waters, though it has been some years. I spend most of my time in Scotland."

"My cousin has come to Town to seek a bride," Lady Dorburton added.

Catherine jerked, the memory of the garden as fresh in her mind as newly turned earth. He was watching her, and possession simmered in his eyes for that one, fleeting moment, leaving her feeling branded.

Leaving her feeling *his*.

"How delightful!" Mrs. Waters brightened. "You must tell us which social events you will be attending so we can be certain to meet again."

As if he had not just scorched her with a glance, he smiled at the other ladies with considerable charm. "You may be assured of that."

"I must introduce my cousin to a few more people," Lady Dorburton said. "Do excuse us."

"'Twas a pleasure," Gabriel said with a bow, then allowed Lady Dorburton to lead him away.

Catherine watched him go, helpless to look away, every fiber in her body longing to follow.

"My goodness." Beth sighed. "He is the most handsome man I have ever seen."

"Scotland," Mrs. Waters said in a considering

voice. "He has a title, but I do not fancy my daughter living among the barbarians."

"Oh, Mama." Beth turned to Catherine. "What did you think, Catherine? I found him quite civilized . . . for a barbarian."

"He seemed quite unobjectionable," Catherine murmured. Her mind still spun, denying the evidence of her eyes and ears. He was real, he wanted her, and in his presence the voices stopped. *How was this possible?*

"I expect you did not notice his charm," Beth said slyly, "since you and Lord Kentwood were smelling of April and May not ten minutes ago."

"Beth!" Catherine flushed, wondering what Beth would think if she knew the truth.

"Is there something you would like to tell your dearest friend?" Beth continued, ignorant of Catherine's torment. A playful smile curved her lips. "Do you expect an offer in the near future?"

"I cannot begin to anticipate," Catherine said firmly.

"A wise answer," Mrs. Waters proclaimed. "Beth, do not tease Catherine. I'm certain that should she receive an offer of marriage, we would be the first to know. Ah, look. They are ready to begin the launch. And here comes Lord Kentwood."

"My apologies for leaving you for so long, ladies." Lord Kentwood bounded over, his excitement contagious. "Come closer. This will be an amazing display." He grinned at Catherine. "Allow me to escort you, Miss Depford."

She nodded, grateful to have some direction. But even as she placed her hand on his arm, a sensation of disloyalty made her want to snatch it back. She took a deep breath, forcing calm. For the moment, the voices were gone and she was in control of her faculties. "Lead the way, Lord Kentwood."

Chapter 5

With much fanfare and a great cheer from the attendees, Mr. Brown maneuvered his balloon into a slow ascent. The breeze caught the device, aiding it in its bobbing climb, rippling along the sides of the silken sack of air.

Lord Kentwood watched with the fascination of a young boy. Under other circumstances, she would have found his reaction charming. At this moment in time, however, she was more concerned with the Scotsman who stood a short distance away.

Staring.

Butterflies danced in her stomach at the heat of his gaze. It astonished her that she did not burst into flame from his intense regard, but what shocked her even more was the nearly irresistible desire to walk away from Lord Kentwood to be with Gabriel.

Not Gabriel, she corrected herself. *Lord Arneth*.

Anyone else might refer to such a reckless craving as madness, but having experienced *real* madness, she could only attribute this to some sort of wild physical attraction. She could not explain why she dreamed of the Scotsman when she had never laid eyes on him before, much less why her dreams had taken on such a scandalously erotic tone. Or why the voices in her head stopped their chanting in his presence. The only explanations that came to her were wild flights of fancy—that he was a sorcerer or some nonsense of that ilk.

But he was a real flesh-and-blood man, which meant, of course, that his talk of marriage in the garden was real, too. And as much as it thrilled her to know he desired her so intensely, her path was clear. She meant to become Lady Kentwood before the madness stole her wits completely. She could trust Lord Kentwood to care for her with as much diligence as he did his beloved mother, even if she became completely incoherent. She did not have as much confidence in the bold, unnerving Scotsman.

She glanced at him again, and the naked hunger in Gabriel's eyes sent gooseflesh rippling along her skin. Her secret places ached for him in a way that should have shattered her ladylike sensibilities, but instead she could barely restrain the impulse to run into his arms.

This had to stop—dreams or not, voices or not. She could not let this man get in the way of her goal to become Lady Kentwood, not when it was so close.

Lord Kentwood smiled at her just then, a soft, intimate smile that she fancied a man might give his wife across the breakfast table. Her own lips curved in return, and then she modestly lowered her eyes.

She *would* become Lady Kentwood. She simply needed to explain to the Scotsman that he must turn his attentions elsewhere, even though the mere thought of him looking at any other female the way he looked at her made her want to scratch that woman's eyes out.

But in battle, sacrifices had to be made. This was her battle for a secure future, and she intended to win.

The launch of Mr. Brown's balloon thrilled the onlookers, from duke to peasant. Following the event, George Depford invited his more elite guests to a comfortable picnic in the gardens at Farlan House, while the lower orders went back to their ordinary lives, full of stories about the amazing feat they had just witnessed.

As her father's hostess, Catherine made certain the servants were organized and the food plentiful.

Luckily she had learned her role early in life and was able to carry it out without much concentration.

Her entire focus remained on finding a way to speak to Gabriel in private.

With Lord Kentwood safely occupied in conversation with a group of gentlemen, she watched Gabriel—*Lord Arneth*—as he partook of the feast and chatted with the other guests. Lady Dorburton, having performed her familial duty by introducing him to others, now kept company with society matrons on the opposite side of the garden. Gabriel was instead accompanied by a dark-haired man she did not know, dressed neatly but not nearly as elegantly as the Scottish lord.

The voices remained blissfully silent, and when she saw that Gabriel and his companion were temporarily alone, she put her newly formed plan into action.

Hiding behind her role as hostess, she made her way with some resolution to the two gentlemen, who stood apart from the other guests. A footman trailed behind her with a tray of lemonade. "I hope you enjoyed the balloon launch, Ga— er, Lord Arneth."

"I did indeed, Miss Depford." Her name fell from his lips like a caress, and her body tightened in response.

She broke eye contact and glanced at his companion. "Would either of you gentlemen care for some lemonade?"

"I would love some," the other man said.

"Excuse my manners," Gabriel—*Lord Arneth*—said. "This is my brother-in-law, Mr. Brodie Alexander."

"A pleasure to meet you, Mr. Alexander."

"The pleasure is certainly mine, Miss Depford."

Catherine waited until Brodie had been served a glass of lemonade. The footman turned away, and Catherine stepped closer to Gabriel, finally gathering the courage to look into his eyes. Still, the jolt of attraction shook her.

"A pleasure to see you again, Lord Arneth." With a discreet touch, she pressed a note into his palm, then turned and followed the footman to the next group of guests.

Brodie chuckled. "Aye, that lass will make the stormiest courtship worthwhile."

"She's a Farlan. Did you expect anything else?" Turning his back on the crowd, Gabriel unfolded the note and scanned the contents, then stuck the piece of paper into his coat pocket.

"What is it?" Brodie asked.

Gabriel grinned. "The lass has finally come to her senses."

*   *   *

"Cat, what has come over you?" Beth's shocked whisper echoed in the empty hallway as Catherine pulled her along. "What are we doing inside?"

Catherine stopped outside the yellow parlor, which had once been her mother's sewing room. "Beth, I need you to help me. Please."

Beth narrowed her eyes, then folded her arms across her bosom. "Catherine Depford, what is going on?"

"Please, Beth. There isn't much time." Glancing up and down the hall to be certain they were alone, Catherine opened the door and pulled Beth in behind her. Then she eased the door closed.

"Cat—" Beth began.

"Wait." Catherine held up a hand. "Do you recall at the ball last night, you asked me if I was meeting a suitor out in the garden?"

"Yes." Suspicion shadowed her friend's face. "You said you were not."

"Well, I was."

Beth's mouth fell open. "You lied?"

"I was afraid you would be cross with me." Catherine touched her friend on the arm, praying Beth would believe the small fib. "I was worried you might think me fast for taking such a chance with my reputation."

"You would be correct!" Clearly outraged, Beth opened her mouth to lecture, then paused. "Why are you telling me now?"

"Because I do not want to risk my reputation for a man."

Beth gave a sharp nod. "I should say not!"

"But there *is* a man I must speak to. Alone. And I need your help."

"What?" Beth squeaked. She reached for the doorknob.

"Beth, please." Catherine caught her before she could open the door. "Please help me. This is most important."

"Have you taken leave of your senses?"

"Shh. Lower your voice, lest the servants hear us."

Beth clamped her lips shut and glared.

Catherine sighed. "Fine, then do not forgive me. But I must speak to Lord Arneth alone—"

"Lord Arneth!" Beth exclaimed. "What about Lord Kentwood? I thought you had set your cap for him."

"I have."

"Then how can you be meeting Lord Arneth? Especially when you have only just been introduced to him?"

Catherine winced. "It was he I met in the garden last night."

Beth gasped, her hand going to her throat. "You did no such thing!"

"I did."

"Alone?"

"Yes."

"Did he kiss you?"

"Beth!"

Beth gave her a hurt look. "It is a logical question."

"If you must know, no, he did not kiss me."

"Thank goodness for that. You are my best friend, Cat, but I do not approve of your careless disregard for Lord Kentwood. I believe he fancies you."

"I have no intention of hurting Lord Kentwood in any way." Catherine paused, knowing she had to say something that would make Beth relent, for if Beth knew of Gabriel's ardor, she would never leave the room. "Lord Arneth has some knowledge of my mother," she lied.

"Oh! It would make sense, I suppose, that since he is from Scotland, he might know something of your mother's family."

"Yes. Exactly. And in order to speak to him without risking my reputation, I need you to stand outside this door and be my chaperone."

"I should stand *inside the door*, Catherine Depford, if I am to be any sort of chaperone!" Beth pursed her lips.

"You are right, of course. But Beth . . ." She took Beth's hands. "You know the stories about Mama. I should hate to have some gossipmonger overhear my conversation with Lord Arneth."

Beth's expression softened, and she squeezed Catherine's hands. "I understand."

"Then you will help me? And you will come fetch me if anyone comes near the room?"

"You can be certain I will."

"Very well, then."

"Very well." Beth tilted her chin. "There is one thing I must insist."

"And that is?"

"The door must remain open. It is the only way to preserve your reputation, Catherine."

"But—"

"The only way."

Recognizing the glint of stubbornness in her friend's eyes, Catherine nodded in defeat. "As you wish."

A soft knock came at the door. Both girls jumped, then Catherine opened the portal a crack and peered through.

Lord Arneth looked back at her. "I am expected, I believe?"

"You are." Catherine opened the door, and he slipped through quite gracefully for such a big man.

"Miss Waters, I take it you are the chaperone?"

"I am." Beth's watchful demeanor melted a little beneath his warm smile. "I will be just outside."

He bowed. "I will remain a gentleman at all times, I assure you."

She pinkened. "See that you do." With a quick warning look at Catherine, she stepped out into the hallway, leaving the door standing half open.

"Come away from the door," Catherine said, and walked to the center of the small room, where a table stood with a vase of flowers. The muffled thuds of his footsteps made the flowers quiver as he followed her.

She turned to face him, one hand on the tabletop. His mere presence filled the tiny parlor with an energy that flirted along her skin like the vibrations of harp strings.

How many times had those arms held her in her dreams? How often had his lips caressed her skin? Just the memory of things that had happened only in her imagination was enough to rouse her body to complete alertness.

"You wanted to speak to me, lass," he reminded her, a smile playing about his lips.

"Yes." She licked her suddenly dry lips. "I just do not know where to begin."

"We might begin with the dance you promised me. The one you have yet to grant me."

"Oh." Heat flooded her cheeks. "I apologize. I suffered the headache and needed to leave the ball immediately."

"Convenient, that." He raised a brow. "A man would think you were trying to avoid him."

"Not exactly." She fiddled with the ivory roses in the vase. "I would like to speak with you about our conversation in the garden last night."

"Indeed?" He leaned against the back of an armchair, only a small area rug spanning the distance between them, and folded his arms. "I would be most interested to discuss that topic."

She poked at the roses again, strangely reluctant to send him packing. "You said you came to find a wife."

"So I did." He watched her intently as he said, "And I've told you you're the one I want."

She stilled, her breath caught in her lungs.

He gave a nod at her reaction. "Aye, I came here for you, Catherine Depford. You might say we are destined to wed."

"What?" Her arm jerked, and she accidentally yanked one of the roses from the vase. The bloom flew across the carpet and hit him in the chest. "How can we be destined to wed if we have only just met?"

"I know your family, lass. It has long been the custom for the Farlan women to marry the Mac-

Braedon men." He pushed away from the armchair and scooped up the rose from the floor, then presented it to her with a flourish. "They've asked me to fetch you home."

She took the rose from him and lifted it to her nose. The sweet scent calmed her thundering heart. How ironic that her lie to Beth had suddenly become truth. "Who are you then to be trusted with such an important task?"

"Gabriel MacBraedon, chief of clan MacBraedon, though in England it suits me better to be Lord Arneth." He grinned. "Or rather, it suits the English better."

"Are the Farlans part of your clan?"

He laughed out loud. "Hardly, though we have depended on each other for some generations now."

The temptation to know more about her mother was irresistible. Perhaps she could finally obtain answers to her questions! "I had not considered that my mother's family would want to meet me. I have never corresponded with them."

"Indeed? So you know nothing about the Farlans?"

"No."

"None of the legends or family stories?"

"None. My father did not allow contact with my mother's family." She brushed her lips against the silky petals and cast him an apologetic look. "He does not like the Scottish."

Gabriel snorted. "Well, they've little fondness for him, I can tell you that."

"Why do you say that?" The hand holding the flower stilled with the bloom against her cheek.

"The Farlans promised their daughter, Glynis, to the MacBraedon chief. But she ran off with your father and broke the word of her clan."

Her mouth fell open. "I can hardly credit it! My mother? And the chief . . . would that have been your father?"

"My uncle."

"I see." At least this much made sense! Her father's dislike of the Scots, the lack of communication from her mother's family.

"So you see, according to family tradition, we are supposed to wed." He reached out and took the rose from her. "You're the bride for me, Catherine Depford, and I've come for you."

She laughed. "Here in England, simply claiming a woman is not done." She sucked in a breath as he trailed the rose down her throat. "A . . . a gentleman must first court a lady and then obtain her father's permission to wed her."

"Is that how it is done?" He touched the bloom to the hint of shadow between her breasts.

She forgot to breathe. "What are you doing?" she whispered.

"Not nearly what I want to be doing." His eyes glittered. "You were teasing me with this simple flower, sweet Catherine. And now I want to drive you mad with it."

Boldly, he trailed the blossom across her bosom. Her body woke with a vengeance, nipples hardening to peaks beneath her chemise, breasts swelling in clothing that suddenly felt too tight.

"This is not why I asked you here," she managed to say.

"Ah, but this is why I came. To be alone with you again." He took a step closer, trailing the rose down her torso. "To convince you to be mine."

She stepped backward but bumped into the table. She gripped the surface with both hands. "Lord Arneth—"

"Gabriel."

"Gabriel," she murmured. "I have more questions."

"I will answer all of them." He slid an arm around her waist. His warm male body pressed against hers in an intimacy she had never felt before.

Except in dreams.

Terrified, excited, her breath caught. "When?"

"In time." He dropped the rose back into the

81

vase, then tenderly stroked his fingers down her cheek, his mouth grim with the strain of self-control. "I didna intend to do this." His gaze followed the path of his fingers as he trailed them down her throat. "I'm not a barbarian to be tossing a lass over my shoulder and carrying her off. But something about you, sweet Catherine, tempts me to forget that."

"My father would come after me." She sucked in a quick breath as his curious fingers traced along the top of her bodice. Immediately her body responded, her breasts aching within the stiff confines of her clothing. Her eyes slid closed, her mind lost in new sensations.

His touch. At last.

"He would indeed," he murmured. "But would you want to leave me?"

His thumb brushed her nipple through her clothing, and she gasped, opening her eyes again.

"What are you doing to me?" The plaintive longing in her voice surprised her. She struggled for reason, but the surging emotions battering her senses would not let her form a coherent thought.

He dipped his head, his mouth lingering just above the flesh of her throat. "What are you doing to *me*?"

She met his gaze with total candor. Said nothing.

With one agitated movement, he slid his hand to the back of her neck and brought his lips to hers.

His mouth—ardent and insistent—demanded capitulation. His hand held her head still while he took his fill of her. Everything female within her opened, offered, gave. He took, his body hard and hot against hers.

Dear God, she wanted . . . too much.

Surrender slackened her limbs. It was wrong, this was wrong, the situation was wrong. But sweet heaven, such hunger! She'd never known such a thing existed. She wanted more, and still it was not enough.

He nibbled at her lips, urging them to part, deepening the kiss with male demand.

More, his kiss insisted. More and more and more.

Everything, her body agreed.

Then a footstep sounded outside the door. The rustle of petticoats, a woman humming. Loudly.

He jerked his mouth away. His fingers flexed against her nape as he struggled for control, his breathing ragged. Their gazes met, and except for his arm at her back, she would have staggered at the hot need blazing in his eyes.

"I will see you again." With this harsh whisper, he stepped away from her. She stumbled against the table, nearly knocking over the vase, but his hand at her elbow saved her from falling as her knees refused to support her. "I will come to call tomorrow. Go driving with me. Four o'clock."

She nodded her agreement. Her body throbbed, and for the first time in her life, she longed to strip off her restrictive clothing, to be naked with him in broad daylight.

That thought alone brought her back to herself with a nearly audible snap.

"You had best return to your guests before I find another use for that table." He growled the sinful promise as he backed up another step.

Beth chose that moment to return to the room. "Catherine, we should return to the garden. Now."

Catherine nodded. "You are right, Beth." She started toward her friend, rather shocked that her legs were working correctly.

Beth gave her a searching look, then said, "You might want to look in the mirror before you return to the gathering."

"I will."

"Miss Depford."

Catherine paused and looked back at him.

"See to it that you are nae feeling poorly tomorrow afternoon." The warning in his voice matched the heat in his eyes.

A quiver of excitement rippled over her at the way he looked at her. "I promise."

With a bow to both ladies, he strode from the room.

"My goodness!" Beth laid a hand over her heart. "Such a man!"

"Yes, he is very striking." Catherine frowned at the open doorway, going over their conversation in her mind. She had not gotten nearly all the information she wanted. What about the voices? The dreams? This man was somehow involved with the whole of it. He knew her mother's family. Did he also know of the Farlan curse?

"I admit I am aghast at your boldness, Catherine, but having seen this gentleman, I must concede that I myself might have been moved to take such a risk with my own reputation." Beth fanned a hand near her pink cheeks. "Though I believe I have never seen you behave so very fast."

"Fast!" She goggled at Beth. "I was the picture of submission and deference!"

"You conversed for more time than might be considered proper," Beth corrected. "In fact, I believe there was a certain familiarity in your manner toward Lord Arneth."

"That is neither here nor there. I did not accomplish my purpose." Catherine marched over to a mirror on the wall and gasped as she viewed her own reflection—cheeks pink, eyes glittering, her bonnet askew. Quickly she straightened the straw confection, tucking her curls beneath the brim.

"He asked you to go driving with him," Beth said.

Catherine sighed. "I know. I did not have the opportunity to refuse."

Beth rolled her eyes just in the slightest. "If you had not been *kissing him*, then you might have been able to voice an objection."

Catherine propped her hands on her hips and looked at her friend. "You have made your disapproval quite clear, Beth."

Beth bit her lip. "I do not wish you to be cross with me, but you are my dearest friend, and I want what is best for you."

Catherine sighed. "I know."

"And what about Lord Kentwood? You should not lead him to believe his attentions are welcome if you have feelings for another man."

"His attentions *are* welcome!" Catherine shook her head, fighting to regain her common sense. But Gabriel's touch had left her feeling anything but sensible.

Beth gave her a chiding look. "Then you must discourage Lord Arneth from calling on you tomorrow."

"Help me, Beth. I cannot be at home when Lord Arneth arrives."

Before Beth could comment, a quiet knock on the open door had both of them turning to see Catherine's father standing in the doorway.

"Here you are, daughter. What are you doing all the way back here?"

"Just seeking a moment of quiet conversation with Beth." Sending her friend a warning glance, Catherine went to her father's side and patted his arm.

"We have guests, daughter, and Lord Kentwood specifically inquired after you."

Beth arched her brows, but Catherine ignored the look and said, "We are finished here. Come, Beth."

For a moment, she thought Beth would refuse, but then she came forward. "Indeed," Beth said, casting a glance at Catherine. "I should not like to keep Lord Kentwood waiting."

Catherine ignored the implied jibe and took her father's arm. "Lead on, Papa."

"I am a lucky man to be able to escort two such lovely ladies." Oblivious to the undercurrents, Catherine's father cheerfully led them back to the party.

Chapter 6

Gabriel presented himself at the Depford home at precisely four o'clock the next day. His stylish phaeton would have cost the earth under normal circumstances, but he had won the vehicle in a card game the night before, neatly avoiding spending any of his rapidly dwindling funds.

When one wooed an heiress, it helped to look as if her fortune was unnecessary.

He knocked at the door, which was quickly opened by a very correct butler. The old fellow's face was set in lines of utter blankness designed to impress and intimidate.

He was impressed. How long would it take Donald to learn something like that?

"Yes?" the butler intoned.

"Lord Arneth to see Miss Depford."

"I am sorry, my lord, but Miss Depford is not at home. Would you care to leave your card?"

"Not at home?" His jaw dropped, but he quickly snapped it shut. "What do you mean, she's not at home?"

The butler did not flinch. "As I said, my lord, she has gone out. But you may certainly leave your card."

"I'll not be leaving my card, blast it!" Rage roared through him like a boiling burn. This was the second time she had fled from him.

"If you will not leave your card, my lord, I regret that I cannot help you."

Gabriel struggled for patience. "Do you know where she went?"

"Miss Depford is out with friends. Good day to you, my lord." The butler started to close the door.

"Hold!" Gabriel stuck his booted foot in the doorway. "She and I had an appointment. She must have forgotten."

"I cannot say. Now good day, my lord!"

His boot still wedged in place, Gabriel leaned into the doorway as the little man tried a second time to shut the portal in his face. "It doesna matter to you that your mistress does not keep her commitments?"

This time a flash of something—outrage, annoyance—flickered across the butler's face. "I regret Miss Depford is not home, my lord; now do allow me to close the door!"

"Not until you tell me where she is."

Gabriel laid more strength against the door, reluctantly impressed when the elderly man managed to hold fast against him.

"My lord, please desist!" the butler gasped. "I have told you all I can!"

"Stodgins!" came a voice from inside the house. "What are you doing?"

The door was suddenly yanked open, and Gabriel stumbled forward a step into the foyer. He grabbed the doorjamb to steady himself and looked up to meet the displeased expression of Catherine's father. Behind Mr. Depford, the old butler leaned against a table, gasping for breath.

"Who might you be?" Depford demanded.

"I am Lord Arneth." Gabriel straightened, brushing at his coat. "I came to call on your daughter."

"She is not at home." Depford gave him a considering look. "Arneth, eh?"

"Aye."

"I have never heard of you." Depford scowled. "You're a Scot."

"I am."

"And you came to call on Catherine."

"And didna I just say that very thing? We were to go driving at four o'clock."

"She went shopping." Depford turned away and began walking down the hallway. "Come with me, Lord Arneth. I should like to speak with you."

Gabriel cast a bemused glance at the butler, who simply closed the door and turned a stoic look him. "This way, my lord."

Gabriel followed the elderly servant down the hall. Depford's study was a comfortable room with soft carpeting and a huge mahogany desk that dominated the space. The man himself sat in a massive chair behind it and waved a hand for him to enter.

"Sit down, Lord Arneth."

Gabriel sat, curiosity more than anything driving his compliance.

"So," Depford said, leaning forward and folding his hands on his desk. "You came to call on Catherine today."

"As I told you already."

"Why do you court my daughter, Lord Arneth?" The sudden hardness in his eyes belied his casual pose.

Gabriel stiffened, braced for battle. "She's a bonny lass, as you must know."

"Aye, my daughter is lovely. She looks much like her mother, who was a Scot like yourself."

"Was she now?"

"She was." Depford slowly leaned backward, gripping the arms of his chair. "And she pined for

Scotland her entire life, until she went mad with it."

"I am sorry for your loss."

Depford raised a brow. "Thank you, but I do not recall telling you that my wife died."

Gabriel shrugged. "'Tis common knowledge."

"Yes, I suppose it is." Depford sighed.

"Mr. Depford." Gabriel waited until the man met his gaze again. "I'll have you know that my intentions are honorable. I am seeking a wife."

"I feared as much. I do not want my daughter going off to Scotland, to pine for her home as her mother did before her."

"Ah." The truth glimmered in his mind. "Do you worry that your daughter might go mad as well?"

"Do not even say that!" Depford slapped a hand on the arm of the chair. "Just know, Lord Arneth, that your suit is not welcome. Should you offer for my daughter, your offer will be refused."

Silence descended. The two men regarded each other as the blunt statement vibrated through the room.

"You canna protect her forever," Gabriel finally said.

"'Tis not your affair."

"Indeed, 'tis more my affair than you ken."

"Stay away from my daughter, Arneth. She's not for the likes of you."

Gabriel jerked to his feet, pride stiffening his spine. "The likes of me? I am chief of my clan, Depford, and an earl as well. I'm told you want a fine title for your daughter. Mine is nae good enough?"

Depford rose as well. "Yours will take her off to the wilds of Scotland. Catherine is a lady and belongs here in London among civilized company."

Gabriel leaned forward, bringing him eye to eye with the older man. "And was that what you thought, George Depford, when you stole Glynis Farlan from her promised bridegroom and carried her off to England?"

Depford jerked back in shock. "How the devil can you know something like that?"

Gabriel barked a laugh. "Because that bridegroom was my uncle. And I—" He jerked a thumb at his own chest. "I am the MacBraedon."

"MacBraedon." Depford whispered the name, and the hint of fear tracing the syllables made Gabriel's blood sing. "Is that why you have come for Catherine? For revenge?"

"She belongs with her people, Depford. 'Tis . . . tradition that the Farlan women wed the chiefs of clan MacBraedon. And your daughter is a Farlan, despite your Sassenach blood."

"No. Never." Depford backed away, his face darkening with rage and fear. He stumbled into his chair, caught himself. "You'll not take my daughter, MacBraedon. I don't give a hang for your family traditions."

"You made that clear enough when you stole Glynis away."

"Glynis went willingly," Depford snapped. "She did not love the man, and she wanted to live a life of comfort and wealth in a civilized city, not your Highland village."

"She had a duty to perform and broke her word. And you helped her. My people have suffered for it, and they willna forget that."

"You do want revenge, don't you?" Depford yanked open a drawer in his desk and grabbed a small pistol. He pointed it, his hand steady. "Get out, blast you! You'll not take my daughter, do you hear?"

Gabriel looked from the pistol to Depford's panicked eyes. "I tried to court her like an English lady, but like her mother, she seems to have no idea of how to keep her promises."

"Go back to Scotland," Depford demanded. "Leave us be."

"I would that I could do just that," Gabriel replied. "Your city smells of refuse, and you English lie to each other with every breath. But I canna return to my people without my bride."

"You will not have her!"

Gabriel grinned. "We will see about that." He turned on his heel, unconcerned with the pistol Depford still aimed at him, and stalked out of the study.

Her head throbbed. The quiet, steady chanting filled her ears and mind until she could barely see straight. Catherine closed her eyes, heedless of the crowd jostling through the linen draper's shop.

A broken vow when peace was sworn . . .

"Do tell me, Catherine, do you prefer the peach silk or the blush?"

Catherine stared blankly at the two pieces of material Beth displayed for her. "What did you say?"

The price shall be a daughter born . . .

"Which one do you think looks better with my complexion?" Beth held one delicate sheet, then the other, near her cheek.

Of Farlan blood to wed our chief . . .

"They look the same." Catherine turned away, focusing on a bolt of soothing blue. The voices in her head grew louder, more insistent. Images followed, scenes from her dream.

"Similar but not the same." Beth contemplated the rainbow array before her. "Perhaps a willow green."

An elderly woman with wild silver hair . . .

Each generation, no relief . . .

"Or maybe a bold jonquil?" Beth reached for a bright yellow roll.

A dagger . . .

Thunder . . .

A red-haired woman crying out in pain . . .

The dagger is her mark of grief . . . the girl who's born to wed our chief . . .

"I just cannot decide," Beth said with a sigh.

The chanting came faster, stronger, louder. Catherine reached out to grip the edge of the display table. Her head spun with images, words, demanding voices.

By eighteen years the girl shall wed . . . else madness comes and sees her dead.

Why had she left her home? Why had she thought it wise to avoid that persistent Scotsman?

The vision of him rose in her mind, and again he reached for her. The voices changed . . . a chaotic chorus of chanting. The words ran together, tumbled over one another, clashed and careened in her head.

He could make the voices stop. Only him. Always him.

"Catherine." He said her name, reached out a hand. "Come home with me."

She whimpered, closing her eyes and pressing her fingertips to her temples. "No. No, I cannot."

"Catherine. You are mine." His words overrode the chanting, which had turned into a tornado of banshees in her brain.

"No. I cannot. No!"

"Catherine." He kept his hand extended, his blue eyes hot with need and knowledge. "Surrender."

"No!" She howled the word, falling to her knees. "No! Stop!"

"Catherine . . ."

"I will not go! I cannot!"

"Catherine!"

"Nonononononononono . . ."

"Catherine!" Someone grabbed her arms, shook her. She opened her eyes and saw Beth's worried face.

"I cannot," she whispered.

"Cannot what?" Beth pleaded.

"You can." Gabriel's voice drowned out the others that haunted her. In her mind, he put his arms around her and held her close. "Come to me, and I will protect you."

Blackness closed over her, and the world faded away.

"Beth, really, I do not need you to accompany me into the house. I am fine." Catherine climbed out of the Waters carriage with the assistance of a footman and headed for the steps. The voices had subsided to a quiet murmur, but the humiliation of fainting in public still burned hot and bright. "Go home. I shall see you at Vauxhall tonight!"

"You had *the vapors*, Cat. That has never happened to you before." Beth held out her hand so the footman could assist her to the ground, then hurried after her and caught up as Catherine lifted her foot to the first stair. "I am coming inside with you, and that is that."

"Not necessary." Catherine marched up the steps. "Go back to the comfort of your carriage."

"I will not." Beth trotted right beside her. "Something is amiss with you, Catherine, and since you are my dearest friend, I am honor-bound to discover what it is."

Catherine stopped two steps from the top and faced Beth. Never before had she seen such determination in her friend's eyes. "No, please, Beth." She bit her lip and glanced at the people strolling by on the street. So far no one paid the two of them any mind, but she lowered her voice anyway. "I know you intend to tell my father what happened today. I would prefer you did not."

"I am quite certain you would prefer that; however, I am worried about you." Distress melted some of the resolve from Beth's expression. "Talk to me, Catherine. Tell me what is wrong."

"Nothing is wrong." Catherine turned to

resume her ascent. "Every young lady experiences the vapors on occasion."

"Not you. You are of substantial constitution and have never succumbed to so much as a sniffle."

"It is nothing."

"It is *something*." They reached the top step, and the butler opened the door. Beth caught Catherine's arm as she made to step through. "Please, Cat. Tell your father what happened or I will."

"I do not want him to know."

"You do not want me to know what, daughter?"

Catherine jerked her head up in alarm and saw her father standing in the doorway. "Papa, I did not realize you were at home."

"I have been waiting for you." His severe expression did not lighten. "Miss Waters, thank you for seeing my daughter to the door."

"But—"

"Good day to you, Miss Waters. Please give my regards to your mother."

Beth swallowed hard and bobbed her head. "I will. Good-bye, Catherine. Mr. Depford." She hurried down the stairs toward her carriage.

George Depford took a step back into the foyer. "Come inside, Catherine."

Slowly, Catherine complied. "Is something amiss, Papa?"

"In my study." As Stodgins closed the door, her father gestured for her to precede him.

She walked down the length of the hallway, very conscious of her father's heavy tread behind her. His stern visage had not changed since he had opened the door. Something was very wrong.

Did he know, somehow, about her dreams? The voices? Had the servants told him about her midnight wanderings?

They walked through the open study door, and he closed it behind them, sealing them in privacy. He swept a hand toward an empty chair in silent command, and as she seated herself, he took his position behind his desk.

"What is this about, Papa?" She curled her fingers around the ends of the chair arms. "Has something happened?"

He leaned forward, folding his hands on the desk. "You had a caller while you were out. Lord Arneth."

She couldn't read his tone or mood. "My heavens! I cannot believe I forgot about that engagement. I'm such a goose!"

"So you *were* scheduled to go driving with him?"

"I was. So silly of me to forget."

"Hmph." He leaned back in his chair, dropping

his hands to his lap, and regarded her carefully. "I am surprised at you, daughter."

Catherine shrugged and gave him a guileless smile. "How so, Papa? I did not intentionally forget the appointment."

"I believe you did, but that is not what surprises me. I am astounded that you would accept a Scotsman as a caller at all."

She frowned, dropping the pretense. "What do you mean? You said you wanted me to become a countess, and Lord Arneth is an earl. I would think you would be in raptures at his interest in me."

He slammed his hand on the desk. "I will not have my daughter running off to the wilds of Scotland! You will wed an Englishman, by God!"

Catherine drew back at the thunderous outburst. "I had no idea you felt so strongly about the subject."

"Stay away from the Scotsman."

His demand only stiffened her spine. "How can you object to a Scottish suitor when you married a Scot yourself?"

"That is *why* I object," he said, pointing a finger at her. "I have told you many times that the Scottish are too emotional, too uncontrollable. I loved your mother, Catherine, but the marriage was an utter disaster."

"Because she went mad."

He sighed. "It was not simply that. She became obsessed with returning to Scotland. I cannot tell you the number of times she nearly lost her life attempting to escape back to the Highlands. I do not want that for you."

"Which?" she asked. "You do not want me to pine for my home, or you do not want me to go mad?"

He sucked in a breath. "Just do as I say."

She nodded slowly. "That is what you fear, isn't it? You are afraid I will go mad as Mother did, so you want me to stay here, close to you."

He pressed his lips together. "I worry about my only child. There is no wrong in that."

"Not at all. But you know more about what happened to Mother than you have ever told me, Papa."

"It is nothing for you to worry about."

"Do not dismiss me!" The sharp tone of her voice had her father raising his eyebrows. She took a deep breath and struggled to calm herself. "I apologize, but this is very frustrating for me. Clearly you are worried that I may go mad as Mother did. Do you not believe I have the right to know the whole of it?"

He regarded her in heavy silence for several long moments. Finally he nodded. "I forget sometimes that you are a grown woman, but as your father, I want what is best for you."

"The truth is what is best for me." She met his gaze steadily. "Tell me about the Farlan curse."

He blinked. "Where did you hear that term?"

"From Mother." She swallowed past the sudden tightening of her throat. "She spoke of it the day she died."

"Dear God." He closed his eyes for a moment, then opened them. "I did not know."

She took a deep breath. "What is the curse?"

"She never told me. And once she got . . . worse, I could not trust what she did say."

"I understand." She gripped the chair arms with clenched fingers. "So Mother married you against her family's wishes and then . . . regretted it?"

"I suppose that is true." He swiped a hand over his jaw. "Her family came after us, tried to carry her off the day we were to wed. But we escaped them."

"Obviously you were able to marry."

"Yes. It's easy enough in Scotland. And when we stepped from the parson's house where we had said our vows, her family stood waiting. They spoke of doom and disloyalty to the clan and a curse. Soon after your birth, the madness began."

"Is that the curse then? The madness?"

"I do not believe in any curse, though I suppose

that is as good a name as any for the condition. Perhaps it is some physical ailment particular to your mother's family. But I do know this—you must stay away from this Scottish earl, Catherine. And you must resist the call of your Scottish blood and maintain decorum at all times."

"I have never done otherwise."

"It is more important than ever now that this man has come courting you." He caught her gaze with his. "What happened today?"

She managed to maintain a calm she did not feel. "Beth and I went shopping."

"That is not what I mean, and well you know it, Catherine. What was it that Miss Waters wanted to tell me? The secret you did not want me to hear?"

"It was nothing." With a casual shrug, Catherine stood. "Perhaps I should consult with Peg on what I will wear to Vauxhall tonight."

"Sit down."

She hesitated, then slowly lowered herself back into her chair.

"Tell me what happened, Catherine, or I will summon Miss Waters and ask her myself."

Catherine sighed. "I simply swooned, Papa. It was nothing of consequence."

"Swooned, eh?" He regarded her with a critical eye. "Perhaps I should summon the physician."

"No! There is no need." Agitated, she rose to her feet again. "Young ladies swoon all the time."

"True, most of them do. But not you. Perhaps you should not attend Vauxhall tonight. I will send our regrets to the Waters ladies."

"But . . . Lord Kentwood said he would attend."

"I am aware of that." He held up a note bearing a flowing feminine script. "But this must take precedence. It arrived today. Lord Kentwood's mother has invited us to tea tomorrow afternoon at her home."

Stunned, she stared at the pale stationery as if it were made of gold. "Such an invitation is unprecedented. Could it mean . . . ?"

"That Lady Kentwood would like to meet you? That her son is seriously considering offering for you? I believe so."

She placed a hand on her bosom as if she could stop her fluttering heart from leaping from her chest. "I am overwhelmed."

He stood up. "You understand now why you must be at your best tomorrow. So you will go to your chamber now and remain there for the rest of the evening. I will send our regrets to the Waters ladies and to Lord Kentwood for this evening."

"But—"

"That is the end of the matter." He slashed

his hand through the air. "You have been acting strange of late, daughter. Very distracted and unfocused. Trust me when I say that you will benefit from the rest."

She nodded, and turned away to obey her sire. She was trembling from head to toe, both from the possibility that Lord Kentwood might soon ask for her hand, and from the knowledge that she must not have been hiding her recent difficulties as well as she had thought if her father had noticed enough to comment.

The question was, did she have enough time to become Lady Kentwood before anyone guessed the truth?

Chapter 7

Gabriel stormed into the house like an ocean gale, his mood black and his pride smarting.

"What foul wind has sent you flying through the door without so much as wiping your feet?" Donald stepped into his path and scowled at the scuffed marble floor of the foyer. "We dinna have maids to clean up after you, *Your Lordship*."

Gabriel glared at the elderly man. "Keep a civil tongue in your head, old man. We've more to worry about than the bloody floor."

"Do we now?" Donald bristled. "I'll thank you to remember who you're talking to, laddie."

"Believe me, I canna forget it." Gabriel took off his hat and tossed it on the table. "Your lass is playing games with me, Donald. Today she wasna home when I went to fetch her."

Donald shrugged. "Farlan women are known to change their minds with the wind."

"Aye, and we all ken the consequences! Look at where we are now because of a Farlan woman."

Donald's blue-gray eyes glittered with the light of battle. "Dinna bring up Glynis, Gabriel."

"How can I not, when her Sassenach husband has told me that no daughter of his will be marrying a Scotsman?"

Donald sucked in an outraged breath. "He didna dare!"

"Aye, he did. He said Catherine Depford is not for the likes o' me and willna be running off to the Highlands with an uncivilized man such as myself."

"As if a Farlan lass would find London more to her liking!" Donald scoffed.

"Indeed." Gabriel flexed his shoulders. "To give the man credit, he fears for the lass. He worries that she will go mad like her mother."

"And so she will until you wed her. Bloody interfering Sassenach!"

"He doesna know about the curse."

"And would probably dismiss it if he did!" Donald made a fist and shook it. "He doesna ken who he is dealing with."

"Aye, he does."

"Oh really now?" Donald grinned with unholy glee. "Did you tell him then?"

"I did."

"I wish I could have seen that." Donald gave a wicked chuckle.

"Hey now, what's all the ruckus?" Brodie and the twins came out of the library with Patrick trailing behind.

"Depford claims that a MacBraedon isna good enough for his daughter," Donald said.

All four men scowled as they came near. "Does he now?" Brodie said softly.

"Indeed," Gabriel said. He met Brodie's gaze in a moment of perfect understanding.

"Is he still breathing?" Patrick asked, eyes narrowed and hands fisted.

"He is," Gabriel said.

"I suppose we'll be paying a visit then." Brodie grinned and glanced at the others. "'Tis a good thing, since we've all been sitting about getting fat this past week."

"Speak for yourself," Donald grumbled. "I've fetched and carried for the lot of you!"

"I've tried to win the lass by English rules," Gabriel said, "and for that, all I've gotten was the door closed in my face."

"Ha!" Brodie smacked his hands together. "Carry her off, will you? I'll fetch the rope."

"I dinna know if it's come to that yet."

"What?" Brodie stopped mid-step. "If you'll not court her like an Englishman, then the other option is to simply take her."

"Unless she comes willingly."

"But will she?" Angus asked. "Or does she feel as her father does about the Scots?"

Donald thrust out his chest. "No Farlan lass would turn her back on her people!"

They all stared at him.

Donald sighed, deflating. "Except for Glynis, I suppose."

"We willna know until I ask her." Gabriel clapped a hand on Donald's shoulder and looked at his men. "But understand this. If the lass resists, then I *will* do what is right for our people and carry her back to where she belongs. Maybe if she sees the damage the curse has wrought, she will be moved to put things to rights."

"Or maybe her rich father will come after you with a noose in his hand," Patrick grumbled.

"That may yet come to pass," Gabriel agreed. "But once we're home—in the Highlands—none can best us."

"Aye, 'tis true." Brodie thrust his fist in the air and roared the battle cry of the MacBraedons. Patrick, Angus, and Andrew threw back their heads and echoed the call.

While Gabriel simply grinned at the antics of his

men, Donald snorted in disgust and waited for the uproar to settle. When it did, he looked at the four of them through slitted eyes. "Do I need to remind you that we're still in London and canna be reiving away the lass as if she were simple cattle?"

"We can indeed, Donald," Gabriel assured him.

"'Tis a simple thing," Patrick chortled, then subsided at a warning look from Gabriel.

"And how do you mean to be accomplishing that wee miracle, Gabriel MacBraedon?" Donald demanded.

"Donald, do you nae want to get the best of the Englishman?" Angus challenged.

"I do, I do. But I willna have the lass hurt or frightened in the doing of it." Donald stared them down as if he were still a young man, well muscled and battle ready. "It willna do Gabriel a bit of good if the girl refuses to marry him after all the trouble."

"She *will* marry me," Gabriel said. "Have no fear of that, Donald."

"But I do have fear of it," Donald retorted. "You mean to raid Depford's home and steal the lass away and marry her by force if necessary!"

"What else am I to do?" Gabriel demanded. "My people are starving. *Your* people are starving, Donald Farlan. And the only way to make it stop is for me to marry your granddaughter!"

Stark silence followed his thunderous tone.

"I ken the ways of the curse, Gabriel," Donald finally said, "for wasn't it my own daughter who broke her word and doomed us to this cause?"

"'Twas indeed," Gabriel agreed. "And 'tis my duty as chief of the MacBraedons to wed this lass and put things to rights." He softened his tone, well aware of his men watching the exchange. "She'll be no prisoner, Donald, but a cherished wife who will bear me sons. And the curse will be appeased, and prosperity will return to the land."

"But for how long?" Donald asked. "How many generations can we live like this, slave to a curse?"

Gabriel barked a laugh that held no humor. "'Tis I who am slave to the curse, not any of you."

"Both clans—" Donald began, bristling.

"*My* clan." Gabriel stabbed a thumb at his own chest, silencing the other man. "Since the moment my father died, *I* became heir to my uncle and inherited this responsibility. *I* am the one who must wed a lass with the mark of the dagger, no matter my feelings, to keep our people from dying."

Donald scowled. "Are you saying you dinna care about the lass?"

"Perhaps in time, some feeling may grow between us," Gabriel said. "But nonetheless, I will treat her with all the honor due a chief's lady. This I swear to you."

Donald glanced at the now silent MacBraedon men, then back to Gabriel. "See that you do, else you will get no more help from me."

"Agreed."

Donald nodded once, then turned and left the foyer, leaving the MacBraedon chief alone with his men to plan his battle strategy.

The clock chimed eight, and Catherine looked up with some surprise from the novel she had been reading. It was nearly suppertime, and Peg had not come to help her change for dinner.

With a frown, she marked her page and set the book down, then rose and pulled the bell. Her head still felt foggy from her fainting spell earlier in the day, and the voices continued to whisper in the back of her mind, like the quiet burble of a distant brook.

She cast a glance at the clock. Five minutes had passed, and no one had replied to her summons. She went to the door, hoping there was a chambermaid or other servant out in the hall who would go to fetch Peg for her.

But the knob did not turn.

She grabbed it with both hands, hoping the door was simply stuck, and tugged, rattling the portal on its hinges. Had they locked her in? Was she now a prisoner in her own home?

She slapped the door with the palm of her hand. "Peg, where are you? Peg!"

No one responded.

She banged again, fear rising into her throat, seizing her like an invisible fist. "Peg, come open the door! I am locked in!"

Still silence. No one heeded her cries.

She clenched her fingers and pounded on the door with her fist, not wanting to be like her mother. No, not like Mama, whom they locked away and tied to the bed to keep from hurting herself. Not like Mama, who had talked in riddles and sang strange songs. Not like Mama, who had jumped to her death with an unholy smile on her face . . .

Numbness swept through her, and her knees weakened. She sank to the floor, one hand sliding along the wood of the door in entreaty. She was locked in. Imprisoned. Would they tie her down, too?

Her breath shuddered from between her lips. Perhaps it was simply a mistake. Perhaps the lock was faulty or had triggered on its own. Her father did not think she was mad, only feared that it might happen. She could not blame him for the thought; didn't she believe the same thing?

She sat on the floor, her back against the door. Or was it already too late? Had she gone completely mad and they were simply too kind to tell her? Was she doomed to live as her mother had, confined to her rooms and bound for safety, babbling in tongues to people no one could see?

A sound came from the hallway, and Catherine froze, holding her breath, as she identified the swish of a skirt and the scuff of a slipper. Someone was outside the door.

Should she call out? Or would her visitor simply pass by, ignoring the chamber where the madwoman lived?

The clank of silver on china reached her ears through the portal. Then the clinking of keys. She scrambled to her feet, awkward, her skirts catching beneath the heels of her slippers. As the key turned in the lock, she stumbled backward, her gaze locked on the slowly turning knob.

The portal cracked open, then wider as Peg put her head in. "Oh, you're awake!" she exclaimed. A bump of her hip had the door swinging wide open to reveal the tray she held, which was laden with food. "Your father thought you might be more comfortable eating supper in your room tonight."

"I feel quite well," Catherine said, watching as Peg carried the tray over to a small table. "I can certainly go down to the dining room."

Peg turned away from the food and frowned at Catherine. "You will do no such thing. Your father wants you well rested to call upon Lord Kentwood's mother tomorrow."

"I was supposed to see Lord Kentwood at Vauxhall *tonight*." She came forward. "Peg, what is happening?"

"What do you mean?" Glancing away, Peg made herself busy setting out dishes from the tray. "Come and eat your supper now."

"Peg, tell me." She laid a hand on Peg's arm. The maid froze in the act of setting out the silverware. "Did someone lock me in my room?"

Peg took a deep breath and finally met Catherine's gaze. "Your father wants the best for you."

"And he believes locking me away is best?" Catherine squeezed her eyes shut for a moment. "What have I done to deserve that?"

"Fainted clear away at the linen draper's, that's what. Miss Waters sent a note around, and your father turned three shades of white when he read it."

"Oh, for heaven's sake! Show me a woman who has not had the vapors at least once in her life."

"You're looking at her," Peg said, throwing back her shoulders proudly. "Not even when my babes were birthed."

"Well, this is the only time it has ever happened to me, and I think locking me in my room out of some mistaken sense of panic is simply ridiculous."

"He's only trying to do the best by you." Peg pulled out the chair and gestured to the hot dinner spread out on the table. "Sit now and eat. You must keep up your strength."

Recognizing defeat, Catherine sat. "I am fine, Peg. There is nothing wrong with me."

"I know, Miss Catherine."

"You would tell me, would you not, Peg? If I appeared . . . different."

Peg gave an insulted sniff. "And haven't I cared for you well enough these past weeks since Mellie left you?"

"You have," Catherine agreed. She lifted her spoon and tasted the soup. Onion and beef exploded on her tongue.

Peg busied herself by collecting Catherine's pelisse, which was draped over a chair, and hanging it in the wardrobe. "Your father is doing what he thinks right to care for you, and it seems to me that you could take advantage of the opportunity and get lots of rest and eat a good supper. Then tomorrow he can see that you are right as rain."

Catherine took another sip of soup, smiling at the simple logic of the idea. "You are a wise woman, Peg Ross."

Peg gave a chuckle and shut the wardrobe. "Now if I could only get my sons to understand that."

* * *

After Catherine had finished her meal, Peg helped her change into her night rail and then left with the empty tray. To Catherine's relief, the maid did not lock her in this time. She took comfort in the servant's kindness.

Though the hour wasn't all that late, not even ten o'clock, black night had fallen. Twisting the curling end of her single braid, Catherine wandered over to her bedroom window and looked out over the small garden behind the town house. Fat storm clouds blocked the moon and stars, casting a shadow over the earth. Here and there a light could be seen from a distant building, but otherwise the night hung pregnant with a predatory stillness that foreshadowed the brewing storm.

She opened the window and let in the air, breathing in the sweet fragrance of the flowers below. A gentle breeze stirred the lace at her wrists and brought with it the tang of impending rain. The distant sounds of carriage wheels and horses' hooves reached her from the street, but they seemed very far away. From another world.

How simple life would be if this were just any other night, and she just any other woman.

With a sigh, she turned from the window but left it open, better to enjoy the scent of the approaching squall. She blew out her candle and climbed into bed and watched the white curtains billow with the breeze as she waited for sleep to claim her.

But her mind would not quiet.

She had not been ready for her condition to attract her father's attention, and she certainly did not want to jeopardize Lord Kentwood offering for her. These episodes of madness—along with a certain persistent Scottish lord—set obstacles in her way that only made the whole situation more difficult.

Her greatest fear seemed imminent, that Papa would lock her away permanently as he had Mama. That she would have no kind of life, imprisoned in the four walls of her room. That she might die there while yet a young woman. Tonight had been the mere shadow of what might come.

She wanted to live, by God. She wanted a husband who would care for her, someone kind and trustworthy who would see to her comfort even if the madness took her. She wanted children—to see them laugh, to watch them grow. But what kind of mother would she make? How could she condemn innocents to share such a life? No. She didn't want to chance it. But if she wed a man of Lord Kentwood's prestige, he would need heirs.

The minutes ticked by, and then an hour. Her eyelids grew heavier, her thoughts flitting into the silly fantasies somewhere between awake and asleep. The whispering in her mind, so quiescent until now, slowly increased in volume. Chanting that verse. That curse. But she was too tired to fight it. She let the voices wash over her, growing louder and more insistent, and she let them carry her away as if on an ocean wave. Weightless. Carefree. Surrendering.

> *A broken vow when peace was sworn,*
> *The price shall be a daughter born*
> *Of Farlan blood to wed our chief—*
> *Each generation, no relief.*

She floated through the familiar dream like a ghost, watching the action as she had so many times before. And this time, when the mists parted and he came to her, she stepped into his arms before he could reach for her.

"My love." He caressed her face, and the witch and the words faded away, leaving only the two of them.

"Gabriel." She whispered his name, glorying in merely saying the word. A word, a name that meant all that was joy and freedom to her.

Again he wore nothing but a plaid wrapped around him. Eagerly she traced her hands over his bare chest, her fingers shaking. This need . . . so uncontrollable. It swept her along like liquid fire. Her body hungered for him, for all the things he could teach her.

He brushed her hair back over her shoulder and bent to nibble her throat, his mouth caressing that tender place where neck and shoulder met. He held her fast against him with strong hands, and she could feel the heat of his body through the thin cotton of her night rail.

"Gabriel," she murmured.

He raised his head. "I am here, lass." Like a conqueror, he took her mouth as if he had a right to. As if it belonged to him.

And she only wanted him to take more.

Around them the night burst into fury, thunder booming and lightning flashing. Wind whipped at their garments, all but shredding her thin nightclothes. She clung to him, grabbing at his muscular arms lest she get lost in the storm.

"You belong to me." He captured her gaze with his, hot and hungry. "Say it. Tell me."

"I am yours." She shuddered at the mere words. Her body felt like someone else's, so swollen and hungry, so aching with need.

He wrapped his arms around her, held her fast as he kissed her again. She groaned with the pleasure of it, tipping back her head, letting him have his way with her mouth. Anything he wanted. Anything.

A huge boom of thunder jerked them apart. Suddenly they stood on the edge of a cliff . . . and she was slipping!

She cried out and reached for him as the dirt beneath her feet crumbled. He shouted her name, grabbed for her, but the pebbles and soil fell away. With a cry, she fell.

Into blackness.

An abyss.

A nothingness.

"Catherine!" His voice echoed after her, despairing.

"Gabriel!" she cried out—and woke herself with the terror of it.

She jerked straight up in bed, sobs trapped in her throat, tears trickling down her cheeks. She wrapped her arms around herself, shaking, utterly destroyed by the loss of . . . something. Outside, thunder and lightning raged.

"There now, lass, dinna cry so." Gabriel's voice came to her out of the darkness. "I'm here."

With a sharp gasp, she shrank back into the pillows. "You cannot be here."

"But I am." A shadow moved away from the billowing curtains of the open window.

Her hands shaking, she reached for the lamp beside the bed. It took two tries to strike the tinder and light the wick. When the glow lit the room, she looked toward the voice, afraid of what she would see.

Gabriel MacBraedon stood in the middle of her bedchamber, dressed in trousers and a simple white shirt that clung damply to every sculpted muscle of his fine form. He reached up with both hands and slicked back his dripping hair. "'Tis a wretched night to be paying a call, I wager, but I couldna wait another moment to see you, sweet Catherine."

She gaped. "How did you get in here?"

He gave her a wicked smile that did nothing to dispel her scandalous longings. "A man can do anything for the right reward."

"What reward?" She jerked the coverlet to her throat, nervous and excited both at once.

"To look upon your beauty, of course."

"Rubbish."

He started toward the bed. "'Tis God's truth."

"Stop, or I will scream."

He paused, grinning like a pirate. "And when your father comes bursting down the door to save you, then you'll be compromised, won't you? And you'll finally be mine."

Anticipation battled with morality. "I am not yours."

He took the final step to the edge of the bed and reached out to toy with the end of the braid hanging over her shoulder. "Aye, you're mine, Catherine Depford. And after tonight, you'll be the first to admit it."

Chapter 8

She shoved his hand away. "I am sick to death of everyone telling me what I will do or what I will feel. My life is my own!"

Gabriel retreated a step back. "I wish that were true, lass. For both of us."

"What do you know of it?" She pushed the blankets away, heedless of her mode of undress, and stalked past him to the chair where her wrapper lay. Shrugging into the garment, she turned to face him as she tied the sash, jerking the ends tightly. "I do not notice you discomfited by wild dreams and crazed voices in your head." She stopped, listening. "They are gone."

"What is?"

"The voices. Again."

His brows came together in concern. "Lass, I fear for you, to be sure."

"Well, do not." Lifting her chin, she sat down in

the chair. "Now tell me what you are doing in my bedchamber, Gabriel or Lord Arneth or whatever you are calling yourself today."

Irritation flickered in his expression. "Either will do well enough. I've come to talk to you, Catherine. To tell you the truth."

"That," she snapped, "would be a distinct change."

"It has come to my attention that you dinna ken the forces at work between us."

"There is *nothing* between us. It may come to your attention that I was not at home to go driving with you this afternoon."

His expression darkened. "I noticed," he growled.

"That is because I did not want to see you, Lord Arneth. You tricked me into allowing you to call."

He stiffened. "There was no trickery involved, Catherine Depford. 'Tis attraction, pure and simple."

She blew out an impatient breath. "I have an understanding with another gentleman, Lord Arneth. It is very bad *ton* to accept calls from one gentleman when another is on the brink of proposing marriage."

"*I did propose marriage.*"

"You consider that a proposal? That *command* to wed you?" She gave a disparaging sniff.

"Who is he? Is it that puny Englishman I saw you with at the balloon launch?"

"Yes. Lord Kentwood. We will suit quite well."

"Will you now?" He came over to her, his very posture all possessive male. "I offered first. And I think you know by now how well *we* fit together."

"If you wish to wed me, then speak to my father."

"I already have, and he told me no suit of mine would be accepted."

"There you are then. We cannot wed."

"We *can*, and we *will*."

"This is getting us nowhere." Unnerved, aroused by his nearness, she folded her arms across her body so it would not betray her. "What is this truth you came to tell me?"

He considered her for a long moment, blue eyes hot with need and frustration. "Verra well. Perhaps you will come to your senses when I tell you the tale."

"Then by all means, tell the tale. But do hurry, as I find I am growing sleepy."

He scowled at her. "There is much to tell, lass. Starting with the curse."

She jerked straight up in her seat. "The Farlan curse?"

He snorted. "Farlan curse, is it? 'Twas cast by a

127

MacBraedon because of Farlan betrayal. I'd say 'tis a MacBraedon curse."

She narrowed her eyes at him. "Oh, really."

"Aye, 'tis true. Generations ago the MacBraedons and the Farlans were enemies. There were many battles between the two."

"It seems the MacBraedons cannot get along with anyone."

"We are warriors, lass, and believe in fighting for what we want."

She swallowed hard, not in the least naive about what this warrior wanted.

He continued. "Peace was to be sworn between the two clans, by way of wedding a Farlan lass to the MacBraedon chief. But the Farlan chief never intended his daughter to wed his enemy and tried to kill the MacBraedon on the night before the wedding."

"Did he succeed?"

He cast her a look of annoyance. "Of course not, else I would not be here now."

She held up her hands in surrender. "It was a simple question."

"You do not take this seriously." He strode over and leaned down, trapping her in her chair with his hands braced on the arms. His blue eyes burned with a ferocity that sent goose pimples prickling along her arms. "Listen well. *A broken vow when peace was sworn—*"

"*How do you know that?*" Struggling to breathe, she shoved at his chest, but he did not budge.

"*The price shall be a daughter born of Farlan blood to wed our chief—*"

"How do you know that? Stop it! Stop it!" She pummeled his chest and shoulders, panic all but choking her.

"Hush." He grabbed her flailing fists in one hand and placed a finger over her lips with the other. "Now will you listen?"

She nodded, quietly sobbing, unable to stop her trembling.

"There's a lass." He caressed her lips, then stepped back.

"How do you know those words?" she managed.

"'Tis the curse, Catherine. Cast some three hundred years ago by a MacBraedon crone who practiced the old ways."

"Those words . . . that is what the voices say."

"What voices, lass? You mentioned them before."

"In my head." She squeezed her eyes shut. "Over and over, all the time. I hear voices chanting those words." She opened her eyes and looked at him for answers. "Except when you are here."

"Now that's an interesting puzzle."

"So you do not know why that might be?"

He shrugged. "I expect 'tis part of the curse."

She sucked in a shuddering breath. "Tell me what you know."

He gave a nod. "Back to history then. When the Farlan chief tried to kill the MacBraedon, the crone cast the curse to force peace between the clans. Every generation a Farlan lass must wed the MacBraedon chief to keep that peace."

"What happens if she does not?"

"If she doesna wed her destined husband, then the prosperity of the MacBraedons will suffer. The clan will starve."

"I see. And the Farlans?"

"The clan shares in the poverty that follows." He paused, then said gently, "And the Farlan lass goes mad."

She gasped, covering her mouth with her hands. "My mother was supposed to marry the MacBraedon chief," she choked.

"Aye, she was."

"But she wed my father instead. And—"

"She went mad," he finished for her. "'Twas the curse."

"Dear Lord." She closed her eyes for a moment as she struggled with the implications of his words. "It is a fantastic tale."

"I know you dinna ken aught about this." He crouched before her and tenderly took her hands. "Had you been raised with the clans, you would have known the whole of it from your birth."

"But I was not raised in Scotland. I never understood why my mother went mad. I thought it was some sort of family illness."

He gave her a crooked smile. "That it is, in a manner of speaking."

"Do not joke about this."

The smile melted from his face. "I assure you, Catherine, I take the welfare of my clan very seriously." He released her hands and stood. "For nearly twenty years, my people have lived on the brink of starvation because of your mother's actions. 'Tis my duty to set things to rights again."

She narrowed her eyes in realization. "You are the MacBraedon clan chief. That means you need to marry a Farlan to break the curse."

"Break the curse? Nay. The way to do that is nigh impossible. But appease the curse? Bring prosperity back to my lands and food to the bellies of my clan? Aye, 'tis the only way."

"You said you wanted *me* to be your bride!"

"That I did."

"Impossible. You are mad." She scrambled out of the chair, pushing past him to head for the bell-pull. "I am calling for my father."

"Nay, you willna do any such thing." He caught her around the waist with one arm, pulling her back against his warm, damp body. "'Twas your mother who broke her word, Catherine Depford, and now 'tis your duty to balance the scales."

She curled her fingers around the muscled band of his arm and tugged, but the result was like a butterfly pulling at a bull. Nothing. With a sigh of surrender, she let her body sag back against his, trying desperately not to enjoy the scandalous contact. "I will not be forced into marriage to pay for my mother's mistake."

"There willna be any force." He nuzzled her ear, tugging her a hint closer. "You'll be coming to my bed willingly enough."

She sucked in a breath as his teeth touched her earlobe. "I remind you, I am a virtuous woman, Gabriel MacBraedon, and such talk is . . . inappropriate."

He chuckled, the vibration in his chest rumbling against her shoulder blades. "I intend to wed you, sweet Catherine. You had best accept that."

"I will not." She dug her fingernails into his arm. With a hissed curse, he released her, and she spun to face him. "Find yourself another Farlan woman. I will not wed you."

He rubbed at his gouged flesh and gave a dark chuckle. "Oh, sweet Catherine, you are indeed a true Farlan woman, and I'll have no other."

"You must. I will not marry you." She folded her arms to emphasize the point.

"You didna let me finish my tale." He eyed her, then took a step toward her. She moved to the side, but he paced her, curse him. "I canna marry any lass but you. God's truth."

"You mean you *will* not." She dodged in a different direction, but he matched her again, seeming to anticipate her moves.

"I mean I *canna*." He followed her as she took another step in a different direction.

She found herself in a corner between the wall and the bed. Trapped, she folded her arms again and tried to project an air of strength. "Have you taken a vow? Were we betrothed from birth? Why can you not wed someone else? Someone who was raised a Farlan?"

"Because of this." Bold as you please, he stroked a finger along the outside of her left breast. "This mark determines the chief's bride."

She nearly choked. "How did you know—wait. No. This cannot be happening."

"The dagger is her mark of grief, the girl who's born to wed our chief."

"Stop that!" She covered her ears. "It must be too late. I must be mad already. That is the answer. This is all in my imagination."

"Nay, lass. You have a birthmark here—" He touched her again. "'Tis shaped like a dagger."

She simply stared at him. "Have you been spying on me?"

He shrugged. "My clan has been looking for my bride for some time now."

"I see." She took her hands from her ears and took a slow step back. "I thought I was going mad, but now I know the truth. *You* are the one who has no concept of reality."

"You may well be going mad," he said. "I recall you just celebrated your eighteenth birthday."

She lifted her chin. "And if I have?"

He shrugged. "'Tis when the madness begins, unless you've wed the chief."

"How convenient."

"'Tis the truth."

"Your truth."

He rolled his eyes. "Blessed saints, woman, why will you not accept what is?"

"Well, what do you expect? You come to my bedchamber with this unbelievable Banbury tale and expect me to believe you! How do I know you are not taking advantage of me? How do I know you do not want to wed me for my fortune?"

"How else did I know what was happening to you?" he countered. "And what about the mark? I know where it is and what it looks like."

"You managed to get into my room," she shot

back. "Perhaps you found some way to spy on me in the bath!"

He rolled his eyes and glanced toward heaven. "God's teeth, but you're a devil of a woman! Come with me back to Scotland and see for yourself."

"I am *not* going to Scotland."

"Not even to meet your kin?"

"My kin?" She frowned at him.

"Your family, lass. The Farlans."

"Oh." She turned away, arms folded across her stomach. "I must admit, that is a tempting thought."

"Come with me." He came over to her and rested his hands on her shoulders. "Come meet your family and let *them* tell you about the curse."

She flashed him a scowl over her shoulder. "I do not believe in curses."

"Don't you now?" He traced a finger along her spine. "You wake a hunger in me, Catherine, that I havena felt before. Never in my days. How can you deny there is a curse?"

She shrugged away from him. "That sounds more like lust, Gabriel MacBraedon."

He chuckled. "There isna much difference between the two, to my way of thinking."

"How can you expect me to believe this?"

"Dinna think about it right now. Think about

135

meeting your family. About having your questions answered."

"You would have me believe the answer is a curse."

"I believe it is, but if you meet the Farlans, they might tell you otherwise." He gave her a coaxing smile. "You can give me your decision tomorrow."

"A generous allotment of time," she tossed back.

"I will come again tomorrow for your answer."

"I can give it to you now. N—"

He cut her off. "Think about the possibilities. This is a chance to take back the control of your life."

Poised to make a comment, she hesitated at his words. "Control," she murmured.

"Aye. You claim you hear voices. You fear that every man who courts you fancies your fortune rather than you. You intend to wed a pasty-faced Englishman rather than a vigorous man like myself who will make your marriage a pleasure beyond bearing." He lowered his voice to a coaxing tone. "Make your own decisions, Catherine Depford. Decide what you will do and what you will not. Learn the truth."

"I cannot listen anymore." She covered her ears with her hands and shut her eyes.

He chuckled. "Is that the way of it then?"

She opened her eyes to glare at him. "One of us is mad, Gabriel MacBraedon. I just do not know if it is you or me."

"Come with me and find out."

"I think you should leave now." She hugged herself and watched him with solemn eyes. "You have told me so many things tonight. I must think about them clearly."

"I will be back tomorrow night for your answer, lass." He narrowed his eyes. "Dinna make me hunt for you."

"As long as you promise to abide by my answer, then I will do as you wish."

"We are agreed then." He stepped forward, his gaze settling on her mouth. "A kiss good-bye, sweet Catherine?"

She backed up a step. "I do not believe—"

"Psst! Gabriel!"

The loud whisper came from the direction of the window. A young man leaned into the room with his elbows on the windowsill, damp hair clinging to his scalp. As they watched, he swayed, grabbed the sill with both hands, and looked down into the night below. "Have a care, Angus!" he hissed.

"Patrick, what deviltry are you about?" Gabriel demanded. "Get down from there!"

Catherine sent him an arch look. "You know this young scalawag?"

"He's my brother," Gabriel grumbled.

"Good evening, miss." Having gained control of his perch, Patrick gave her a respectful nod, then looked at his brother. "The storm is breaking, so we'd best be on our way."

Gabriel put his hands on his hips. "Are you in charge now, to be telling the MacBraedon when to go and when to stay?"

"No, *your lordship*. 'Twas Brodie who did that." Patrick gave a quick grin. "'Tis just that I am the lightest."

"How did you get up here, young man?" Catherine moved over to him and looked out her window to see a human ladder lined up along the wall beneath. "My heavens!"

"Angus is at the bottom," Patrick told her. "And Andrew on top of him and Brodie on top of him . . . and then me." He gave a quick glance at her attire, then jerked his gaze back to her face, his cheeks reddening. "You *are* a bonny lass; Gabriel was right about that."

"Stop your flirting," came a voice from the darkness below. "You may be the lightest of us, Patrick MacBraedon, but you're far from a feather at that!"

"I'm waiting for my brother to finish his courting, Brodie Alexander!"

Gabriel came over to the window, and Catherine

turned to face him. "I was right," she said. "It is you who are mad."

"Not mad at all," Patrick interjected. "Just Scots."

Gabriel cast his brother an impatient look. "Down with you, Patrick."

"Aye, Gabriel. Good night, miss." With a wink of blue eyes so like Gabriel's, Patrick scrambled down the human ladder with all the nimbleness of a circus monkey.

"Until tomorrow," Gabriel said, then pressed a quick kiss to her lips. As she raised her fingers to her tingling mouth, he swung his leg over the windowsill. "I'm coming down, Brodie."

"Come away," said the disembodied voice.

Gabriel swung his other leg over to sit on the sill, then flipped himself onto his stomach, grabbed the edges of the window frame, and carefully lowered himself until he hung from the sill, facing her. "Until tomorrow."

"You are mad, all of you." With this pronouncement, she closed the windows, narrowly missing his fingers, and flicked the lock.

His laughter echoed back to her.

Catherine woke the next morning to bright sunshine and sweet birdsong. The storm of the night before—and her visitor—seemed like part of a dream.

Peg bustled in while Catherine still lay abed. "Good morning to you, Miss Catherine. Your father would like you to join him for breakfast this morning."

Nodding, Catherine climbed from the bed and stretched.

"I've just pressed your yellow morning dress. It seems quite the thing for a morning as beautiful as this."

Catherine nodded again and made her way to the chamber pot. She took care of her morning ablutions, and only as she splashed water on her face from the basin did she realize that the voices were silent this morning.

What had Gabriel done to her to wreak such a miracle? Had it been his kiss?

Nonsense. Only in fairy stories did a man's kiss cause a miracle. And only one from a true love at that. She would never have considered Gabriel MacBraedon to be her true love. He was too bold, too passionate. He had no respect for the proper etiquette of things, just pushed his way through like a general commanding the troops. His domineering actions vexed her on a basic female level.

Even though when he touched her, her entire body surrendered to him without question.

She reached for a cloth and dried her face, then regarded herself in the mirror. The man was daft;

there was no doubt of it. All his talk of curses and destiny. All his proclamations that she was fated to be his wife because the mystical forces declared it so. How could he expect her to believe such a tale?

So far Gabriel MacBraedon had not shown her anything beyond hot passion to make her consider him a possible mate. Could she trust him to care for her properly? Of course not. Not like Lord Kentwood.

Gabriel had mentioned something about his people starving. If his clan needed the money that much, then he could not be wealthy in his own right. And while she did not object to her fortune being used to help those in need, the question still came back to his level of devotion to his wife. Would he put his clan first over her needs, no matter what happened to her? How could she trust him?

Lord Kentwood was a man who understood responsibility. Even if she were completely addled beyond all hope of sanity, she knew he would treat her with the dignity due his wife.

Catherine came out from behind the screen and made her way to the stool in front of the vanity table.

"There you are," Peg said, turning to Catherine with her jewel chest in her hands. "Will you be wearing the pearls today or your locket?"

Catherine glanced at the primrose yellow dress hanging on the door of the wardrobe, then back to the maid. "The locket today, I think. Unless you feel the pearls would be more the thing."

Peg gasped, her eyes widening with shock. The wooden chest fell from her hands, bursting open as it hit the floor. Jewelry spilled out, glittering in the morning sunlight.

"Peg? What is the matter? Are you ill?"

Peg swallowed hard before answering. "Miss Catherine," she said slowly, "when did you learn to speak Gaelic?"

Chapter 9

"What are you talking about, Peg?"

Slowly the maid bent to pick up the jewel chest. She scooped the gems into the box, then closed the lid and stood again. "You're speaking Gaelic, miss. The language of the Scots."

"What?" Catherine jerked out of the chair, her heart in her throat. "I am doing no such thing!"

"You are." Peg set the jewelry chest on the vanity table.

"I am not! Peg, I do not find this jest of yours amusing."

"I do not know how, but that is the language you are speaking, Miss Catherine."

"Impossible." Catherine leaned on her vanity table and peered at her reflection in the mirror. "I look no different." She jerked away and strode for the door.

"Miss, where are you going? You're not dressed!"

Ignoring her, Catherine yanked open the door and went into the hall. "You there!" she called to a footman passing by. "Where is my father?"

The footman gaped at her attire.

"I asked you a question. Where is my father?"

The servant raised his eyes to her face, confusion evident on his. "I am sorry, miss. What did you say?"

"Where can I find my father?"

The footman frowned and glanced behind her. "What's she saying, Peg? I cannot understand the words."

"How can you not understand me?" Catherine demanded. "How?" His continued puzzlement sent fear fluttering in her belly. She turned helplessly to her maid. "Peg?"

"Is she well?" the footman asked, peering at her with concern. "Shall I fetch Mr. Depford?"

Peg bustled forward and took Catherine by the arms, guiding her back to her room. "Everything is fine, Stephen. Please tell Mr. Depford that Miss Catherine is not feeling well enough for breakfast."

"I will." The footman gave Catherine one last, puzzled glance, then hurried down the hallway.

Catherine allowed Peg to propel her through the doorway and into her bedchamber. Anxiety twisted her insides. "Why did he not understand me, Peg?"

"You weren't speaking English." Peg led her back to the chair.

Catherine sat down, staring blankly at her reflection. "I do not speak this Gaelic, only English and some French." She grabbed Peg's arm as the maid started to turn away. "How is it that *you* understand me?"

Peg hesitated, then admitted, "I speak Gaelic, miss."

Catherine withdrew her hand. "You are Scottish?"

"I am." Peg stepped away to the wardrobe and came back bearing Catherine's wrapper.

Catherine took the garment and spread it over her lap, suspicion twining itself around her thoughts. "Are you a Farlan, Peg?"

"Not at all." Unfazed by the question, Peg set about pulling the rest of the morning's clothing from the wardrobe. "I was born a MacBraedon, but I married a Ross. God rest his soul."

"A MacBraedon." Catherine narrowed her eyes. "Did *he* send you?"

"Did who send me?"

Catherine rolled her eyes. "Gabriel MacBraedon."

"The MacBraedon? No, no. I was sent by the clan, true, but not by the chief himself."

"So you agree you were sent. Why?"

Peg smiled at her, then patted her hand as she

145

bustled past her to lay the garments she had collected on the bed. "To care for you, Miss Catherine, until it was time for you to return home."

"I am home."

"Your home in Scotland is what I meant."

"This is insanity!"

"It's the curse." Peg spread out chemise and stays on the bed. "It's time for you to return to Scotland and do your duty by your clan."

"Not you as well! I do not believe in curses."

"What of your mother?" Peg asked, laying down two silky stockings.

Catherine let out a huff of impatience. "When my mother spoke of the Farlan curse, she was referring to the family madness."

"Was she?"

"I cannot remain like this," Catherine insisted. "I am joining Lord Kentwood and his mother for tea this afternoon. I cannot face them in such a state!"

"I do not know how to help you," Peg said. "For certain, there is no tonic that can cure your ailment—except to return home to Scotland and wed the MacBraedon."

"I can hardly just order the carriage and set out for Scotland!" Catherine protested. "And I have already told your precious MacBraedon that I will not wed him. I believe Lord Kentwood is considering offering for me, and I cannot let any of this lunacy affect that. He holds my future in his hands."

Peg clucked her tongue. "He holds the future you expect in his hands, you mean. What if there is another future waiting for you elsewhere?"

"Like Scotland?" Catherine asked with arched brows. "Do not be ridiculous."

"I'm ridiculous?" Peg threw up her hands. "Which one of us is speaking in tongues?"

Catherine scowled and plucked at the lacy edges of her wrapper. "I have no explanation for that."

"Because 'tis a curse!" Peg's easy London accent gave way to the thicker brogue of a trueborn Scot. She strode toward Catherine, determination etched on her matronly features. "Curses dinna usually have any kind of logic behind them. Nasty, foul things they are, and rather difficult to break."

"This is madness!"

Peg's voice softened. "Aye, it is."

"I do not want this." Catherine jerked out of the chair, throwing her wrapper aside. "I have chosen my future husband. It is Lord Kentwood. And he seems amenable to the idea, else he would not have invited me to tea with his mama!"

"I feel for you, miss, I truly do. Ofttimes, just as you think you have your plans just so, fate comes and turns them inside out."

"Well, I will not cooperate. I will be marrying Lord Kentwood, and that is that."

Peg sighed. "As you wish."

"That is my wish." Catherine gave a sharp nod.

A knock came at the bedroom door. "Catherine? Are you well?"

Catherine gasped. "It's Papa!"

Peg cast her a sympathetic look. "So it is."

The knock came again. "Catherine!"

Peg started to make her way to the door.

"Peg!" Catherine hissed. "What are you doing?"

"I must answer," Peg said. "He's my employer, and I have no desire to be dismissed."

"But—" She clamped her mouth shut as the maid swung open the door.

"Good morning, sir," Peg said, her syllables pure Londoner once more.

Catherine's father strode into the room. "What is this I hear that my daughter is unwell?"

Catherine grabbed her wrapper from the floor and shrugged into it, tying the sash quickly. Now presentable, she opened her mouth to speak, then hesitated, remembering the footman. What if the words came out in Gaelic? How would she explain that to her father?

How could she explain it to herself?

"She is not feeling well this morning," Peg said. "I don't believe she slept soundly at all."

"Catherine?" Her father came forward and took her face in his hands, peering into her eyes. "Shall I summon the physician?"

Catherine shook her head no and gave him a weak smile.

"Perhaps a day of rest," Peg suggested.

Catherine shot her an urgent look.

Catherine's father turned to Peg. "If it is at all possible, I would rather she be ready to meet Lord Kentwood and his mother this afternoon."

"I understand," Peg said. "But what impression would it give to the gentleman's mother if Miss Catherine appears sickly?"

Catherine bugged her eyes at Peg, shaking her head just enough to convey her disagreement without drawing her father's attention.

"What impression would it give if she cancels the appointment?" her father countered. He turned back to Catherine, who managed to smooth her expression just in time. "What are your thoughts, daughter?"

Catherine gave a little smile and shrugged.

"Oh, come now. You must have an opinion on the matter."

She shook her head.

He peered at her, suspicion lighting his eyes. "Why do you not speak?"

Peg stepped forward, the concern on her face a

welcome relief. Catherine had begun to wonder if the maid had her best interests at heart. "A putrid throat," Peg said.

"Indeed?" Skepticism tinged his tone. "Why did you not tell me that from the beginning?"

"I've ordered tea," Peg said. "That should help."

"You did not answer my question, Peg. I asked you what was wrong with my daughter, and you told me she had not slept well."

"And so she hasn't—because of the putrid throat."

"I see." Anger flickered across his face. "I think I should summon the physician after all."

"No!" Catherine cried.

"Ah." Her father clasped his hands behind him. "She speaks. Tell me what this is about, daughter."

Catherine sent a helpless look to Peg.

The maid shrugged, sympathy evident on her face. "Perhaps your father can help."

"Help?" he demanded. "Help with what?"

"You had best tell him, miss. He's your father after all, and he cares for you."

"Catherine, I demand you tell me what is going on here, putrid throat or not. I will wait until you do."

She had no choice. "Papa, please tell me you can understand me."

As soon as she started speaking, his eyes widened. His face grew ashen, and his arms dropped to his sides. "No," he gasped. "No, this cannot be!"

"Do you understand me?" She reached for him. "Papa, do you understand what I am saying?"

"This cannot be happening." To her shock, his eyes grew moist with tears as he came to her and cupped her face. "I so prayed that you would be spared this terrible fate, my daughter."

"What do you know about this?" she pleaded. "Tell me!" She glanced at Peg. "Ask him why he is so distressed."

"I'm sorry to have to show you this, sir," Peg said, completely ignoring Catherine's request. "I was hoping she might come about in time for tea."

Catherine's father stepped away from her and impatiently swiped away a tear from the corner of his eye. "Have things like this happened before?"

"Peg," Catherine begged, "please tell him you can understand me!"

"Not so drastic as this." Peg gave her a pitying glance and went on as if she didn't comprehend a word. "Now and again we have found her going out the front door in the middle of the night, still in her nightclothes. I do believe she was still asleep when she did it."

151

"Dear God." He swiped a hand over his face. The torment in his eyes ripped at Catherine's heart. "It is happening again, just like her mother."

"Oh no." Catherine went to her father and grabbed his arm with both hands. "Oh, Papa."

He looked at her as if she were still a small child, his lips curving with bittersweet remembrance. "I had so hoped this would not come to pass, or at least that it would not happen until I had found her a proper husband."

"She's so young," Peg said. "It breaks my heart."

Catherine whirled toward the maid. "Why are you doing this, Peg? Why are you letting him suffer? Tell him you can understand me, do you hear?"

"She's become agitated," her father said, pulling her into a desperate embrace. "It nearly killed me to lock up her mother, but I feared she would harm herself."

"I completely understand, sir."

Catherine struggled to get free. "Do not talk about me as if I am not here."

"This is how it started for my dear Glynis," her father said, dejection heavy in his voice. "Ranting in the Scots tongue, never speaking English. I did not even know my wife could speak the language, but when the madness first began, it was all she spoke."

"How do you know it is the Scots language?" Peg asked, her face the picture of innocence. "It sounds like gibberish to me."

"I spent many months traveling through Scotland looking to buy wool when I first opened the mills," Papa replied. "I know Scots Gaelic when I hear it." He sighed. "Well, she cannot meet Lady Kentwood in this condition. And as I recall, it was several days before my wife began speaking English again."

Peg wrung her hands. "What shall we do?"

"The only thing we can do. Lock her in her room under guard."

"No, you do not need to do that. I am fine, Papa." Catherine turned pleading eyes to her father. "Please do not lock me away. I could not bear it."

He caressed her hair. "My poor child. I will speak to Lord Kentwood. Perhaps I can convince him to wed her quickly before the madness becomes too much."

"Will he be willing to do that?" Peg asked. "I do not mean to question you, sir, but will an important gentleman like His Lordship be willing to take a mad wife?"

"Traitor," Catherine hissed.

"I will double her portion. Perhaps that will convince him. And if not him, I can think of several other titled but penniless suitors who might be willing to wed her."

"Why wed her at all?" Peg asked. "Why not just care for her yourself?"

"Because I cannot live forever, and I would see her taken care of after I die. The best way to do that is a husband." He pushed Catherine away, holding her at arm's length. "Come take her, Peg. I will summon a couple of footmen to stand guard."

Peg obeyed, taking hold of Catherine despite Catherine's struggles.

"Let go of me," Catherine spat. "How could you do this to us?"

Her father walked to the door. "Once the footmen get here, Peg, make certain you remove anything from the room she could use to harm herself. Letter openers, anything with a sash, such as that wrapper she wears now."

"I will, sir."

"Excellent." He paused at the door, looking twice his age with the grief that pulled at his features. "I leave her in your capable hands, Peg."

He left, closing the door behind him and locking it with an audible snick.

The instant he was gone, Catherine shoved out of the maid's hold. "How dare you! Why did you not tell him you could understand me?"

"Your father does not know I am Scots," Peg replied, appearing undisturbed by Catherine's furious tone. "I would like to keep it that way."

"I will tell him the truth," Catherine snapped.

"Oh, will you now?" The maid chuckled.

Catherine clenched her hands. "You betrayed me, Peg."

"No, I saved you," Peg shot back. "You were dead set to marry that Lord Kentwood, but he is not the man for you. If you want this madness gone, you must wed the MacBraedon."

"Are you on about that curse again?"

Peg let out a hiss of impatience. "Lord above, but you're a Farlan through and through, aren't you? So certain you're right and stubborn with it."

"Believing in a curse is pure lunacy."

"And what is sanity? A girl like yourself speaking a language she never heard before?"

Catherine said nothing, unable to come up with sound rationalization for her situation.

"You have no reasonable explanation for what is happening, Catherine Depford, but *I* can tell you what is what. Your mother bore the mark to wed the MacBraedon chief, but she wed another man instead and was doomed to madness for the rest of her days. I know you bear the mark, for wasn't I the one who helped you bathe these past few weeks? So why do you want to make the same mistake your mother did?"

"Because it is a fantastical notion." Catherine's anger lost steam in the face of the maid's calm demeanor. "If I believed in curses, then what you are saying would make logical sense. But I have never believed in such things."

"Perhaps," Peg said, "'tis time to start."

"It is madness."

Peg shrugged. "They already think you're mad anyway."

Catherine began to pace around the room. "But I do not want to give in to it. And I do not want to go off to Scotland and marry a man I barely know. What if marrying him does not cure my madness? What then?"

"What if marrying him *does* cure your madness, and you're happy for the rest of your days?" Peg countered. "'Tis half of one dozen, six of another."

"Gabriel MacBraedon is a very attractive man, I will admit, but can I trust him to care for me? So far, all I know about him is that he has little use for rules. He has already broken a few key strictures of society and put my reputation in jeopardy."

"And he did this in public? Was there gossip?"

"Well, no," she mused. "He followed me into the garden at Lady Dorburton's and told me he wanted me for his bride. But no one saw us alone. And then later when he came to my room . . ."

Peg gave an appreciative laugh. "Did he? The scoundrel."

Catherine flushed, having forgotten she was speaking aloud. "He came to my room in the middle of the night to talk to me about this curse, but again, no one saw him except his own men."

"And they would die a thousand times before betraying him." Peg picked up the washbasin and went around the room, collecting various items and putting them in the bowl. "The MacBraedon is a man who doesna let anything get in the way of his goal."

"What are you doing, Peg?"

"What your father told me to do. Removing anything that could be considered a hazard to a madwoman."

Catherine pressed her lips together in annoyance. "That is not amusing."

"I am not trying to be amusing. I was given an order, and I must follow it."

"But I am not mad! At least, not yet. It just seems that I am because no one but you can understand me."

Peg paused and looked at her. "For the moment, you are as sane as I am. But the longer you wait to wed the MacBraedon, the worse the madness will become. The curse compels you to your destiny, you see. So if you do not go to Scotland and wed the man that fate has picked out for you, then you will truly go mad, as your mother did, and spend the rest of your life trying to get to Scotland until you finally die of it."

"Is that what happened to her?" Her heart heavy, Catherine sat down at her vanity table as Peg bustled about the room in search of threatening objects. "So that is what she meant by the Farlan curse. She was trying to get back to Scotland, and it killed her."

"Aye." The basin full, Peg set it on top of the vanity. "She was not as lucky as you, however. The last chief was not nearly as strong as the current one. Angus MacBraedon was too proud to go after Glynis when she ran off with your father. It was up to the Farlans to try and get her back, and they failed." She met Catherine's gaze with utter assurance. "Gabriel MacBraedon will nae let you go so easily."

A tremor ran down Catherine's spine at the truth that rang through Peg's words. Not fear, but a bone-deep excitement. To have a man so determined to win her . . . It was flattering and astonishing—and very arousing on an innate feminine level. Heat tinged her cheeks at her own acknowledgment of the shocking feelings.

A knock came at the door, then the snick of the lock releasing as the key was turned.

"That will be the footmen," Peg said. "I'll take the sash from that wrapper now."

Catherine rolled her eyes but untied the thing, handing it to the maid. Peg picked up the basin and dropped the sash into it. "Give some thought to your situation, lass. If you decide you want to go to Scotland and give the MacBraedon a chance, then I will do everything in my power to help you."

"Because your loyalty is to him," Catherine said.

Peg cast her a chiding glance. "Because 'tis my family, too, who are starving. I do what I can, but the curse has a way of making short work of my best efforts to help. In the end, the fate of those people is up to you."

Pulling the door open, Peg greeted the footmen as she left. One of them peered in at Catherine, then closed the door and locked it behind the maid.

Catherine looked around at her room, now stripped of anything that could be considered "dangerous," and realized that her worst nightmare had come true. Her father had declared her mad and locked her away.

A tremble shook her, and she hugged herself, uncertain what do to next—surrender to the looming insanity or take a leap of faith that the Farlan curse was real. That she might yet escape a future of lunacy simply by marrying Gabriel MacBraedon.

She tried to think logically. If the madness had indeed begun to take hold of her as the past couple of weeks indicated, then Lord Kentwood might well be lost to her. As kind as he was, she doubted that his duty to his line would allow him to take on a mad wife. He would need heirs, and she might not be able to provide them, especially if she was under some compulsion to go to Scotland no matter what the cost.

Which meant that her father would betroth her to some titled fortune hunter, who wanted her dowry more than he wanted her. And that was the very situation she had been trying to avoid. She had a sudden mental image of being locked away in a filthy asylum while her erstwhile husband squandered her dowry.

But the alternative—going off to a strange country where she did not know the customs and trusting a man who had no compunction about breaking rules to get what he wanted—that, too, was frightening.

All the Scots she had met so far were loyal to Gabriel. Peg, Gabriel's brother Patrick, Mr. Alexander from the balloon launch. She could imagine that his entire clan, who apparently depended on him to appease the curse and restore prosperity to the land, would be equally devoted. On one hand, perhaps that was a sign that he was a man who did not shirk responsibility (which would include his wife), so that even if the curse was just a piece of superstitious nonsense, he would see that she was well cared for if she went mad. On the other hand, such fidelity to the chief also meant that Catherine would have no allies to aid her, should her interests go against Gabriel's.

Her life in shambles, she fell on the bed, curled into a ball, then cried herself to sleep.

The day passed by in excruciating tedium. Catherine was ignored except when Peg brought her luncheon. The footman stood in the doorway the whole time, watching, so Peg could not converse with her. Catherine ate the light fare, then went back to bed, watching the shadows in her room slowly lengthen and then disappear throughout the hours of the day.

She had fallen back to sleep again when Peg arrived with her supper. She sat up in bed, yawning as Peg led an elderly servant carrying the tray over to the small table and chair by the fireplace. The thin old man set down the tray with an audible clank. Catherine glanced at the doorway, expecting to see the footman.

No one was there.

For a brief moment, she thought of jumping

out of bed and racing through the door. How fast could she run? Could she escape the house before the servants caught up with her? With any luck she could get out to the stables and steal a horse before anyone was the wiser. Then she could ride like the wind, heading north, flying toward home where the heather covered the hills like lush carpet and the water from the snowcapped mountains tasted so fresh and sweet . . .

She was on her feet and headed for the door before she realized it.

Peg gave a gasp, and the elderly servant darted in front of her, blocking her way.

Incensed, she nearly shoved the man to the ground. But his eyes stopped her. Eyes of a peculiar blue-gray that watched her with fear and love and utter joy.

Eyes she saw in the mirror every day.

"Dinna be leaving us so quickly, Catherine Depford," the elderly man said. "We've come to help you."

Her knees sagged, and the old man caught her, guiding her with Peg's assistance to the edge of the bed where she could sit. "Peg, close the door," he said.

Catherine stared as Peg shut the door, and a cry escaped her lips as she realized what had just happened. Dear God, had she just tried to run off to

Scotland? Had she really intended to dash from the house in her nightdress and steal a horse and race for the north?

Tears sprang into her eyes, and she let out a sob, completely undone by the muddle that was her life.

"There, there, lass." Crouching before her, the elderly man presented a handkerchief and dabbed at the tears that trickled down her cheeks. "We're here to help you, Peg and I are."

Once again she was struck by the remarkable familiarity of his eyes. "Who are you?" she managed.

He smiled, tenderness and elation in every line of his face. "I'm Donald Farlan, sweet girl. I'm your grandfather."

Chapter 10

George Depford entered White's with some trepidation. For years he had been denied entrance into the sacred chambers of the most exclusive gentlemen's club in London. Membership at White's depended not on how shiny your gold was but how blue your blood. And as a common merchant, his blood was a simple red.

How ironic that it was here where he would settle his daughter's future.

His heart grieved for his little Catherine. How he had prayed she would not inherit her mother's lunacy. But today he had been confronted with undeniable proof that she was indeed going mad, just as Glynis had. God save them both.

He followed a servant through the rooms of the club, more than aware of the stares and whispers that followed him. *That's right. Look at the commoner in your midst, you bloody nobs. Take his money at the card tables, but never let him set foot in this establishment reserved for the highborn.*

He longed to clench his fists. To rail at these genteel pretenders. Most of them could not run a business if it were handed to them. They whittled away their useless lives at the tailor's or the brothel or the gaming hells. Or their club, that sanctum of peace safe from the feminine influence.

Yes, he wanted to clench his fists and demand they acknowledge that he was as good as they were. Perhaps better, since he had earned his place in the world, whereas they had simply been born to it. But that would only reveal his vulnerability to them. Better they thought him arrogant as he strolled proudly past all the curious eyes hidden behind daily newspapers.

He knew he wasn't accepted—but he had hoped that his daughter would be. That her beauty and fortune would win her an entrée into this elite society.

Kentwood had made him doubt his dreams. Now he did flex his hands as he remembered his meeting with the young earl.

Kentwood had outright refused to wed Catherine quickly.

He had declined again when George had doubled her dowry.

He had then had the audacity to dismiss George

Depford, implying quite clearly that he thought the reason Catherine needed to wed in such haste was that she was expecting a child.

George had very nearly planted him a facer.

But really, he couldn't blame the man. Kentwood had noted Catherine's odd behavior and had heard the tale of how she had fainted while out shopping with Beth. Then George had arrived and tried to convince him to wed Catherine quickly. What else was a man to think?

No, Kentwood would never offer now. He had ruined that for his little girl, feeding the man's suspicions with his longing to see Catherine settled before she grew too addled to say the vows.

So he had done what he had sworn never to do. He had made an appointment with Viscount Nordham to negotiate terms to sell his daughter into marriage.

The servant stopped at two chairs tucked away in a corner far from the others, where two men might discuss business without being overheard. Nordham rose and gave a nod of acknowledgment. The tall, black-haired man had a sleek handsomeness that tended to attract the ladies with its element of danger. And often did, earning him a reputation as a rake. He drank, gambled, and wenched to excess, but he had a title and was in dire need of funds.

The perfect groom for a hasty wedding.

Nordham dismissed the servant with a casual wave of his hand, never breaking eye contact with his visitor. "Sit down, Depford."

George sat, and Nordham signaled to another servant, who brought forth two glasses of brandy.

"Drink up," Nordham said, seating himself and downing half his portion in one swallow. "Then we can commence negotiations."

Depford pushed the goblet away. "No, thank you, Lord Nordham. I prefer not to drink spirits when I am conducting business."

Nordham shrugged and sipped his brandy. But his dark eyes glittered. "As you wish."

"You know why I am here. I would like my daughter to be a lady, preferably a countess."

"I expect my father to cock up his toes at any time," Nordham said. "That would make me an earl, with the family fortune at my disposal."

"But until then, you are dependent on your father's largesse." Confident now, George sat back in his chair with a small smile curving his lips. "I understand he has been somewhat difficult of late."

Nordham pressed his lips together and set his goblet on the table with a click. "What do you want?"

"I want you to obtain a special license and marry my daughter within the week."

Nordham's features sharpened into a frown. "Why the haste? I warn you, I will be father to no man's bastard."

With effort, George controlled his anger. "That is not the situation at all."

"Forgive me." The smooth apology was not reflected in his eyes. "Usually there is but one reason to wed so quickly."

"My daughter has a . . . condition. Not fatal, but one where she will need care as she goes on in life."

"Ah." Nordham drew out the syllable. He leaned back in his own chair, a knowing smirk curving his lips. "She has inherited your wife's madness."

This time George did clench his fist. "Yes."

"You want me to take on a mad wife, knowing full well that I must produce an heir."

"Her illness is progressive. She will be able to bear you children before she loses her faculties." His throat clogged just speaking about his daughter in such a manner.

"Mad children, perhaps."

George did not allow his annoyance to show. "It was my understanding you are a gambler, my lord. I am willing to settle thirty thousand pounds on her upon marriage, and she will remain my sole heir to the rest of my wealth and properties. Is that worth the risk?"

"Good God!" Nordham goggled at the princely sum.

"In addition," George said, "I have taken the liberty of buying your gambling vowels from those to whom you were indebted. Should you wed my daughter, I will destroy them, and the debts will cease to exist."

"That's nearly twenty thousand pounds," Nordham whispered.

"Nineteen thousand, eight hundred, and forty-seven, to be exact." George chuckled, sensing victory. "I do not estimate when it comes to money."

"You present a bargain that is hard to refuse, Depford."

"I married late in life, Lord Nordham, and I would see to my daughter's future before it is too late."

"I can tell you I am intrigued. Your daughter is quite beautiful for a woman of her class." Nordham tapped his fingers on his goblet. "Madness or not."

"I can have the papers drawn up and sent to your home this evening."

• Nordham hesitated, then nodded. "I am no fool. I accept your terms."

"Excellent. I warn you, there will be specific instructions regarding the care of my daughter should her illness progress. I would expect you to follow them to the letter and spare no expense."

"Agreed."

George stood. "We will speak again when the papers are signed. You will be a very rich man, Lord Nordham, and not have to depend on your father ever again."

"Something which brings me no limit of joy." Nordham stood, his entire demeanor celebratory, and lifted his glass. "To a successful contract."

George smiled and reached for his own goblet. "That is something I can drink to."

"You understand me." Relief made Catherine's limbs weak. "It is a horrible thing not to be understood."

"I speak Gaelic," the old man said, tucking the handkerchief in her hand. "And so do you, I see."

"'Tis the curse," Peg said, still standing near the door. She opened it a crack and peered out.

"Oh." Sadness filled the old man's eyes. "So it has begun."

"And you are my grandfather?" Catherine asked.

"I am." Donald stood. "Your mother was my daughter, poor soul. I couldna save her, but I will save you, God willing, if it takes my last breath."

Catherine studied the thin old man, imagining

that once he had been fairly tall before age took its toll on his body, shrinking his height and curving his once broad shoulders with the burden of the passing years. His eyes were the same shape and blue-gray color as her own—as her mother's had been. His silver hair tended to curl at the edges, and a neatly trimmed beard gave him a distinguished look. A bold blade of a nose added to the impression of strength despite his half-starved appearance.

"Do you mean save me from this curse?" she asked, surprised at her own acceptance of him.

"And what else do you need saving from? Except this filthy city." He wrinkled his nose. "I'm missing the fresh air of home, God's truth."

"Peg tells me that the only way to break the curse is for me to marry Gabriel MacBraedon."

"So it is. Though you'll not be breaking the curse so much as satisfying it."

"I do not understand."

"If you wed the MacBraedon, the blight will be lifted from the lands of MacBraedon and Farlan alike. And you, lass, will nae suffer the madness that took your mother from this world."

"But that is not breaking the curse?"

"No. Another lass is already marked to wed the next generation of MacBraedon chiefs. And so it has been for some three centuries now. And so it will be for generations to come." He grinned, showing her teeth that had seen better days. "But your future will be assured, and that is our purpose for the moment."

"Enough of this jabbering." Peg came over, hands on her hips. "I gave the footmen enough herb in their soup to put them to sleep, but they willna stay that way forever. The lass must make her choice."

Catherine got to her feet. "What choice?"

"We've come to rescue you," Donald said. "The lads are waiting outside to take you home to Scotland."

She stiffened. "Scotland has never been my home. *This* is my home."

"So it is," Peg said, flashing Donald an impatient look. "But Scotland is home to your family and to the MacBraedon."

"Will you come away with us, granddaughter? Will you follow your destiny and end the torment of our kin?"

"You want me to run away to Scotland with you? Right now?"

"Indeed." Donald nodded.

"Oh." Her stomach did a little flip, and she sank back down on the edge of the bed.

"Your grandfather is here to look after you on

the trip," Peg said. "What choice do you have? Would you rather stay locked in this room until your father chooses some greedy brigand of a husband for you? Or will you take your future in your own hands and choose your own path?"

Catherine looked from one to the other, then settled on Donald. "You will be my guardian?"

Donald nodded. "I will."

She curled her fingers into the coverlet, hardly able to believe she was even considering the idea. "And you will not force me to marry Gabriel MacBraedon?"

"Force? No. Encourage? Perhaps, but only because 'twill be the salvation of us all." The twinkle in Donald's eye coaxed a smile from her.

"Go with them, child," Peg urged. "If nothing else, you will be out in the fresh air."

"If I go," Catherine said, "I am going so I can meet my family." She turned her gaze to her grandfather. "Perhaps on the way you can tell me more of this madness that plagues our family."

"I will tell you everything you want to know."

"I am comforted to hear that. But there is one answer I need from you before we proceed further. Why have you waited until now to come see me? Why have I not met you before?"

"Oh, my sweet girl. Many's the time I wanted to

come and have words with your father on that very subject. But he would have had me hauled away had I dared darken his door."

"I know he does not like the Scots, but—"

"Not like us? Sweet heaven, the man detests the very air we breathe. Why have I not come to you before now? Because your father wouldna let me, that's why. He and his money made a formidable blockade. 'Tis only recently we were able to get Peg a position in this household to watch over you for us."

"We knew where you were, dear," Peg said. "We just couldna get close. Not until Mellie left a few weeks past and I was able to take her position."

Catherine looked from one to the other, torn. Then she took a deep breath. "I will go to Scotland."

"Saints be blessed!" Peg exclaimed. "Come, let me help you dress. Donald, you watch the door."

"I will."

Peg urged Catherine over to the wardrobe. "You've made the right choice, my dear."

Catherine glanced at her grandfather, who studiously kept his gaze on the door, as Peg pulled out a sturdy riding habit from the wardrobe. "I hope so."

"What the blazes is taking so long?" From the shadows of the garden, Gabriel looked up at Catherine's window. "Peg and Donald have been gone an age."

"Perhaps the lass is stubborn." Brodie grinned, his teeth a flash in the darkness. "She is a Farlan you know."

"Aye, well do I know it." Gabriel rocked on his heels, gaze fixed on the brightly lit window.

"Why does the curse have to pick your bride for you?" Patrick grumbled. "Why can you nae pick any Farlan lass you choose?"

"It doesna work that way."

"I know that." Patrick kicked a pebble, sending it skittering through the brush.

Brodie hissed at him. "We dinna have the rain to hide us today, young Patrick, so have a care."

Patrick scowled. "I'm tired of England. I want to go home."

"We all do," Gabriel said.

"I just wish you could have married Jean," Patrick said. "Then we wouldna have had to come here."

The dart hit his heart dead center, though Gabriel doubted Patrick even realized the weapon he had wielded.

His brother continued, "I would have liked Jean for my sister."

And Gabriel would have liked her for his wife.

An image of her flashed through his mind, all

dark eyes and black hair and sunny smiles. Her well-rounded figure had tempted him into her arms more than once. Even though he knew they could not be. Even though she knew it.

But she had not borne the mark, so they had been forced to walk away from each other, both of them knowing he might well be moving toward a marriage that had no love.

"I would have been happy to marry Jean Farlan," Gabriel said quietly, touching his thumb to the band of his ring. "But she knew my duty was to wed another."

"Stupid curse," Patrick muttered.

Gabriel sucked in a breath, trying to soothe the wound that still throbbed, even after three years. "Aye."

"Enough talk of the past," Brodie hissed. "We're standing on enemy land, in case any of you have forgotten."

"I've forgotten nothing," Gabriel snapped. "Come, lads. Donald has been gone too long."

They broke from the bushes and hurried to the wall of the house. One by one the men climbed on top of one another to form a human ladder. Once everyone was in place, Gabriel hoisted himself onto the first man's shoulders and began the climb up to Catherine's window.

When he reached the top, he peered inside, expecting to see Donald surrounded by Depford's men. Instead he saw Catherine, clad in just a shift, raising her arms so Peg Ross could fit a corset around her tiny waist.

He could not deny that fate had sent him a bonny bride. With her pale skin and hair like flame, she drew him with her siren's lure. Her soft curves—especially those pretty, plump breasts—whetted his lusty appetite. The shift she wore was of the sheerest cotton, accenting rather than hiding her charms.

Peg tugged the laces of the corset, narrowing Catherine's waist even more and plumping her breasts up like an offering from the gods, the lacy edge of the garment barely covering her nipples.

She was his, marked so by destiny, yet his blood raged with the undeniable need to claim her. To take what was his in a way no man could dispute.

Hardly aware of his actions, he climbed through the window and dropped lightly to the floor. Despite his care, Catherine heard his entrance. She glanced over at him and gasped, grabbing for a discarded wrapper draped over a chair.

"What are you doing here?" she cried, using a clenched fist to hold the silky creation against her. Despite her attempt at modesty, the full-length mirror behind her revealed a tantalizing view

177

of milky shoulders, a tiny waist, and a sweetly rounded bottom.

Peg gasped. "Miss! You spoke English!"

"I did?" Catherine said.

"You did indeed." Peg finally glimpsed him. "Good heavens! You scoundrel! The lass isna dressed yet!"

"I can see that." He approached slowly, his heart pounding, his body tight with desire. "But certainly, as her betrothed, I may savor the beauty of my bride."

Donald turned away from the door to face him. "MacBraedon, what the devil are you doing here? You were to wait for the signal."

"I was concerned that something had gone awry." Gabriel focused on Catherine, on the way her fiery hair fell over her smooth white shoulders, how her pretty bottom curved in the reflection of the mirror, how delicate were the bones of her ankles.

Aye, there might be no love in this union, but there would be passion aplenty. A man could be satisfied with that.

Donald came forward, stepping into his path. "Have some respect. The lass isna your wife yet."

"And I have not said I shall be," Catherine retorted.

Gabriel gave her a slow smile. "You will be."

"Be off with you so Miss Catherine can finish dressing," Peg said.

He eyed Catherine again, this time from the angle of practicality. "She canna wear that for the journey we're to make."

"She'll wear her riding habit," Peg said. "'Tis the only thing suitable enough."

"Then find another garment. We will be several days ahorse, living off the land. She willna be comfortable in that, and we canna afford to stop to soothe her ills."

Catherine raised her chin. "I can ride quite well, thank you, and the habit is designed for horseback."

He chuckled. "A leisurely trot through Hyde Park, perhaps, but not galloping like the devil to the border. And you willna be riding sidesaddle, my love. You'll ride astride or you'll ride with me."

"Ride with you! I will not!"

"You will," he shot back, "if that's what it takes for us to make it to Scotland ahead of your father's men."

"We dinna have the time to find other clothing," Peg protested.

"Then I suppose she must wear the habit for now. But do away with the corset, woman. We canna have the girl fainting along the way."

Catherine's mouth fell open. "I cannot go about without a corset!"

"You can and you will." Gabriel turned his attention to Donald, leaving Catherine spluttering. "Donald, make your way down and wait for us at the bottom."

"I dinna want to leave the lass. I promised I would be her guardian."

Gabriel laid a hand on his shoulder. "And so you shall, but you're no longer a young man, Donald, and 'twill take you longer to get to the ground. Peg and I will watch over Catherine."

"Go on, Donald," Peg said, busily untying Catherine's stays. "He'll behave himself, or he'll hear about it from me."

Donald gave Gabriel a hard stare. "Treat her with respect, MacBraedon. She'll be yours soon enough."

"Not necessarily!" Catherine tossed out. Peg shushed her, and she pressed her lips closed, but those gorgeous eyes spoke volumes.

Gabriel grinned. At least his life would not be boring. "Go, Donald."

Donald gave a nod, then glanced at Catherine. "I'll be waiting for you outside, granddaughter. Have no fear."

"I do not fear this oaf."

"Oaf, is it?" Gabriel came closer. Her scent teased him, clouded his thinking.

Chuckling, Donald climbed out the window and onto the shoulders of the top man in the human chain.

Catherine barely noticed her grandfather's departure. "Yes, oaf. What else would you call a man who tosses about orders as you do?"

"A clan chief."

She put her hands on her hips. "Well, I am not part of your clan."

"Not yet."

"Not ever." Peg brought over the midnight blue riding habit, but Catherine held out a hand to stop her from coming any closer. "No, Peg, I have changed my mind. I will not be going to Scotland."

"What!" Peg exclaimed.

Gabriel scowled. "Of course you will go."

"I will not. I can speak English again." She sent him a look of fury that should have scalded him but only made him want her more.

"But for how long?" Peg asked. "The curse can strike when you least expect."

"It does not signify."

Gabriel stepped closer, looming over her. He itched to touch her but dared not, not when he was trapped between anger and lust. He clenched his fists at his sides. "You will go with us, Catherine Depford. People are dying, and you can save them."

She did not back down. "*I* will make the choice." She turned away, then slid him a glance over her shoulder. "Perhaps I shall send around a note to Lord Kentwood."

Jealousy roared through him, gripping him with wicked claws. He grabbed her, jerked her against him, and ground out, "The hell you will."

Dragging her with him by the arm, he reached the bed in two steps and yanked off the coverlet. Her eyes widened, and she tried to break free. "No," she panted, "I will not go with you!"

"People risked their lives to find you, Catherine Depford. You *will* go to Scotland tonight." He threw the coverlet over her head, then bent down and lifted her over his shoulder. She let out a soft oomph as her stomach made contact with hard sinew. He straightened, locking an arm around her thighs to keep her balanced. She began to squirm, and he swatted her on the bottom.

An outraged yelp reached him from beneath the blanket.

"Dinna struggle or you'll kill us both!"

Peg watched him with rounded eyes, one hand over her mouth in shock.

He paused to give his clanswoman an apologetic smile. "'Tis the only way, Peg. She's a Farlan through and through."

Peg nodded and watched silently as they headed toward the window.

Brodie leaned with his folded arms on the sill, grinning. "I told you we should bring the rope."

"You did. Next time I will listen."

Gabriel peered down at the human ladder. Catherine squirmed again, and he gave her a hard squeeze. "Stop your thrashing! Do you want to fall out the window, woman?"

She said something to him, and even though the words were muffled by the blanket, her irate tone was not.

"You've made yourself a marriage bed of thorns, Gabriel," Brodie observed with a chuckle.

"So I have." He glanced at Peg. "Is Depford at home?"

"No, my lord."

"That's fine then." He looked at Brodie. "Send up Angus and Andrew. Then you and Patrick and Donald bring the horses round."

"You dinna mean to walk out the front door?" Brodie asked, astonishment clear on his face.

"The kitchen door, actually. We'll not get my bride out this way, not without one of us breaking our necks."

"Agreed." With a sigh, Brodie began climbing down. "Remake the ladder, lads. The MacBraedon would like Angus and Andrew to clear his way through the house."

In mere minutes, the ladder had been formed again, this time with Brodie and Patrick on the bottom and Angus and Andrew near the top. Angus was the first to climb through the window, then reached down and assisted his brother.

Andrew scrambled through the window, then found his footing.

"Depford is not at home," Gabriel said, "but I expect the servants willna want us to escape with my bride. 'Tis up to the two of you to clear the way."

"Understood," Angus said. He smiled at Peg and gave a little wave. "Hallo, Mum."

"My boys." Peg came over, and the twins each bent down to kiss her cheek. "Take good care of Miss Catherine now."

"We will," Andrew said.

"Lead on," Gabriel said, tightening his grip on a wiggling Catherine. "Your mother will be safe enough here."

"I'll be fine," Peg said. "Go. Save our people so I can come home to you."

With identical waves of farewell, the twins strode forward, their long legs eating up the length of the room in seconds. Gabriel followed, balancing his woman on his shoulder.

"Angus!" Peg hurried after them, the riding habit in her hands. "Take this with you. The lass needs something to wear besides her shift!"

Without breaking stride, Angus took the clothing and draped it over his shoulder, then followed his brother out into the hallway. Gabriel waited for a soft whistle—the signal to proceed—then went after them.

Several footmen and one intrepid housekeeper attempted to stop them. Angus and Andrew made short work of the footmen and locked the housekeeper in a closet before she could sound the alarm. The kitchen was all but deserted, with one lad sleeping in a corner. The trio of Scotsman walked softly past the young page, never disturbing his slumber.

By the time Gabriel walked out the kitchen door, he was quietly cursing the bundle of female flesh slung over his shoulder. She had squirmed and wiggled and struggled the whole way, tiring his muscles with the need to keep her in one place.

This could have been a simple matter to resolve. If she had only come willingly as she had said she would . . . But no, God forbid a Farlan keep her word. So they were reduced to outright abduction.

He trotted to the stable area, Angus before him and Andrew behind him. Astride his own mount, Patrick clutched the reins of Gabriel's horse, while

Donald and Brodie gripped the others. Gabriel turned to Angus. "Hold her," he commanded. Angus wrapped his arms around the twisting bundle of woman and held her with easy strength as she tried to free herself.

Settled in his saddle, Gabriel reached for her again. Angus handed her up, and Gabriel managed to get her situated in front of him on his horse. She slipped a hand from beneath the blanket and yanked it off her head.

"You will pay for this," she snapped, eyes molten with fury.

He nodded. "I will. From the moment we speak our vows."

She let out a sound of frustration, then burrowed back into the folds of the blanket against the wind as he urged his horse into a gallop toward the Highlands.

There was no escape now. She was his.

Chapter 11

S he must have dozed, for when Catherine awoke the group of clansmen had stopped in a clearing near a stream. Gabriel had just begun to hand her to one of the others. Disoriented by the sudden downward movement, she threw her arms around his neck, clutching at him with sleepy panic.

"There, there, sweet Catherine," Gabriel murmured. "I've got you."

"Where are we?" Still muddled, she rested her head against his chest. His heart beat strongly beneath her cheek.

"We've stopped for a rest. 'Tis almost dawn."

"Have we ridden all night?" His body gave off a toasty warmth, and she cuddled closer.

"We have." He tucked her more comfortably against him. "As much as I enjoy having you in my arms, fair Catherine, we must allow the horse to rest."

She came fully awake at that, flushing with humiliation. What was wrong with her, clinging to him like a wanton? "Let me go."

He chuckled. "As you wish."

He allowed her to slide down off the horse, and the well-trained beast remained still as she dropped to the ground. Her blanket slid from her shoulders. With a gasp, she realized that she was yet in her unmentionables—and had been riding with him in such a state for hours!

He burst out laughing and dismounted.

Her face burned. She shoved her tangled hair back and lifted her chin. "This is not amusing. You have abducted me!"

"I dinna think that's accurate."

"How else would you describe it? You carried me out of my house on your shoulder like a bag of grain."

He stepped closer, holding her gaze. His blue eyes never failed to incite that melting sensation in her belly. Frustrated with her own inability to resist this wild attraction, she held the contact with stony resolve.

"You agreed to come with us," Gabriel said. "'Twas merely your fierce temper that resulted in your method of escape."

"*My* temper?" He was right, curse him, but she was not about to admit it.

"Aye." He leaned down so they were practically nose to nose. "You're a passionate woman, Catherine Depford. 'Twill make for a pleasant wedding night for the both of us."

Did he never admit defeat? "I have not yet agreed to marry you."

"True." He stroked a hand down her cheek, and her pulse skipped. "But a man can hope."

Before she could respond, he turned and walked away, leading his horse toward the stream.

She could only stand there, watching his retreating back, conflicting emotions battling inside her. Why did her heart soften in his presence, even as her temper boiled? What was it about this stubborn Scotsman that made her so vulnerable to him?

Could they be connected somehow through this curse everyone seemed to believe in?

Donald came over to her. "Come, granddaughter."

"Where are we going?" Finally noticing her surroundings, Catherine tugged her blanket more closely around her and looked around. "Is there no inn where we might refresh ourselves?"

"An inn?" Donald chuckled and shook his head. "No, we've no coin for such places."

"What? But where . . ." She stumbled over the words and lowered her voice to a whisper. "Where shall I go to . . . take care of my needs?"

"Ah." Glancing away, Donald cleared his throat. "We will find you a bit of privacy." He began to lead her toward a stand of bushes near the water's edge.

"Where are you going, Donald?" Brodie called out.

"The lass needs—" Donald waved his hand toward the bushes, at a loss for words.

"Ah." Brodie nodded. "Have a care she doesna slip away from you, Donald."

"Have no fear of that," Donald snapped.

They reached the bushes, and Donald gestured toward the shrubbery. "You can go behind there. I'll make certain that no one bothers you."

Catherine hesitated, put off by such primitive accommodations. The mere thought of taking care of her body's needs out in the open with a band of Scotsmen standing only paces away shocked her. But what choice did she have?

She looked at her grandfather. She did not know him, had not had the time to come to trust him. Yet Gabriel had been right. Her temper had gotten the better of her, and she had arrived at this place through unorthodox means. Nonetheless, she had indeed made the choice to leave behind everything familiar, to travel to Scotland on the frailest bit of hope that she might be able to make some sense of the recent events in her life.

Kentwood was lost to her, and her father's reaction to her madness still stung with betrayal. What did she have waiting for her in London? Nothing. She could only continue forward and hope to find answers in Scotland.

"Grandfather," she said. Joy lit his eyes at the address, and her heart squeezed in response. He seemed such a dear man. "Will you please find my clothing for me?"

"I will."

"Thank you." With as much dignity as she could manage, she slipped behind the bushes.

"What are you about, letting the woman wander freely?" Brodie asked, standing beside Gabriel as they both watered their horses at the stream.

"She willna go far. At least not the way she's dressed now. Besides, Donald will watch after her."

"Will he? Then why is Donald talking to Angus?"

Gabriel glanced around and saw Donald was indeed conversing with Angus, and Catherine was nowhere to be seen. "Bloody hell."

"Go on and find your bride," Brodie said with a grin. "I'll watch the horses."

Gabriel stalked over to Donald, who was just turning away from Angus with Catherine's riding habit in his hand. "Donald! Where is Catherine?"

"She's seeing to nature." Donald began walking toward the bushes on the far side of their camp.

"And the dress?"

"My granddaughter asked that I fetch it for her." Donald stopped and faced Gabriel with a scowl. "You canna have the lass running about naked as the day she was born."

A pity, that.

"I'll take the dress to her." Gabriel held out his hand.

Donald narrowed his eyes. "She's done what you asked and come with us, Gabriel. Dinna shame her."

"I'll remind you, Donald, that she didna come quietly."

Donald hesitated, then handed him the dress. "Dinna make me regret my part in this, MacBraedon."

"I intend to wed her, Donald. She's under my protection." Gripping the dress, he made his way to the cluster of bushes. "Catherine," he called softly.

"Do not come closer," she squeaked. "Where is my grandfather?"

"He's nearby. I've brought your clothing."

Silence.

"Catherine?"

"I want my grandfather," she said in a small voice.

"He canna come. Do you want your dress or no?"

"I do."

"Then take it."

She peered out from behind the bushes, clenching the blanket closed at her throat. "Give it to me," she said, reaching a hand around the branches.

"And how will you fasten it?" he asked.

"I will manage."

"I can help you."

She clenched her outstretched hand. "I do not want your help."

"You're a stubborn woman," Gabriel said.

"No more so than you."

"'Tis my duty to protect you. I willna harm you." He handed her the riding habit. "Take your clothing. I stand ready to assist you."

She snatched the dress away from him and ducked behind the bush again.

"This is no way to start a courtship," Gabriel said.

"Courtship?" she scoffed. Rustling indicated she was trying to dress. "Nothing that has happened between us could be considered a courtship."

"All the more reason for us to start again."

She let out a hiss of exasperation, followed by more rustling of fabric and branches. "I do not recall that we truly 'started' at all."

Gabriel rolled his eyes. The woman could talk coins away from a blind man with her manner of circling her words into a muddle. But he'd not fall into her trap of twisted language this time.

"Trust me, Catherine," he said quietly.

"How can I?" she replied, her tone just as somber. "I do not know you."

"Will you at least allow me to fasten your dress? I have no desire to share your beauty with my men."

She hesitated.

"Catherine, be practical. If you were at home, you would need your maid to assist you."

"Yes, I would," she replied, sounding pensive.

"Let me help you."

Another long moment of silence.

"Very well," she said.

"I'm coming back there." He walked around the bushes and found her with the riding habit half on, trying to keep the blanket around her at the same time. "I canna help you if you dinna let go of the blanket."

She stood perfectly still, watching him with distrustful eyes. Farlan eyes. "You will be a gentleman?"

"What kind of man do you think I am?"

"I do not know what kind of man you are. I do not know *you*."

He took a deep breath to hold back his ire. The lass surely could not know how close to danger she trod with such blatant attacks on his honor. Hadn't he left behind the woman he'd chosen in order to wed this ungrateful Farlan that fate had gifted him?

"I am the MacBraedon," he said stiffly. "My duty lies with my clan. You, Catherine Depford, are destined to be part of my clan, whether you understand that or not."

She studied his face, her own giving nothing away. Finally she slid the blanket from her shoulders and set it on the ground. Holding the dress in place, she turned her back that he might do up the dozens of fastenings.

There was something tantalizingly intimate about helping a woman dress. He looked at the creamy flesh of her shoulders, at the tissue-thin cotton of her shift, and relished the notion that he was the only male here to enjoy such a sight. Aye, she was a beauty, this bride of his. As he fastened the hooks and buttons, he thought about how much he would like to perform this task in reverse.

"I do not mean to be troublesome," she murmured.

Her soft words jerked him from his fantasy of getting her naked. "What was that?"

She turned her head sideways, but did not look

all the way back at him. "You said once I was troublesome. I do not mean to be."

"Well, that was different. You were nae troublesome on the ride here."

She gave a chuckle. "I was asleep!"

"Aye, dozing in my arms like an angel."

She flushed, and he watched with fascination as the pink swept across her fair cheeks and down her neck. "I hope you were not uncomfortable."

"Hardly." He finished fastening her dress and laid his hands on her shoulders. "I am an honorable man, Catherine. You must learn to trust me."

"Trust." She sighed and turned to face him. He let his hands slide from her shoulders. "I trusted my father, and he betrayed me by intending to sell me like a prize cow."

"He didna ken the curse."

"*I* didna ken the curse, either."

He chuckled at her attempt to imitate his manner of speech. "How could you? You didna grow up amongst your clan as you should have."

"I must say, unconventional as it was, I enjoyed the best sleep I have had in weeks while riding with you from London."

He gave a slow smile, wondering if she was thinking what he imagined she was thinking. "How so?"

"Because I did not dream, and I did not hear voices chanting in my head."

"Oh." Perhaps the ride had not been as stimulating for her as it had been for him. He'd had to spend several minutes after dismounting contemplating the cold stream before his body had settled down.

"Why do you suppose that is?"

He jerked his attention back to her. "Why what is?"

"Why all the symptoms of insanity seem to disappear when you are near me. Yesterday I was speaking Gaelic all day despite never having learned the language. Then I started speaking English again as soon as you arrived."

He shrugged. "Perhaps 'tis because the curse knows I will be your husband."

She sighed, weariness more than exasperation filling the sound. "You do not give up easily, do you?"

"A MacBraedon doesna surrender."

She laughed, but it had a bitter edge. "So I have observed. Listen to me, Gabriel." She laid a hand on his arm, trapping his attention with her soft gaze. "I am not going to Scotland to marry you. I am going there to meet my family and find the cure for this madness."

"The cure is marriage."

"Perhaps. But I will not be forced into any union against my will." She dropped her gaze, then glanced away to the stream running beside them. "Even though I thought to marry Lord Kentwood, I did not select him because he was the richest or most important man. I chose him because of how he treated his mother."

"What does a man's mother have to do with marriage?"

"The tender way he cared for her." A wistful smile curved her lips. "I thought perhaps if I ended up a madwoman that he would care for me just as kindly."

"If you wed me, you willna become a madwoman at all."

"Because of the curse, correct?" He nodded, and she gave him a doting smile. "What if I do go mad, Gabriel? Would you treat me well? Could you be the man I wanted Lord Kentwood to be?"

And just how was a man supposed to compare himself with the likes of the lady's favorite suitor? "I dinna know. Perhaps the man you want isna real."

"I thought that about you once. That you were not real. Could not be."

He chuckled. "You have a vivid imagination."

"Perhaps. But what is a girl supposed to think

when she dreams of a man one night and then meets him at a ball the next night? Of course I thought you were my knight come to save me."

"You have exalted expectations," he said. "A husband is just a man, and none are perfect."

"Perhaps." She folded her arms, hugging herself. "But the husband I would have chosen is lost to me, and you insist on taking his place."

"Neither of us has a choice in this matter, Catherine."

Something in his voice must have given him away. Her head came up, curiosity flickering in her eyes. "Was there someone for you, too, Gabriel?"

"Once." He shrugged, uncomfortable with the direction of the conversation. "But I know my duty. I will make you a fine husband."

"Only if you can prove to me that you know how to put others before yourself." She gathered her red hair at the nape of her neck and twisted a bit of ribbon torn from her habit into the mass of tangled locks.

He struggled not to take offense. "I came to England for you, did I not? And I tried to win you by English means. Does that prove nothing?"

"It proves you are very determined."

He gave a sharp nod. "I am at that."

"I cannot promise I will ever marry you, Gabriel. Once we reach your home, I will know more."

"You're foolish indeed if you believe you can refuse me."

A knowing smile curved her lips. "It is a woman's prerogative to refuse any offer she wishes."

"Too true." He cast a swift glance down her sweetly curved body. "I'll convince you to wed me, Catherine. You will beg to be my bride."

She licked her lips. "I cannot imagine that will happen."

"After we reach my home, after you see the suffering the curse has wrought." He slid his thumb along her damp mouth. "After you realize the passionate lover I can be, that is when you will accept me."

Her lips parted. "I already realize it, if my dreams are a true reflection of you."

A breath hissed from between his teeth. "Dear God, woman, I am only human."

She squeezed her eyes shut, then opened them. "I apologize, Gabriel. I should not have said that."

"Do you ken the effect you have on me?"

Her reply came so softly he almost did not hear it. "The same you have on me."

"Then why will you not accept me? Be my wife, Catherine."

She shook her head, regret soft in her eyes. "I cannot. At least, not yet."

"I willna stop asking."

"I know."

"I want you badly."

She sucked in a breath, pleasure flickering across her features. "I want you too, God help me. But we must think about this with calm reason."

He curled his hands into fists. "Blasted curse. It even manipulates our attraction to each other."

"How do you know it is the curse?"

He let out a disbelieving laugh. "What else could it be?"

Her lips curved in a smile as old as Eve. "Us."

Chapter 12

Us.

That one word haunted Gabriel for the rest of the day's travel as he and his clansmen thundered for the border. Catherine curled against him, the swift pace preventing any conversation. She had buried her face into his chest, her blanket pulled up around her, and he could tell from the relaxation of her limbs that she had fallen asleep again.

The softness of her body played havoc with his concentration.

Of course this immediate, fiery need between them *had* to be driven by the curse. Such violent attraction rarely occurred outside of legend, and certainly not to ordinary people.

He had come close to such a union once, with Jean. He had loved her as he had loved no other woman, and passion had smoldered hot between them. Even knowledge of his destiny had not deterred him from falling for her charms. But they had known each other all their lives. Their desire for each other had grown over time.

The bittersweet tang of regret swept over him. If his duty had not commanded he marry Catherine, he would have wed Jean Farlan years ago. But the curse declared he would have no choice in his bride, so they had parted with heavy hearts.

Now he finally had his bride in hand. He would overcome her uncertainties and convince her to wed him, and his people would be saved from the curse.

He had to believe that once she saw for herself the ravages cast on his people by the curse, she would find the compassion to wed him and end the suffering. All that talk of her perfect husband . . . surely that was just a young girl's fantasy. He was an honorable man who would cherish his wife and take his vows seriously. What more could a woman ask?

At least she had not spoken of love. For that was the one thing he did not think he could give. He had only ever loved one woman, and even though they could never be together, he did not believe he could feel that way for another. Passion and respect would be enough.

It would have to be.

* * *

The ransom note never came.

George Depford stared blankly at the new contracts for the mill, unable to concentrate on a single word. Nearly two days gone, and no word about his daughter's abduction. What sort of fools were these brigands who had taken her? When he had returned home from his meeting with Viscount Nordham, he had found the house in an uproar and his daughter taken.

The housekeeper had been locked in a closet. Several of his footmen had been bruised and knocked unconscious. Poor Peg, Catherine's maid, was beside herself. Stories abounded of how these men had wrapped his daughter in a blanket and forcibly carried her from her home. She had been struggling, he was told. Protesting. Fighting this injustice.

Good girl.

Of course she must have been taken for ransom. He was a wealthy man, wasn't he? Why else would someone come into his house and carry off his daughter if not for a rich reward? And the Bow Street Runners had agreed with him. Wait for a ransom note, they had said. But nearly forty-eight hours had passed, and no demands had come.

How could he know where to look for her if no one contacted him?

He gave up on the contracts and sat back in

his chair, staring at the ceiling. He was a man of action, and this helplessness did not sit well with him. Even Bow Street had not been able to discover anything.

A knock came on the door to the study. "Come!" he barked.

Stodgins opened the door. "Viscount Nordham to see you, sir."

Ah, blast. "Send him in."

"Very good, Mr. Depford." Stodgins backed out of the doorway to let Viscount Nordham enter.

The viscount strode into the room, his pace urgent. "Well? Were you going to tell me at all?"

George shrugged. "I take it you have heard."

"That your daughter—my betrothed—has been abducted? Of course I have. It is all over London."

"Bloody gossips." George waved a hand at a chair. "Sit, Lord Nordham."

"What is the ransom?" Nordham demanded, seating himself. "Who has taken her?"

"I have not yet received a ransom note."

"What?"

"It is true. I assumed one would come, for why else would someone abduct my daughter if not for money? But alas, there has been nothing."

"The devil you say. So there is no hint of who took her, no idea at all of what ordeal she is going through?"

"None." George gave him a sad smile. "Though I do appreciate your concern."

"It concerns me as much as you. I would like to know if my future wife has been violated."

George shuddered. "Dear God, let it not be so."

"Indeed. I would know which heirs are mine."

George sent him a look of disgust. "Must you be so indelicate?"

"The entire situation is indelicate, Depford. Even if she has not been ravished, her reputation is now in shreds—which then reflects on my good name."

George rolled his eyes. The Nordham name was not exactly exalted in some circles. "My daughter was stolen from her home by force, Lord Nordham. I hope you will not expect her to pay for something which was beyond her control."

"Of course not. She is but a woman in the hands of merciless men." He fixed George with a hard stare. "It is you who will pay, Depford, and handsomely, for me to take her off your hands."

"What nonsense is this?"

Nordham leaned back in his chair. "I am already taking on a wife who will most probably go mad. Now there is the chance she will come to me as used goods. If you want me to wed her, you will need to make it worth my while."

"Of all the—you, sir, are an unconscionable rogue!"

"Perhaps." Nordham smirked. "But apparently I am the only man in London who will take your daughter to wife. Pity that she has no other suitors."

"If she did, I would sooner see her with one of them—" He stumbled to a halt as an idea struck. Good God, could it be? He shoved back his chair from his desk and stood.

"What is it, Depford?" Nordham got to his feet.

"An urgent matter. I will have Stodgins show you out." George hurried to the door.

"But we have not yet completed our negotiations."

George opened the door to the study and gestured for Nordham to leave. "Since there is no information right now about my daughter's whereabouts, we have nothing to discuss. As soon as I have the facts, I will contact you."

Nordham approached the doorway slowly, a calculating look on his face. "You know where she is."

"I have an idea. I must investigate further."

"What do you suspect?"

"I would rather gather the facts and present them to you instead of speculating," George said. "Where can I reach you tonight?"

"I shall be at my club."

"Very good then. Stodgins!"

Nordham paused before exiting the room. "You had best share every fact with me, Depford, for I shall find out the truth in the end."

"I am an honest businessman, Lord Nordham." Stodgins arrived, and George said, "Please escort Lord Nordham to the door, Stodgins, and then call for my carriage. I will be going out."

"Very good, sir. This way, my lord."

Nordham sent George one last look. "I will expect to hear from you this evening, Depford."

"I shall contact you at White's," George agreed. "Good day to you."

Nordham spun on his heel and marched after Stodgins. George stepped back into his office, shutting the door with a soft click. Then he leaned against it, closing his eyes.

How could he have missed it? How much time had he wasted waiting for a ransom note that might never come?

Other suitors. Heaven help him, but he had forgotten about the Scotsman. Arneth. Hadn't he come sniffing around Catherine, looking to court her? Hadn't he accused George of stealing the old chief's bride? No doubt he had been furious to be run off at the point of a pistol.

George swiped a hand over his suddenly dry mouth. Revenge. That's what it was. It was the nature of Scotsmen to take what they wanted, damn the consequences. He had flat-out told the fellow his suit would never be accepted. So the Scot had carried off Catherine. It was the only explanation that made sense.

If other brigands had carried her off for riches, they no doubt would have taken advantage of being inside the home of a wealthy man and helped themselves to some of the valuables throughout the house. But nothing was missing. Not a single candlestick or silver spoon. Hardly the work of money-hungry villains.

But an angry Scot who held a grudge—who had attempted to court his daughter and been rejected—now that made sense.

Dear God, what was wrong with him? Why hadn't he thought of Arneth straight off? He should never have overlooked such an important clue. Even now his mind moved slowly, as if he were under some kind of spell. He shook it, struggling to think clearly. Arneth. Of course. He should have realized that at once. Gad, how much time had he wasted? Why hadn't he remembered?

Stodgins tapped at the door. "The carriage is here, sir."

"Excellent." He jerked open the door and stormed down the hallway, fury growing with each step. So the Scotsman thought to take what he wanted, did he? Thought to carry off a man's daughter like she was one more sheep or cow to be added to his herd. Well, he would soon rue the day he had stolen the daughter of George Depford.

Servants stood by with his hat, walking stick, and greatcoat. He accepted all three, his temper nearly boiling over as he considered how frightened Catherine must be. Had the man taken advantage of his captive from the first night? The idea could not be borne. That her innocence should be ripped from her by some savage—

Stodgins opened the door, but George paused for a moment, sucking in deep breaths to calm his raging fury. He needed to think clearly and not jump to conclusions. As a man of the world, he knew what horrors could await a young, innocent girl in the clutches of men with no morals. The type of men to steal a girl from her bed in the middle of the night. But if he thought about them now, the atrocities that could be visited on his only child . . .

He needed to be in control of his emotions, to use his wealth and influence to find his daughter and bring her home. He would deal with the aftermath as it came.

He strode from the house, down the stairs, and

into the carriage. Seating himself, he barked the direction to the driver.

"Dorburton House."

"Tell me about my mother."

Donald paused in his task. They had stopped for the night, again setting camp beside water, even though there was a village a short walk away. Donald and Catherine sat alone by the fire. Gabriel, Patrick, and Brodie had gone to the village to see about spending a few coins on some vegetables to have with their meal—freshly caught rabbit that Donald was currently skinning. Angus and Andrew were a few yards away, taking care of the horses.

The past two days riding with the Scotsmen had earned her some much-needed rest, peaceful slumber undisturbed by maddening dreams or disembodied voices. Despite the urgent speed of their travel, she now felt steady enough to ask some of the questions that had been haunting her.

After all, who better to tell her about her mother than her grandfather?

"What would you like to know?" Donald went back to work on the rabbit, but she could tell his mind was not completely on the task.

"I do not know much about her. She died when

211

I was very young. And the short time I did know her, she was not well."

"Aye, the madness." He sighed, shook his head. "We tried to warn her, to stop her from wedding your father. But she was a determined one, that daughter of mine. When she made up her mind, there was no stopping her."

"I know she was supposed to marry Gabriel's uncle."

"Aye, she was. She had the mark, just here on her shoulder." He touched just above his collarbone, careful to keep the gory knife from staining his clothing. "I've been told you bear the mark as well."

"Yes." Her face warmed, and she was grateful he did not question where it was located. "I assumed I inherited it from my mother."

"The mark doesna always fall in the same family. 'Tis not something passed from mother to daughter, for what a muddle that would make!"

"I do not understand."

He paused in his work to gather his thoughts. "If the girl with the mark marries the chief and then her daughter bears the mark, what happens if the chief and his wife also have a son, who will become the next chief? A sister canna wed her brother."

"I see the problem."

"The lass with the mark—we call her the Bride—is always of the Farlan clan, though sometimes she doesna bear the Farlan name, like yourself."

"So I bear the mark, but I was born a Depford. That means my child will not bear the mark after me?"

"Not at all. Another child born of a Farlan woman already carries that burden, destined to wed the next chief. If Gabriel doesna have sons, then Patrick will be the chief. The lass would marry him."

Catherine frowned as she tried to sort it out in her mind. "What if a Bride is born but the chief is already married? Does she still go mad?"

"No, thank the Lord. The curse seems to know what 'tis about in that respect." When he fell silent, she continued to watch him expectantly. He finally gave a put-upon sigh and added, "If there isna a chief to wed, the curse leaves the girl be. Still, a Bride is born every generation just to be safe. 'Tis why we came looking for you, granddaughter. We couldna find Gabriel's Bride."

"What about the other girl? The one you have already?"

"Ha! She's but six years old. Our people are starving. We couldna wait another ten years, not when there was a chance there was a Bride of Gabriel's generation to be found."

Uncomfortable, Catherine glanced away. "The rules of this curse are very intricate."

He snorted. "Rules? We've only learned this from observation over the past three centuries. The crone who cast the curse didna write down a rulebook for us to follow." He turned his attention back to the rabbit, his movements agitated and jerky.

She hesitated to ask, but the question burned inside her. "Have there been any other brides who did not wed the chief when they should have? Any others who . . . who went mad?"

"Only Glynis." He discarded some unwanted parts and turned the animal over. "In three hundred years, she was the only one to try and run from her fate. The poor lass. She always wanted more than we could give her."

"So my mother was the first bride to go mad."

"She was."

"And up until now, all the other brides married as they were supposed to."

"Aye. Because they knew what would happen if they didna do their duty."

"They would go mad."

"Not just that." Donald set aside the meat he had carefully sliced and picked up the stewpot beside him. He looked up, his eyes blazing. "'Tis nae just the fate of the Bride that matters, granddaughter. There are other repercussions. The curse steals away any bit of prosperity the two clans have enjoyed. Every man, woman, and child experiences hardship and starvation."

"I understand."

"Do you? Even now the clans are suffering, and 'twas my daughter who caused it. She didna want to live simply, as our ancestors have lived for generations. She wanted more, riches and fancy clothing, and she defied centuries of tradition to get it." He stood, the stewpot in hand. "She died for it, poor soul, and others have died since then because of the curse. Because she didna believe. She thought the curse was just a legend—and her lack of faith killed her."

He stalked away, heading for the pond.

Catherine watched him, her heart aching. She wanted to apologize, but she wasn't certain what she had said that had sparked his temper like that.

"He doesna mean to hurt you with his words." Gabriel stepped out of the shadow of the trees, a sack in his hand. "His wife—your grandmother— died because of the curse. She fell ill, and nothing we did could heal her."

"Oh." Tenderness welled in her heart. "Of course he believes in the curse. He must blame something for taking his wife from him."

He gave her a reproachful look. "Catherine, we

all believe in the curse. We've seen too much not to."

"I do not want to argue with you." She stood and shook the dust from her skirts. "I cannot blindly believe in something so fantastical, no matter how much I want to."

"Perhaps when we reach my lands, you will change your mind."

"Perhaps," she agreed.

Donald came back from the pond, hauling the water-filled stewpot. "Have you brought the potatoes?" he demanded.

"I have." Gabriel handed over the sack. "Keep the fire low, Donald. We're nae home yet."

"I know, I know." Donald grabbed the sack and began taking out the few vegetables the men were able to purchase, muttering as he did so. Gabriel walked away from the fire toward the trees. Catherine hurried after him.

"How long until we reach your home?" she asked.

"Several more days."

"And why must my grandfather keep the fire low?"

"Because we might be followed." He stopped walking a short way into the thicket, just far enough to give them privacy, and turned to face her. "You may forget that you left no note for your father. I assume that 'twill take him a short while to discover where you are, but then he will come after us with all the forces his money can buy."

"I had not considered that." Yet the more she thought about it, the more it made sense.

"You didna consider that your doting papa would come all the way to Scotland to fetch you home? I thought you were more intelligent than that."

She stiffened. "There is no cause to be insulting."

"Did you think there was some other reason we were riding like the wind for the border?"

"You said you are eager to marry me. I assumed you intended us to wed at Gretna Green."

He laughed. "Are you daft? I intend to wed you in the MacBraedon family chapel and have the union blessed by a priest."

"Well, you did not share your plans with me." She folded her arms.

"'Twas an oversight. We're nae wed yet."

"And may never be," she snapped.

"Dinna start that talk again. We *will* wed, Catherine Depford, so you'd best get used to it."

"Give me one good reason to marry you."

"This." He pulled her into his arms, his mouth hot and hungry as it covered hers.

She made a tiny whimper in the back of her throat, then surrendered to the kiss, to the wild magic that swept over her whenever he touched her. She didn't understand it, didn't want to accept it. But she could not deny it, either. The power of the passion between them swept away doubt and hesitation and defiance.

He stepped deeper into the woods, dragging her with him. In a moment he had her backed up against a tree, trapped there with his body. He took her wrists in one of his big hands and pinned them above her head, then looked into her eyes, his breath hard and fast.

She could have struggled. Could have screamed. But even though he infuriated her, even though she still believed she had some choice in wedding him, she could not resist him.

Could never resist him.

"This is why we will wed," he whispered, stroking the back of his hand down her throat. "This heat between us canna be cooled by pretending it isna there." His hand slid lower, gliding between her breasts, lingering there. "I want you badly, Catherine. And you want me."

"I do not want to," she murmured. "God as my witness, I wish I had the strength to resist you."

His mouth quirked in an indulgent smile. "But you canna resist this, can you, lass?" He moved his hand, cupped her breast, and stroked the nipple with his finger.

A quick gasp escaped her lips, and her eyes closed

halfway as pleasure began to build. "Gabriel . . ."

"Aye." He bent down and nuzzled his mouth against her throat, continuing to massage her soft flesh. "Say it again, sweet Catherine. Say my name." He rubbed against her, showing her without words how strongly she affected him.

"Gabriel," she sighed.

"There's a lass." He slid his hand downward, stroking her hip, and leaned in to take her mouth in yet another heated kiss. She opened to him, let him feast at her mouth. He let go of her wrists, and she wrapped her arms around his neck, clinging in helpless capitulation.

Another tug at her skirts, but she barely noticed. Cool air brushed her legs. Then his hand, warm on bare flesh, gliding along her thigh.

Between her thighs.

His fingers touched her, and she gasped, her eyes popping open to meet his. He took advantage of her gasp and deepened the kiss, stroking his tongue into her mouth much as his fingers stroked her damp, feminine flesh. All the while he kept his eyes open and watched her, drawing her into this heady intimacy.

Her head spun. She had never felt this before, not outside a dream. Her heart pounded; her blood raced. Her flesh quivered with this new experience, demanding more. She could not look away, could not tell him to stop, even when he ended their kiss and buried his face in her neck.

"This is what I can give you," he murmured against her flesh. "This is why we should wed. This fire between us . . ."

He caressed her feminine folds with a gentle, knowing touch that shattered any doubt still lingering.

". . . this is something rare. Precious."

Tension wound tighter and tighter. He knew just where to touch. And how. And when. Whimpering sounds escaped her throat. She pressed her head back against the tree, trusting that he would not let her fall, and gave herself over to this wicked, delicious sensation.

The climax hit suddenly, startling a cry from her that he quickly stifled with his mouth. Her body quivered, the sharp release tossing her high into bliss, then letting her tumble down to utter contentment. Her muscles hummed; her body sang with exaltation. She sagged in his arms, bemused and deliciously sated.

And wondered, as he pulled her into a strong and comforting embrace, where this left them now.

George Depford strode into his home, practically throwing his hat and walking stick at the servants. His visit with Lady Dorburton had been enlightening indeed, and his mind had snapped back to its normal quick pace. Whatever malaise had affected his memory seemed to have been cured, like a spell that had been broken.

How dare he? How dare that Scots rogue carry off his daughter after his suit had been refused?

He stormed up the stairs to his bedchamber, calling for his valet.

He should have expected this sort of behavior. No man liked being told he was unsuitable, especially at the point of a pistol. He should have known a proud man like Lord Arneth would not simply walk away without a whimper. Hadn't he himself spent years working with the Scots, bargaining with them for their wool? And hadn't he learned in all that time that a clan chief was the most arrogant of all men? That they got what they wanted, no matter what the method?

Arneth had wanted Catherine, so he had taken her.

He was gone from London. Lady Dorburton had confirmed that. And his men with him, including the identical twins described by his servants.

And Catherine.

His thoughts were racing with full strength, planning and rejecting strategies. Fury boiled through him, and he again bellowed for his valet. This time the little man came running.

"Yes, Mr. Depford?"

"Pack my bags, Bloodworth. We are going to Scotland immediately."

"Will you be hunting or will this be a business trip, sir?"

"Both." George let out a wicked laugh. "I will be traveling by coach with my fastest team. Pack appropriately."

"Yes, sir." Bloodworth raced from the room.

"Take my daughter, will you?" George spat. He pulled a packet of papers from the pocket of his greatcoat, tossed them on the bed, then shrugged off the coat itself. "You shall pay for that, you blasted Scot! See if you do not."

He picked up the papers from the bed and glanced through them. There was only one thing left to do.

Stalking over to the desk, he took the quill and scrawled his signature at the bottom of the paper with Lord Nordham's.

He would set out for Scotland tonight, and when he caught up with the villains who had abducted his daughter, he would see them all arrested and transported at the very least. As for Catherine, he had no doubt she would be thrilled to see him. He dared not imagine the indignities she must have suffered at the hands of the Scots.

Luckily Lord Nordham had been agreeable—

based on a substantial increase to Catherine's marriage settlement—to taking to wife a young lady who had been through such an ordeal.

He folded up the papers again and set them on the desk where he would not forget them when he left for Scotland. With any luck, his daughter would be a viscountess by the end of the week, and he could rest easy at last, knowing he had provided her a future of comfort and security.

He just hoped this experience did not send her over the edge into complete madness.

Chapter 13

After several days of travel, Catherine felt wrung out and completely filthy.

She woke with Gabriel pressed up against her back, his arm slung over her waist. The rest of the camp was still asleep. Quietly she sat up, resting her back against a fallen log. Gabriel shifted slightly but did not wake. Her determined suitor had tied a rope around her ankle that fastened to his wrist. Though the rope wasn't particularly thick, the knots were complicated and tight. Had she been determined to escape, it would have taken her hours to undo them.

But escape seemed a foolish notion. Where would she go, back to London? Back to madness and a marriage to a man who loved her fortune more than he loved her?

At least in the company of the Scotsmen, the madness abated. And she had *chosen* this path rather than having a future foisted upon her.

Her gaze drifted to Gabriel. Days had passed since their encounter in the woods when he had shown her a glimpse of what it could be like between them. They had not spoken about it, and nothing of that nature had happened again. Yet every time he looked at her, she was transported back to that moment. The temptation to repeat the experience was nearly irresistible. Even now she trembled just to think of it.

He surely was a handsome fellow. Her gaze slid over his face—his lashes looking so silky compared to his masculine features. A sharp blade of a nose, prominent cheekbones, a dent in his chin. And his mouth. His lips looked soft and lush from where she sat, the little scar at the corner only adding to the appeal. The attraction between them burned hotter than any dream she had ever had, and she imagined for a moment what it would be like living as his wife. Given his lusty nature, no doubt he would bed her often and get her with child very quickly.

Just the thought sent a surge of warmth through her private places. Yes, there were worse things in marriage than having an enthusiastic and robust bridegroom.

The muffled sound of horses' hooves jerked her out of her fantasies. She huddled down behind the log and peered over it to look off into the trees toward the main road. After a few moments, two men leading their horses came through the woods.

"Well, well," one said softly. "A flock of chickens ripe for the plucking."

The other shook his head. "They look to be Scots barbarians. They might kill ye as soon as look at ye. I'd leave them alone and look elsewhere to water your horse."

Catherine slowly sank down farther behind the log. The rope tying her to Gabriel did not allow her to go far, but she managed to curl herself around him. Perhaps if these newcomers saw everyone sleeping, they would go on their way.

And maybe she would grow wings and fly home to London.

The two brigands tied their mounts to tree branches near the water so their animals could drink and crept back toward the slumbering travelers.

Catherine snuggled closer to Gabriel, her mouth near his ear. "Gabriel, we are not alone."

He made no noise. No grunting, yawning, or startled yelp. One moment he was sleeping, and the next he was wide awake. He turned his head slowly so he could look into her eyes.

"Fine horseflesh," the one thief said. "They would fetch a pretty penny."

Gabriel narrowed his eyes. Then he mouthed, "My dagger," and cast his gaze downward. She followed his line of sight and saw the dagger tucked into the sheath at his belt. As silently as she could she eased the weapon from its holder, then slid her hand and the blade beneath the edge of her skirt.

Footsteps approached and stopped.

"Bloody hell, Martin, they have a woman with them!" came the hoarse whisper.

"Is that so?" The other man came over. "Look at that hair. They say redheads enjoy a tussle more than other wenches."

"I say we slit their throats, then take their purses and their horses. And the woman."

"Agreed." One of the men stepped closer to Gabriel. The quiet hiss of a blade leaving the sheath echoed in the clearing.

Gabriel jumped to his feet. One arm came up and sent the villain's knife flying. A well-placed elbow sent the fellow sprawling. Gabriel's other arm stretched awkwardly, still bound to Catherine. "The rope!" he barked.

She brought out the knife and slit the rope with a single slice, freeing him as the other brigand charged him. His fist came around and met the man's jaw with a crack.

Hands grabbed Catherine from behind, and she screamed.

"Hush now, 'tis only me." Donald dragged her backward, away from the fighting. Brodie, Patrick, and the twins had jumped to their feet and were charging into the fray. "Come away with me now so you dinna get hurt. The lads know what they're about."

With her grandfather's help, Catherine struggled to her feet and hurried away from the brawl. The old man gripped a dagger of his own as he led her by the hand at a run into the trees nearby.

"What about Gabriel?" she panted, leaning against a tree trunk when her grandfather stopped.

"Dinna fash yourself. 'Twill be over in moments." His gaze was fixed on the fight where he could see it through the leafy branches.

She could not see anything. The awful sounds of flesh hitting flesh reached her ears, followed by cries of pain. Who was winning? She could not tell, and she worried that the thieves would somehow overwhelm Gabriel's men and come looking for her. She glanced at her grandfather. He grasped his dagger with the ease of long experience, but he was still an old man. She clenched her fingers around the handle of the blade she still held. She would protect him if need be.

After a few minutes, silence settled over the area.

"Catherine?" Gabriel called.

"Here." She stumbled forward, astounded at how her heart had leaped at the sound of his voice. She shoved her way through the saplings, one branch snapping back and whacking her in the eye with a large leaf. She shoved the bough aside, blinking frantically as tears welled from the sting.

"There you are." Clothing and hair askew and blood trickling from the corner of his mouth, Gabriel held out a hand to her.

She reached for him, then stopped short as her leg caught. Glancing behind her, she saw the rope tied to her ankle had gotten tangled around a thorn bush. A growl of frustration escaped her as she marched back to deal with the situation.

He chuckled, then arrived at the thorn bush in three long strides, just before she did. Reaching his callused hand into the spiny overgrowth, he swiftly untangled the rope.

"There, you are free."

She said nothing, just bent down, lifted the edge of her skirt, and tore a thin strip from the edge of her shift. Letting her skirts fall back into position, she reached up and dabbed at the blood on his lip with the makeshift bandage. "Does this hurt?"

"'Tis nothing." The look he gave her shook her to her toes. Possessive. Hungry.

She froze, the scrap of cotton still pressed to

229

his warm mouth. How easily she had stepped into such a wifely role.

Too easily.

Intimacy wound around them like smoke.

He took her hand in his larger one and brought it to his lips. His kiss was as gentle as a butterfly and as forceful as a boiling spring. "You tore your garment for me, lass, and I canna afford to buy you another."

"It does not matter," she murmured. She could not look away from his eyes, so blue and warm. His prowess in laying low the thieves had affected her as if she were a green girl, all awkward silence and self-conscious blushes. How ridiculous was it to be impressed by male grace and a muscular form? Did her thrill at his victory make her weak and foolish?

There was more to a man than physical strength.

Nonetheless, his knowing smile made her heart do a slow turn in her chest.

"It does matter," he said, squeezing her hand. She quickly snatched it away. "You must have a care with your belongings. I am not a rich man."

"I am wealthy enough for the both of us."

He frowned. "Your father willna pay your dowry to the man who doesna have his approval."

"Meaning I am nothing without my father's money?"

He chuckled and tapped his finger on the chin she had raised in ire. "You are much more than a rich man's daughter, Catherine Depford."

The admiration in his tone silenced her.

Brodie came over to them, a small leather bag in his hand. "Let me see to that wound, Gabriel."

"I already . . ." Her words faded as Brodie turned Gabriel around. A long, nasty cut gashed the back of his arm halfway from his shoulder to his elbow.

She swallowed hard, unable to look away from the blood oozing from the slash. It trickled along his arm and dripped to the ground.

Brodie withdrew a needle and thread from the bag. He glanced at Catherine and scowled. "If you canna stomach the sight of blood, turn your back, lass."

Gratefully, Catherine turned away.

She found herself surveying the camp. Patrick had one thief lying facedown on the ground with Donald sitting atop him, binding the brigand's hands with rope. Mere feet away, Andrew sat on top of the other miscreant. Angus approached his brother from the direction of the horses, a coil of rope in his hand.

"What will happen to them?" she asked, not daring to look at Gabriel.

"We'll bring them to the magistrate and let justice have its way." He hissed with pain, and she couldn't stop herself from glancing over. Steady as an oak, Brodie methodically pushed the needle through Gabriel's flesh over and over and carefully closed up the wound.

"Is there anything I can do to help?" she surprised herself by asking.

Brodie glanced up at that. "I'll be finished in a moment. I've done this before, you ken."

"'Twas a lucky blow is all," Gabriel said, grinning over his shoulder at Catherine. "We'll break camp when Brodie is done."

Unable to watch the unorthodox surgery unless absolutely necessary, Catherine turned her attention back to the thieves. Patrick and Donald had bound their captive, who squirmed on the ground in frustration.

Donald watched the man's antics with a grin of unholy glee. "Madmen they were, to attack a party of Scotsmen, and them outnumbered," he said with a chuckle.

A few feet away, Angus and Andrew tied the last knot on their own prisoner, then pushed him into a sitting position against a log. The fellow attempted to get up, and Andrew shoved him back down with a boot against his chest. Angus produced a lethal-looking blade and loomed over the thief in silent threat.

Catherine stood helplessly, lost in this alien world of male violence and casual cruelty.

"Done," Brodie said, snapping the thread.

"My thanks to you," Gabriel said.

Brodie nodded, then walked away. Gabriel turned to face his men. He sent a smile at Catherine, but she couldn't respond. Perhaps she was simply undone by the attack; she wasn't certain. Perhaps *bewildered* was a better word. Or *shocked*.

"Here now, you needn't watch this." Apparently reading her mood, Gabriel took her by the shoulders and turned her away from the scene, leading her back to the log where their blankets were. "The men have the situation under control. Are you hungry?"

"A little."

"I've a bit of bread." He crouched by his rumpled blanket and opened his satchel.

"They meant to kill you." She sank down on the ground, her knees suddenly weak as water. "They would have killed all of you and ravished me."

"They're just simple thieves. I've handled worse." He sat beside her, resting against the log, and unfolded a square of cloth to reveal a heel of bread.

"I have never seen anything like that before." She took the bread and broke off a piece, then rolled the bit between her trembling fingers and thumb,

233

too distracted to eat. "You were quite brave in your defense of us."

He shrugged, reaching to rip off some bread for himself. "Perhaps 'twill make you feel safer with me."

"Perhaps." Contemplative, she popped the bread into her mouth.

She could not deny that he had warded off the thieves with little effort. Obviously he was perfectly capable of protecting her physically. But what about emotionally? Would he have a care for her heart, or would he treat it with the same indifference as he did the thieves?

She wished there was some sign that she was doing the right thing by journeying to Scotland.

An insect buzzed around her head, and she slapped at it, missed, then succeeded in swatting it flat against her arm. The sight of the squashed bug smeared over her flesh made her stomach lurch.

"I need a bath," she announced, scanning for something to wipe her arm. "I look as if I live in the sty with the pigs."

Gabriel produced a handkerchief and cleared away the remains of the insect. "You look fine. We're almost to the border."

"I do *not* look fine. My dress is filthy and my hair is attracting these insects." She swatted at another one. "I used to bathe every day and change my clothes at least three times before supper. My current state is unacceptable!"

"You wash your face every morning."

"That is not enough. I need a bath, I tell you." Panic rose inside her. Suddenly a bath was the most important thing in the world to her, as foolish as it seemed. She needed to feel clean again. "I smell terrible."

"You're welcome to bathe in the burn there."

She flushed. "I cannot bathe in that stream without seriously compromising my modesty. There are hardly any bushes along the edge."

"I could tell the lads not to look."

"Will you *stop*!" She got to her feet. "You seem amused by my state, Lord Arneth. I, however, am not! Can we not once stay at an inn for the night?"

"No, we canna stay at an inn. Your father is bound to be at our heels as it is!"

"My father probably does not even know where I am."

Gabriel folded his arms behind his head and leaned back on the log. "I would say he does. We had words, he and I."

She narrowed her eyes. "What words?"

"I told him I meant to wed you, and he told me 'twould never happen. Oh, and he had a pistol."

"What!"

He shrugged. "'Tis true. So aye, I expect your father is most probably after us, so the sooner we get to MacBraedon lands, the safer we will be."

"I never expected him to follow us."

He barked with laughter. "What did you think he would do once his precious daughter went missing?"

"I did not think about it at all. I was angry at him. I did not even consider how my disappearance might affect him."

"A fine daughter you are," Gabriel chided. "One disagreement doesna mean he stops loving you. I imagine he was mad with panic when he found you gone."

This news did not sit well with her already frazzled composure. How could she have not realized? Of course Papa would be worried about her. "I am afraid I have been so caught up in my own affairs that I did not consider how this would affect Papa."

"Aye, you do tend to be concerned with yourself."

Her mouth dropped open. "What a horrible thing to say!"

He shrugged. "'Tis true. You plotted to marry Kentwood, all the while wanting him to take care of you. You never gave a thought to how it would affect Kentwood to have a mad wife."

The truth sliced through the last thread of her control. "That is none of your affair!"

"It is, you ken, because I am the man you were meant to wed."

"According to *you*."

"According to the blasted curse!" He jumped to his feet, anger radiating from every inch of him. "I am destined to marry you, Catherine Depford, and let me remind you that *you* would nae have been my choice if you'd not been forced on me by that curse."

She sucked in a breath, offended. Furious. Her eyes stung. "Then why are you even here?"

"Because I have no choice." His words hammered at her like stones cast from a crowd. "I have people depending on me—on *us*—to save their lives. I have responsibilities I canna ignore."

"So you keep saying."

"And every word is true." His blue eyes blazed with fury, and she suddenly became aware of the rest of the camp watching them. Silently.

He held up a hand and began to tick off his fingers. "My people are starving. My brother has been reiving cattle from our neighbors to try and help feed our clan, and I must settle the debt.

My sister, Brodie's wife, is about to birth their first babe, but he is here at my side, helping his people, instead of with his wife. The twins hadna seen their mother for weeks because she has been working in your father's household to help us get close to you. Your grandfather has lost both a daughter and a wife to this curse, but he is here with us to protect you.

"All of this is caused by the curse, Catherine Depford, and we are all of us here for you, because you are the key to making the suffering stop." He raked his gaze down her form. "Yet you willna make the commitment to wed me. All you can talk about is a bloody bath."

To her horror, tears welled up in her eyes. "I am sorry."

"I will believe that," he said, "when you stand with me before the priest and say 'I will.'"

He turned on his heel and stormed off, leaving her alone in the middle of the clearing, surrounded by clansmen who would not meet her eyes.

Well, he'd made a fine muddle of everything.

Gabriel balanced his dagger, aimed, then let it fly. It landed with a satisfying thunk in the trunk of the dead tree. He stalked forward, retrieved his dagger, then went back to the other side of the clearing and aimed again.

Brodie came out of the trees just as the dagger flew by. Once again it hit the dead oak.

"Have a care with that," Brodie said.

"Dinna walk between me and the target," Gabriel snapped. "Is the camp packed up then?"

"Aye." Brodie retrieved the knife from the tree and brought it to Gabriel. "You said some harsh words to the lass."

"She pricked my temper." He took his dagger and turned it over in his hand. "A bloody bath! People are starving."

"She hasna seen it. She canna know."

"Is she not human then? Has she no compassion?" He aimed, threw. Thunk! Hit the tree again.

"She's young, Gabriel, and has lived a life of luxury we canna even imagine. Heaven help us, but the lass is all a-muddle simply because she's been wearing the same dress all this time."

"Who cares about the bleedin' dress?"

"She does."

"Bah!" Gabriel went to retrieve his dagger. When he'd pulled the blade from the tree, he turned to face Brodie. "She's spoiled is what she is."

"Aye, she is. Spoiled and taken from her home. Gabriel, at least she came willingly."

"You call it willing when I had to carry her out?"

Brodie grinned. "That was just Farlan temper is all."

"She came for herself, to find answers to her madness. Not to wed me. Not to help our people."

"I think she will realize the truth when she sees what the curse has done to the clans."

Gabriel strode over and took his place again. "Why the devil does the curse choose my bride for me? Why can I not simply wed any Farlan woman? I would have taken Jean and been content."

Brodie shrugged. "'Tis a curse, you ken. I dinna believe 'tis supposed to be easy."

"But this one. How can I wed a woman like that? Aye, she makes my loins ache, but other than that—is there no character? Does she think of no one but herself?"

"Perhaps you need to set an example," Brodie said. "If you show her compassion, she might surprise you."

"Perhaps." He pondered the old tree, then considered his future wife. "I will think on it."

"Good. Now come along. We've those brigands to dispatch before we can be on our way."

"You're right." Gabriel slid his dagger back in its sheath. "The sooner we get home, the better."

The Scotsmen made short work of the brigands, tossing the bound men over the backs of their horses. Then they broke camp and set out on the road again, leading the footpads behind them on their mounts.

They reached the magistrate in a little over an hour. The thieves were well known to him, and the magistrate had been hunting them for some while. Gabriel was grinning as he came out of the magistrate's office. He said nothing about what had transpired, merely climbed back into the saddle behind Catherine, pulling her close.

She rode the rest of the day in front of Gabriel, her head in the hollow of his collarbone and her body surrounded by his strong arms. Her hip was tucked into the cradle of his thighs, and she could not ignore his nearness. Yet despite the intimate position, she could feel the wall he'd erected between them. She hated knowing it was there, wholly aware of his low opinion of her. Was she really that selfish? She had only been trying to find a solution to her problem. Perhaps in resolving her issue, she would solve his as well.

By nightfall, she was drooping in the saddle. When Gabriel finally called a halt, she nearly cried with relief.

"Are you certain about this?" Brodie asked.

"Aye," Gabriel said. He dismounted, then caught Catherine as she nearly slid out of the saddle. "Here we are, my girl. Stand up now. There you are."

Catherine swayed on her feet, clutching at his cloak to keep from falling. "Where are we?"

"I've seen to our accommodations tonight," he said. "Look."

She managed to focus. "Good heavens! Are we at an inn?"

"Indeed." A stable lad came forward, but Gabriel waved him off. "Patrick, you and Andrew see to the horses."

"Aye, Gabriel." Patrick took the reins of Gabriel's mount. "Where shall we meet you?"

"In the dining room. There's food a-plenty, I'm told."

"Saints be praised!" Following the stable lad, Patrick led the horses into the stable.

Catherine clung to Gabriel. "I thought you did not stay at inns."

"Tonight we do." He led her inside. Brodie, Donald, and Angus trailed behind.

"Good evening, my lord!" The innkeeper came forward with a huge smile.

"Good evening. Is all prepared?"

"It is indeed, my lord."

"Excellent. Lads." He turned to his companions. "Sit in the dining room and fill your bellies. I will escort Catherine to her room."

"One minute, MacBraedon," Donald said, disapproval creasing his face. "Do you think—"

"—that as her fiancé, I am the only one who should accompany her? You are correct, of course."

"That isna what I was going to say."

"My daughter, Ellen, will be assisting the lady," the innkeeper said. "You, my lord, may escort her to her room, but this is a respectable establishment."

"Of course, my good man," Gabriel said. "I will simply conduct my future wife to her chamber and then return to the dining room for some of your delicious fare."

Young Ellen stepped forward. "This way, my lord."

Gabriel followed the innkeeper's daughter, urging Catherine along before him.

"Gabriel." She paused at the foot of the stairs and lowered her voice. "How can we afford this?"

He nearly smiled at her use of the word *we*. "Those brigands were worth more than my sheep. There was a fine bounty for bringing them to justice."

Delight sparkled in her eyes. "I am so glad some good came of that."

Ellen paused at the top of the stairs. "Miss?"

"Coming!" Catherine hurried up the stairs. Gabriel followed behind her, ridiculously happy at having made her smile. What spell did the woman weave? Or was it the curse again, making him want her more than seemed normal? Even as he relished the attraction between them, he dared not trust it. Perhaps this was the curse's way of bringing the accursed couple together. Would it wear off once they were wed?

He hoped not. It was that promise which made this union palatable to him.

He reached the upper hallway and followed the women two chambers down. Ellen pulled out a key and unlocked one door, then swung it open and gestured for Catherine to enter.

Gabriel reached them just as she started to go into the room. She froze in the doorway. Over her shoulder he could see the candles lit around the large metal tub, steam rising from the water within it.

"Your bath, my lady," he murmured.

She spun around to face him, surprised pleasure lighting up her face. "Oh, Gabriel, thank you!"

He lifted her hand to his lips. "Ellen will bring you a nightdress to sleep in and a clean traveling dress for tomorrow. Good night, sweet Catherine."

She clung to his hand before he could leave. "Thank you, Gabriel. Truly." She tugged him closer, then stood on tiptoe to brush a kiss on his cheek.

His heart squeezed at the first freely given sign

of acceptance from her. "Pleasant dreams," he said, then left her while he still could.

Catherine watched him go, more touched by his kindness than she could express. Perhaps there was some hope for a compatible union after all.

Chapter 14

On the day they reached the MacBraedon lands, Catherine was not certain what to expect. Certainly not an ancient castle built on the headland of a huge lake, a stone wall enclosing the sprawling fortress. A drawbridge spanned a canal in front of the stronghold, leading the way to the strip of land that was almost an island.

They had emerged from a road winding through the mountains to be treated to the stunning view of the glen where the MacBraedon clan lived. Weather-worn cottages and barren fields dotted the landscape, and in the distance stood the castle with the blue expanse of the water behind it. A well-traveled road wound its way to the drawbridge of the castle.

In the distance, a child gave a shout and ran for one of the cottages. By the time the group made their way down the road, the villagers were emerging from their homes and lining the streets. They cheered and waved as the horsemen rode by, some running alongside the travelers as they made for the keep.

Secure in Gabriel's embrace, Catherine could not help but notice the extreme poverty of the people around her. Clothing was threadbare and many times mended. The people were gaunt, a weariness in their postures even as they smiled with genuine pleasure to see their chief. The children hid behind their mothers' skirts, their eyes wide and their silence eerily wrong.

Every once in a while they would pass a cottage with a cow or sheep in the yard. Even the animals looked drained of life, strangely thin and listless in the bright daylight.

The glen looked like a slice of heaven with blue sky, the beauty of the huge lake, and the majestic mountains all around them. The people who lived there should have reflected nature's bounty, and the fact that they did not disturbed her greatly.

Gabriel had warned her that his people were starving, but she had still never imagined this.

They rode across the old drawbridge. The wooden planks creaked as they traversed it, and she glanced uneasily at the water below, wondering if horses could swim. When she looked up again, they were on the other side and riding through the gates of MacBraedon Castle.

A crowd of people met them in the courtyard, cheering and calling out to them as the travelers halted their horses and dismounted.

"Brodie!"

Gabriel was just helping her off the horse when Catherine heard the cry, and as her feet touched the ground, she saw a woman heavy with child throw herself into Brodie's arms. The petite brunette immediately burst into tears, and Brodie's face was a picture of tenderness as he whispered to her, holding her with one arm around her waist and wiping the moisture from her cheeks with his other hand.

"That would be Maire," Gabriel murmured. "Brodie's wife and my sister."

"Gabriel!"

Gabriel turned just in time to embrace the older woman who rushed forward. "Mamaidh," he said. He gave her a squeeze, then turned to Catherine. "Catherine, this is my mother, Fenella."

Fenella smiled at her. Her eyes were the same stunning blue as her son's, and she smiled as she clasped Catherine's hand in both of hers. "My heavens, you look like your mother! I'm pleased to meet you, Catherine, and happier than you know that you've come."

"Thank you." Catherine looked around her, uncomfortable with the light of hope she saw in Fenella's eyes. "The castle is absolutely wonderful."

Fenella laughed. "'Tis spring right now. 'Tis not quite so comfortable in the wintertime. Come." She led Catherine by the hand to where a big bear of a man was hugging Patrick. "Let me introduce you to my husband. Lachlan!"

The older man turned toward them. His green eyes sparkled, and his long hair was a combination of silver with streaks of gold that matched the beard that framed his smile. He was tall and broad of shoulder, but age had added considerable bulk to his belly. "So, this is Gabriel's bride. Welcome, my dear."

"Thank you," Catherine said. Then the man startled her by grabbing her and hugging her tightly. For an instant she could swear she felt his hand brush her bottom, but then he was releasing her with a jolly laugh.

"You're a bonny one to be sure, and that red hair means Farlan or my name isna Lachlan Drummond."

"Her mother was Donald's daughter," Fenella said. Her smile appeared strained, but then she looked at Patrick, and the joy returned to her face. "Patrick, thank God you are safe."

Patrick laughed and hugged her until she squealed in unmatronly glee. "'Twas England, Mamaidh, not the wars."

"Same thing," Lachlan snorted.

249

"Catherine." Brodie came over with his wife on his arm. "Allow me to introduce my wife, Maire."

"I'm so pleased to meet you," Maire said. She was such a tiny woman that her rounded belly took up most of her torso. She wore her dark hair in a knot at the base of her neck, and her hazel eyes sparkled with good humor, even as they were shadowed with weariness. When she smiled, Catherine noted a resemblance to Gabriel's mother.

"Your husband has been most eager to get back to you," Catherine said. "Congratulations on your child."

"Thank you." Maire placed her hands protectively on her belly. "We expect the birth in a month's time."

Gabriel came over to them. "What has happened to me wee sister?" he teased. "I swear you're twice as big as when I left you."

Catherine's mouth fell open at the indelicacy of the statement, but Maire just laughed and swatted Gabriel's arm. "You're a horrible man, Gabriel MacBraedon, to poke fun at a woman in my state."

"'Tis a good thing we are blood kin. You canna do much harm to me without drawing the wrath of the kirk."

Maire rolled her eyes and turned her attention

back to Catherine. "Men are naught but little boys in clumsy grown bodies, dinna you think?"

"I . . . I could not say."

"My betrothed is a virtuous woman." Gabriel slung his arm around her shoulders and gave her a quick hug.

Catherine jumped, startled. How could he call her his betrothed in front of all these people when nothing had been agreed upon between them? She was tempted to correct him, but she had never seen Gabriel so cheerful and was reluctant to ruin his homecoming. In fact, everyone in the courtyard was amazingly loud and laughing and boisterous. So open with their emotions. How could they be so carefree when it was clear that survival hovered on the brink of disaster?

"There's to be a feast," Brodie said. "So your mother tells me. To celebrate the chief's homecoming."

"A feast, is it?" Gabriel asked. "And where will we be getting the fatted calf?"

"Strange as it seems," Maire said, growing more serious, "just yesterday Dougal the Younger caught a magnificent stag and brought it to the castle to share with everyone."

"I canna believe the luck!" Gabriel exclaimed. "Such a feast is truly a blessing."

251

"Perhaps your luck is changing," Maire said with a smile toward Catherine. "Meg—the wife of Will the baker, not the other Meg—said her cow gave milk this morning for the first time in weeks."

Gabriel's mouth fell open in amazement, and then he snapped it shut. "I dinna know what to say."

"I think the curse is pleased with you, brother." Maire laughed and squeezed his arm. "When is the wedding?"

Gabriel shot a look at her, but Catherine could not answer, immobilized with uncertainty. She did not want to disappoint Gabriel's family, but she had not yet decided if they would suit. And wasn't there some old saying about not upsetting a woman who was with child?

Donald came over just then and diverted the conversation. "I'll be leaving you for a short while, granddaughter, to go fetch my own back for the festivities. You'll be safe enough in the castle."

"Do you not live here?" she asked.

Donald choked. "A Farlan chief living in Mac-Braedon Castle? My ancestors would disown me."

"We might have a position open for a butler," Gabriel said, deadpan.

"Dinna turn your gaze on me," Donald snorted. "The lot of you are too slovenly to look after."

The men roared with laughter.

"Grandfather." Unused to such irreverent humor, Catherine grasped his hand between both of his. "Will you be back soon?"

He gave her a tender smile. "Before sundown, my dear. I must go home and fetch your family to you."

Her fingers tightened around his hand, but then she released him. She was nervous to meet her relatives and even more discomfited to be left alone with the MacBraedons. They all looked at her as if she were the answer to their prayers. She hated to disappoint such friendly people, but she had to be true to her heart, whichever direction it led her.

And it might not lead her to the altar with Gabriel.

Donald kissed her cheek and called out his farewells, then got back on his horse and rode out, Angus and Andrew on either side.

"Are Angus and Andrew Farlans as well?" she asked.

Gabriel shook his head. "No, they're going with Donald to protect him. Despite his denials, the man is getting on in years."

"You must be exhausted," Maire said, taking Catherine by the arm. "I'll show you to your room, and you can rest before the feast begins."

"That would be wonderful." As Maire led her away, she glanced back at Gabriel. He merely waved in farewell, then was swallowed up by the crowd of family.

Maire led Catherine into the cool stone castle, and the raucous voices in the courtyard faded to a dim echo. They passed the great hall, then Maire led her up a curving staircase. Brodie's wife took the stairs slowly, clearly struggling with her burden. She paused once, halfway to the top.

"Are you well?" Catherine hovered near Maire where she leaned against the wall to catch her breath. "Shall I fetch someone?"

"No." Maire shook her head, and Catherine noticed the young woman's face was pink with exertion and damp with sweat. "'Tis just close to my time and the babe ofttimes steals the wind from me."

"Let me help you." Taking Maire's elbow, she assisted the woman in her slow climb up the stairs.

When they reached the top, Maire paused again for a few moments, then led Catherine down the hall to the tower at the end.

"This is the best room in the castle, except for Gabriel's," she said. The door creaked loudly as she opened it. "You can see clear across the loch."

Catherine stepped into the room. The tower was square rather than round, and the furniture was simple. There were glass windows on three sides of the room, a strange indulgence compared to the threadbare curtains, and sunlight streamed in to light up the spacious room. The large bed looked quite old and was covered with a handmade woven blanket in a blue and black plaid pattern.

"We hope you'll be comfortable here," Maire said.

"It is a lovely room." Catherine ran a hand over the blanket.

"My grandmother wove that." She suddenly hissed with pain and placed a hand on her lower back. "Heavens!"

"Sit down." Catherine hurried over and helped her get to the stool beside the hearth. "Shall I call someone?"

"Rachel and Flora will be along with some water for you to wash with," Maire said. "We dinna have enough water to spare for a full bath, so 'twill just be for the basin over there."

"I would be glad of it."

Maire gave a weak smile. "I expect them to come at any moment, so I will sit here until they do."

"Are you certain I cannot help you in any way?" Maire looked very pale—too pale as far as Catherine was concerned. "I do not . . . that is, I have never known anyone who was breeding before. I confess I do not know what to do."

"Perhaps 'tis the excitement of your arrival." Maire smiled, and once more Catherine was unnerved by the utter faith and hope in her eyes. "When you wed my brother, you will make things right again."

Unwilling to distress the ailing woman further, Catherine tried to change the subject. "Perhaps I should fetch your mother? Or even your father?"

"My father?" Maire closed her eyes against another twinge of pain. "My father died almost twenty years ago."

"Then who is . . . Your mother introduced me to her husband."

"Oh, Lachlan. Aye, he is her husband but no one's father."

Catherine went to sit on the edge of the bed. "Your family lineage is somewhat confusing."

Maire laughed, and some of the tension faded from her face. "The pain is easing some."

Catherine let out a relieved breath. "Thank goodness."

"I must admit, your arrival was timely," Maire said. "I've been fearful for the child. 'Tis my first."

"Do the women in your family have difficulty in childbirth?"

"No." Maire rubbed her hands over her belly. "'Tis the curse is all. Terrible things happen for no reason at all."

Catherine hesitated before replying. How was

a body supposed to respond to such a statement? *I do not believe in your curse?* And she wasn't even certain that was the case anymore. For some reason, the more time she spent with the Scots, the more real the curse appeared to be.

What if the power to end the suffering of these people was really in her hands? What if all she needed to do to change the direction of all these lives and save her own sanity was to marry Gabriel?

Uncomfortable with this train of thought but needing to know more, she probed, "You said things were better in your grandmother's time."

"Aye. The glen was alive with crops ripening, and there was cattle and sheep aplenty. The wells were full of fresh, sweet water, and the men brought back fish by the net full when they went out on the loch." She smiled, a wistful tone entering her voice. "I remember it a little. I was just a girl when everything changed."

"From what I have been told," Catherine said, watching for a reaction, "the change occurred when my mother ran off to wed my father."

"Aye, 'tis true." Maire nodded, sadness clouding her expression. "Until then all the Brides had married their true husbands, and the curse was satisfied. Glynis Farlan was the first to deny her destiny."

Deny her destiny. Curse or not, her mother had indeed run away from the man to whom she was betrothed. She had spurned her duty. And if Catherine chose to believe in the curse, that was what she was doing by not committing to marry Gabriel.

"The curse takes away all the bounty from the land," Maire continued, apparently not bothered by Catherine's silence. "The crops willna grow and the wells go dry. The cows dinna give milk. The lambs are born with two heads." She swallowed hard, smoothing a trembling hand over her bulging belly. "It has been twenty years since this land has come alive. Twenty years while my people have had to wait for Gabriel to grow into a man and become chief of the clan so he could make everything right again."

"The old chief had no sons?"

"Oh no. 'Tis part of the curse. *Only the dagger will bring him sons; should he wed another, there will be none.*"

The hair on Catherine's arms stood up as Maire easily quoted part of the verse that had so long haunted her dreams. She moistened her suddenly dry lips. "So the chief can only have sons if he weds the right woman."

"Aye."

"And Gabriel's uncle—your uncle—did not wed his Bride, so he had no sons."

"No children at all."

"And your parents were already married."

"Aye, and Gabriel was barely a man full grown when Uncle Angus fell from the battlements and died."

Catherine shuddered; the description of the old chief's death too closely matched her mother's.

A clatter sounded from in the hall, startling both of them.

"That will be the water," Maire said, starting to rise.

Catherine got to her feet and waved the expectant mother back into her seat. "You stay right there, Maire." The knock came, and Catherine called, "Come in!"

Two young girls entered the room. One, a freckle-faced redhead, struggled with a full pitcher. The other was a brown-haired girl with a sunny smile who bore a stack of drying cloths.

"Catherine, this is Rachel"—the dark-haired girl bobbed a quick curtsy— "and this is Flora." The redhead did the same. "They keep the household running."

The girls giggled at that, and Flora went over to the bureau and carefully set her burden beside the plain white basin atop it.

Catherine came forward and took the pile of drying cloths from Rachel. "Help your mistress, Rachel. She is unwell."

The servant blinked. "Oh, she's not my mistress, my lady. You are."

Catherine's mouth fell open as Rachel blithely turned to help Gabriel's sister. Maire chuckled, getting to her feet with the girl's assistance. "You will be marrying my brother, Catherine, which makes you lady of the house."

"But—"

"Everyone here already considers you their lady," Maire continued. "When you wed my brother, you deliver us from the curse."

Flora came back, swinging the empty bucket. "If you call for me before the feast this evening, my lady, I will arrange your hair for you."

"She does a lovely job of it, too." Maire touched a hand to her own hair.

"Thank you," Catherine said, the words tangling with panic in her throat. "That would be lovely, Flora."

"Gabriel will fetch you for the feast," Maire said, making her way toward the door. "You should rest in the meanwhile. 'Twas a long journey from England for you."

"Yes, it was. And you should rest, too."

"Be sure I will." Maire left the room with Rachel.

"Do call if there is aught you need, my lady," Flora said. She sketched another curtsy, then left the room, shutting the door behind her.

Catherine sank down on the edge of the bed, setting the pile of cloths beside her. These people were so nice. So without pretense. And so blindly faithful to the tale of the curse. She hated to crush their hopes and tell them that she had not yet decided if she would marry Gabriel.

Yet at the same time, she could not throw caution to the wind and just wed him so as not to disappoint them. Marriage was forever and needed to be considered carefully, even an arranged union such as this.

But was it selfish to want to wait? Was she a horrible person because she needed time to ponder the most important decision of her life? Another person, a more impulsive person than herself, might be able to wed the man without much forethought. He was a handsome devil and titled with it, and heaven knew there was enough heat between them to singe their flesh without so much as a touch.

Was that enough to sustain a marriage? What about when they grew older and the flames of passion cooled? Would they be content together? They would probably have children. She could find comfort in that.

And what if she did wed him and nothing

changed? She had burned her bridges in England; there was nothing there for her now except her father. And would he even forgive what she had done? Was she completely ruined now, having run off with a band of Scotsmen, even though her grandfather had served as her chaperone?

These people wanted her as their lady. They looked at her with hopeful eyes, and she found herself *wanting* to help them. Even if there was no curse, she was certain she could convince her father to pay Gabriel her dowry. The money alone would go a long way toward helping the clan. And if she did go mad in the end, was this such a terrible place to do so? Better perhaps than London, where every flaw was exploited as fodder for the latest *on dit*. She might be happy here, surrounded by these kind people, at least as long as she could hold on to the memory of helping them.

And when the madness took her, perhaps they would remember what she had done for them with fondness. Perhaps they would care for her with compassion, long after her wits left her.

It was something to think about.

Gabriel sat with Brodie at the table in the great hall, each with a wooden cup of ale.

"This is the last cask of ale," Gabriel said.

"We've none until the crops begin growing again. Or unless we can find the funds to buy some."

"We'd have had the funds," Brodie retorted with a smirk, "except you spent it all on a tub of water."

Gabriel arched his brow and took a sip. "And whose idea was that?"

"I said to show compassion to the girl. Compassion is free, you ken."

"Still, she seemed grateful."

"That you took the time to see that her needs were met? Aye, but was she grateful enough to agree to the marriage before her father comes?"

Gabriel sighed. "Not yet. Stubborn wench."

"And yet you let the clan think there's going to be a wedding."

"I canna disappoint them. And maybe being treated like a bride will help sway her."

"Your mother will ask you to name the day soon enough. The people have suffered under the curse for too long."

"I know it. Between my mother and her father, time is against me."

"Aye. You know he'll be following you," Brodie said, his expression growing serious. "If we hadna pushed the horses to their limits, he might yet have caught us."

"What sort of father doesna come for his daughter when she has been taken?" Gabriel said. "Aye, he'll come."

"Woo her," Brodie said. "There's been naught but fire between you since you met. Have you not considered bringing the lass some flowers or singing a love song?"

"When have I been able to do any of that?" Gabriel said. "First the woman was avoiding me, then we were in a mad race to get back to the Highlands."

"And with Depford on his way here, you're in a mad race again, but now 'tis against time." Brodie took a healthy swallow from his cup. "I saw the look on her face when we got here. She's beginning to feel the suffering."

"I noticed it, too." Gabriel smoothed his thumb along the side of his cup, trying not to look at the ring on his finger—the memory of what he could not have. "Perhaps compassion will move her to accept me."

"You're a braw lad, Gabriel MacBraedon." Brodie grinned. "Surely the lass has noticed."

Gabriel raised a brow. "Not as much as you have, apparently."

Brodie snickered and reached for his ale again.

A soft footstep made both men look toward the door. Maire walked toward them, one hand cupping her belly. She glanced at Gabriel and smiled, then looked at Brodie. Her face glowed. "And here is my fine husband, back from his journey and already tippling the ale."

"'Twas your brother's doing," Brodie said, getting to his feet. "He's a terrible influence."

"I know it." Maire tilted her face for Brodie's kiss and accepted his arm around her waist with obvious gratitude. "Your bride is in the east tower room, Gabriel."

"I thank you for showing her the way."

"She's all a-muddle, but I imagine a wee bit of sleep will fix that. I could use a bit myself." She looked up at her husband with an intimate smile. Brodie touched her cheek and kissed her gently on the lips. For a moment it was as if no one else existed but them.

Gabriel felt like an interloper. The three of them had grown up together, and all of them had always known Brodie would wed Maire. How then could he watch them together after five years of marriage and feel as if he were spying on a courting couple?

He and Catherine might never have that. What they had was sparks to kindling, hot passion that blazed like wildfire between them. But intimacy? No. Love? Definitely not. They would wed to save the clan and find some comfort in each other's bodies. They would have children and make a life together, all without complications of the heart.

Brodie murmured in Maire's ear, and Gabriel glanced away. His gaze fell on his ring, and he clenched his fist around it. If he had been free to wed Jean, would he have had what his sister did with Brodie?

"I believe we're embarrassing your brother," Brodie teased, resting his chin on top of Maire's head with a grin. "Is that a wee bit of pink in your cheeks, my lord?"

"'Tis the ale," Gabriel grunted.

Maire giggled. "Have a care to nae drink so much that you canna please your bride."

"Have no fear of that." Gabriel tossed back the last of his drink.

"Come, wife. Let us leave the chief alone to ponder his courtship." Brodie took Maire's hand and kissed it. "You look a mite weary. I'll see you to bed."

"Such a gentleman!"

"Hardly," he said with a leer, then gave a gentle tap on her bottom.

"Off with the two of you." Gabriel reached for the bottle of ale.

Maire came around and kissed his cheek. "We will see you at the feast later."

"Aye." His heart softened as it always did around Maire, and he squeezed the hand she had placed on his shoulder. "Get your rest, little one."

Maire patted his shoulder as she straightened, then took Brodie's outstretched hand and allowed him to lead her from the room. Gabriel watched them go, jealous as always that duty came before desire and that he would never have that sort of relationship with a woman.

Then he tipped the bottle to refill his cup and drank a toast to the curse that had robbed him of choice and freedom and the ability to do anything but wed a slightly spoiled redhead who would ease his loins but never his heart.

Chapter 15

Catherine slept for several hours and awoke only moments before Flora arrived to arrange her hair. Having discarded her stained and worn riding habit at the inn, she suffered a moment of panic when she could not locate the sturdy gray traveling dress the innkeeper's daughter had given her.

Flora knocked on the door in the middle of her frantic search. Clad in her shift, Catherine wrapped the plaid blanket around herself and called out, "Come in!"

Flora entered the room, her arms overflowing with lovely jonquil material. "Good evening, my lady. The chief sent this to you since we took your other dress for cleaning."

"Is that where it is? I was worried." Catherine sank down on the edge of the bed in relief.

"This was one of the lady Fenella's dresses,

which we've altered for you using your other clothing to measure." She held up the garment by the shoulders so Catherine could see.

"It is lovely," Catherine approved. "Thank you so much for your kindness."

Flora let out a breath and gave her a shy smile. "Some of the ladies were worried you wouldna accept a dress that had belonged to another."

Catherine chuckled. "That would be foolish of me since I hardly have any clothing at all. I do appreciate your kindness."

"And the lady Fenella was thinking 'twould make a fine wedding dress."

Catherine kept her smile in place, despite the feeling of being herded to the altar. "Again, my thanks."

"I can help you dress now and then arrange your hair for you."

"I would appreciate that very much." Catherine rose and set aside the blanket. "I heard music from downstairs. Has the feast started already?"

"The *ale* has started," Flora said with a giggle. She glanced over Catherine's undergarments. "Where's your corset, my lady?"

Catherine pinkened. "I do not have one."

"Oh." The girl shrugged. "I hope the dress fits properly. But it should since we used your other clothing as a model."

"Then it should fit splendidly."

They had just managed to get Catherine into the dress—and it did fit well, despite the lack of corset—when another knock came at the door. Flora left her sitting on the stool by the hearth, her hair half assembled in a flattering disarray of curls, as she went to answer the summons.

"Your aunty is here, my lady," Flora said a moment later from the doorway. "Shall I let her in?"

"My aunt? I did not even know I had one." Catherine's heart fluttered with excitement. "Yes, do let her in."

When the woman walked into the room, Catherine slowly rose to her feet. Her aunt stopped at the movement, and the two ladies simply studied each other.

They had the same shade of fiery hair, the same Farlan blue-gray eyes. She was a tall woman like Catherine, with a Junoesque figure that made her look like an Amazon queen. And while there were subtle differences in her features, her face resembled Catherine's mother's enough that Catherine felt goose bumps prickle along her arm.

Her aunt's eyes teared up as she looked Catherine over. "I am Vivian Alexander," she managed to say. "Your mother was my sister."

"I am Catherine."

"I know." Vivian came closer. "The resemblance is striking."

"I might say the same to you."

"The last time I saw my sister, she was about your age." The older woman took a deep breath and laid a hand over her chest. "Forgive me, but 'tis a shock."

Catherine swallowed hard. "For me as well. You look as she might now, had she lived."

Flora came over, all brisk efficiency. "Why dinna you sit down again, my lady, and I can finish your hair while you talk to your aunty."

Catherine nodded and slowly sank down on the stool. "Would you stay and talk to me while she finishes?" Catherine asked. "There are so many questions I would ask about my mother."

"I will indeed."

Joyful music filled the air, accompanied by shrieks of laughter as the men and women of his clan danced to the lively reel. Seated at the head table, Gabriel watched his people with a curve to his lips. Such abandon had been absent from their glen for too long. It did his heart good to see everyone rejoicing.

The fact that he himself was feeling more maudlin than celebratory was due to a good amount of ale and his bride's stubbornness.

He *should* be celebrating, blast it. He had done what he set out to do, hadn't he? He had gone to London and fetched his bride home to Scotland where she belonged. And he had done so under the nose of her Sassenach father.

Now he simply needed to convince her to wed him.

He took another swallow of ale. Surely Catherine's heart could not be so cold that she could ignore the plight of the people around them. Surely he could convince her to be his wife. He would be a fine enough husband, and their marriage bed would never grow cold. She would be well cared for, if she would only realize it.

He threw back the last of his ale, then perused the bottom of his empty cup. He needed to set aside this mawkish sentimentality. Love was not a necessary ingredient to marriage, and it was a rare couple who found it. Companionship and incredible sex would do just fine.

He glanced at the pitcher of ale on the table, then blinked as a hand came out of nowhere to close around the handle.

"And where is your bride?" Dougal Alexander asked, lifting the pitcher. "I'm eager to see the lass."

Gabriel turned to glance up at Vivian's husband. "I expect she will be coming shortly. Vivian went up to meet her."

"Ah." Dougal nodded, expertly pouring from the heavy pitcher one-handed while standing. "I expect there will be all sorts of wailing and whatnot to get out of the way before she comes down."

"I expect." Gabriel took the pitcher back when the man was finished and tipped some into his own cup. "I must thank your son for catching our supper this evening."

Dougal grinned and sat down beside Gabriel. "'Twas the damnedest bit of luck, that. We've not caught a glimpse of any game in weeks, then suddenly there's that buck, standing in plain sight, almost asking to be taken."

"This was yesterday morning?"

"Aye. We've taken it as a sign of better times to come."

Gabriel felt a tug at his sleeve. He looked down and met the solemn dark eyes of six-year-old Fay Farlan. As always, seeing her pretty, delicate face gave a tug at his heart.

"Good evening to you, Miss Farlan," he said. "And what can I do for you this fine evening?"

She giggled. "'Tis just Fay, my lord."

"And I've told you to call me Gabriel."

Fay shook her head, disapproval clear on her faerie-like features. "No, that wouldna be right."

"Come here, sweetie." Dougal leaned forward. "Because . . ." He made a snatching gesture toward her face, then held up his fist with the top of his thumb peeking between two fingers. "I've got your nose!"

Fay shrieked with laughter and covered her nose with her hand. "Heaven save me," she wailed in mock despair, "but he's stolen my nose again!"

"That's the truth of it." Dougal waved his clenched hand in temptation. "And if you want it back, you ken the cost."

"I do," she said, her voice nasal through her fingers.

"Well, then, let's have the payment."

Gabriel grinned as the little girl came forward and stood on tiptoe to kiss Dougal on the cheek. He gasped and opened his hand.

"'Tis back! My nose is back!" Fay dropped her hand. "'Tis a miracle."

"Indeed." Gabriel picked her up and set her on his lap. "Let's make certain 'tis fastened properly." He tapped her on the nose, eliciting more giggles.

"Fay Farlan, here you are."

Gabriel and Fay looked up at the same time.

"Hello, Mama." Fay grinned at her mother. "Grandfather stole my nose again."

"And so you've brought this grievance to the chief?" A smile on her lips, Fay's mother met Gabriel's gaze. As always, he felt that bittersweet jolt to his heart. "Hello, Gabriel. I'm glad your time away from us proved fruitful."

Gabriel gave a nod of acknowledgment and let Fay slide from his lap. "Hello, Jean."

Dougal cleared his throat and stood, averting his eyes from the reunion. "More ale," he muttered, and walked away with the pitcher.

"Will you play for us, Mama?" Fay asked, tugging at her hand. "Play the song about the shepherd lad." She turned to Gabriel. "And you can sing for us, my lord."

Gabriel saw the spark of interest in Jean's eyes. How many times had they performed that song together? Dozens at least.

"Do sing for us." Fay clasped her hands together in entreaty. "It has been so long since we have had a feast."

"Very well then." He stood. "Jean, are you willing?"

"Aye," she replied softly. "I shall fetch my harp."

When Catherine and Vivian arrived in the great hall, the merriment had already commenced.

"Ah, they brought out the ale," Vivian said. "'Tis a feast indeed."

"Do you not normally drink ale?"

"Oh, indeed we do. Whisky as well. But both of

those require grains, and our crops have been very poor indeed these past few months. 'Tis all we can do to collect enough oats for bannocks."

"I am sorry to hear that."

Vivian shrugged. "'Tis the curse. Once you marry the chief, all will be well again."

Catherine nodded. Though the pressure to wed Gabriel still caused a twinge of apprehension inside her, she was beginning to think it was not such a bad notion. He seemed to be a good and honorable man, if she used his concern for his people as a measure. And he clearly doted on his mother and sister.

What, then, held her back from saying yes?

"There's your bridegroom now," Vivian said, pointing at the head table.

Catherine followed her line of sight and saw Gabriel sitting at the table with a little girl in his lap. The smile he turned on the child made Catherine's heart roll over. He seemed completely enchanted with the dark-haired little girl, and she giggled and squirmed in his lap with no fear of the authority he wielded.

Was this how he would look with their children?

"Come, let's get you to the head table where you belong. I imagine the food will be coming out of the kitchen shortly, and then we feast!"

"The food is not out yet?"

Vivian slid her a sidelong glance. "There isna much food to begin with, and certainly not enough for more than one course."

Catherine flinched. How could she have forgotten that these people were one step away from complete starvation? When she thought of the many balls and dinners she had attended, some of them with as many as twelve courses, she felt ashamed. How could the wealthy gorge themselves when other people did not have enough to eat?

She followed her aunt through the crowd. People shouted greetings to Catherine, and she smiled and waved at all the unfamiliar faces. By the time they reached the table, Gabriel was gone.

The little dark-haired girl sat alone on the bench, swinging her feet back and forth. Her dark brown, threadbare skirts looked to be a little short for her, baring her ankles when she sat and revealing well-worn shoes. She looked up as Catherine came over. Her soft brown eyes dominated her piquant face, and her expression was more solemn than a small child should bear.

"Well, hello, Fay," Vivian said. She held out her arms, and the little girl hopped off the bench and ran into them.

"Grandmama!" Fay wrapped her arms around

Vivian's neck and squeezed her in a hug. "Mama is going to play."

"That sounds lovely." Vivian stood Fay on the bench. "Fay, this is Catherine. She is going to be our lady soon."

"Are you the Bride?" Fay asked.

Catherine could not help but smile at the utter seriousness of the little girl's expression. "Yes, I am."

Fay gave her a wide smile, revealing that she was missing her two front teeth. "Me, too." She lifted her foot. On her left ankle, clear as day, was a birthmark shaped like a dagger.

"My goodness." Catherine looked at Vivian, registered the resignation on her aunt's face. "This is your granddaughter?"

"Aye." Vivian sighed and caressed the child's hair. "That would make her your cousin."

"Mama has fetched her harp," Fay said. "And the lord is going to sing the shepherd song." She turned her gaze to Catherine. "'Tis my favorite song ever."

"Gabriel is going to sing?"

Though the question was directed at Vivian, it was Fay who nodded. "I asked him to and he said yes. He and Mama have sung this song a lot."

"Your future husband is a very talented singer,"

Vivian said with a smile. "From here you will have an excellent view of the performance."

"Will you watch with me?" Fay asked Catherine. "Sometimes I canna see because I'm such a wee little mite."

Catherine chuckled. "A wee little mite?"

"'Tis what Grandfather calls me."

"My husband, Dougal," said Vivian.

Catherine shook her head as if to clear it. "The family connections here are very complicated!"

"That's to be expected. We live in an isolated area, so the families tend to intermarry quite a bit."

"I can sit here on the table," Fay said, taking Catherine's hand. "Or stand on the bench. If you say 'tis all right, that is."

The girl's tiny hand felt as fragile as a bird's wing and just as bony. How long had it been since she had had enough to eat?

She wanted to weep just at the thought of this little girl suffering for survival.

"Of course it is all right." Catherine cleared her suddenly tight throat. "I would be glad of the company."

The sweet plucking of harp strings echoed through the hall. All conversation hushed. There was a dais on one side of the room where the musicians had been playing when she had first entered. Now a beautiful, dark-haired woman sat on a stool, a harp in her hands. She plucked the strings, her head angled toward the instrument, eyes closed and a slight smile on her lips as she tuned it. The notes vibrated through the air. Gabriel stepped up on the dais, and cheers erupted from the throng.

Ignoring the ruckus, Gabriel looked at the woman. She opened her eyes and smiled at him, a smile of fondness and joy, as if he were the only man in the room. He nodded at her, she nodded back, then began to pluck at the harp with her slender fingers.

"That's my mama," Fay whispered.

Catherine nodded, her entire attention focused on Gabriel as he began to sing.

His rich baritone filled the room. The power of it stunned her, his vocal skill more than evident. She could tell this was not the first time he had entertained people by singing. The song was clearly a ballad, given the tone, but the words were in Gaelic so she did not know what it was about. For a moment she wished her madness would come back, that she could understand the lyrics. Then she realized that all hints of madness had vanished since she had come to Scotland.

Was there a curse after all? And had her mere

proximity to Gabriel been enough to subdue the symptoms?

"The song is about a shepherd in love with a lady," Vivian whispered. "Each day he comes to her with a different gift and asks her to be his wife. She takes the gifts but hasna yet said she'd wed him."

"What sort of gifts?" Catherine whispered back.

Vivian gave her a look. "Things a shepherd can give. A bag of pretty stones, a handful of wildflowers. 'Tis not the gifts that matter but his love for her. But she ignores his love and waits for a rich man."

The tempo of the song changed. Gabriel's voice grew harder, the shepherd boy clearly frustrated with his suit not being accepted. Then Fay's mother joined in on the chorus, her sweet soprano blending in harmony with Gabriel's deeper tones. A woman coaxing a suitor.

They looked at each other as they sang, Gabriel's expression blazing with longing, hers flirtatious. Catherine was swept into the story. "What is happening now?"

"The lady has accepted an offer from a rich man and tells the shepherd boy. His heart is broken."

Gabriel gazed into the harpist's eyes now, his voice taking on a hint of yearning. The harpist answered his lyric with one of her own, her tone nostalgic and sad. Their voices rose and fell in unison, as if they had sung this song a thousand times.

"Years later, the lady is unhappy with her husband and wishes she had accepted the shepherd boy," Vivian whispered. "She finds the bag of stones he gave her and treasures them close to her heart for always."

Gabriel's voice rose to a crescendo, the woman's soprano wrapping around it in harmony. They joined together on the last note, holding it. Then there was silence.

And she saw it then, the look Gabriel gave to Fay's mother. A look of intimacy and longing that had nothing to do with the song. The beautiful brunette held that look for a moment, torment flickering across her own expression before she dropped her eyes.

The hall exploded with applause.

Gabriel stepped off the dais. Fay's mother set down her harp and then accepted the hand Gabriel offered to help her down. Was she imagining it, or did he hold the other woman's hand just a hint longer than necessary? The two walked back to the head table, laughingly refusing to perform another tune. The musicians claimed the dais again and launched into a foot-tapping romp that had half the room dancing.

She could tell the moment Gabriel spotted her. He had been listening to something Fay's mother was saying when his gaze lit on Catherine. His expression changed, grew guarded.

Guilt?

"That was wonderful!" Vivian exclaimed. "No one sings 'The Lady and the Shepherd' like the two of you. So beautiful."

"Thank you," Fay's mother said. She stretched out a hand to Fay, who took it and jumped off the bench.

Gabriel nodded at Vivian, then came forward to take Catherine's hand. "You're a bonny one tonight, Catherine. 'Tis pleased I am to see you."

His touch made her quiver, but her head and heart hesitated to trust him. "You have an excellent singing voice, Gabriel. Truly superior."

"Thank you." He turned to Fay's mother. "Catherine, this is Jean Farlan. I see you've met Fay."

"Yes." Catherine smiled at the little girl, then nodded to her mother. "How do you do, Jean?"

"Very well, thank you." Jean said exactly the right thing, and her manner was correct if reserved, but Catherine had the impression that the harpist might be the only person in the glen not happy to see her.

Vivian clucked her tongue. "Here now. So formal? Is that any way for cousins to greet each other?"

Jean shot a quick look at Vivian, and Catherine said, "Cousins?"

"Indeed," Vivian said. "Jean is my daughter."

"Oh!" The pronouncement took her by surprise, and she studied Jean's face more carefully. "I would not have guessed. You do not favor your mother," she said to Jean.

"No, I look like my father," Jean confirmed. Her eyes flickered over Catherine, from hair to hem.

"The Alexanders tend to have brown hair and eyes," said Vivian, oblivious to the undercurrents. "My son, Dougal, is the same."

"I have never known a cousin before," Catherine said, discomfited by the other woman's quiet study. "It is so thrilling to finally meet my family."

"And we are very excited to meet you at last!" Vivian put her arm around Catherine's shoulders and hugged her. "Welcome home, Catherine!"

"Yes, welcome home." Though Jean's mouth formed the words, her eyes remained cool.

A ripple went down Catherine's spine. She had seen that look before, in the eyes of jealous debutantes in London. Perhaps she had *not* imagined the air of intimacy that seemed to exist between Gabriel and Jean.

The idea made her head spin. She had never considered that when she married Gabriel, he might turn to another woman to satisfy his needs. But many men did just that, wed for the sake of their titles or their estates—or in this case, the clan—and found their pleasures elsewhere. Was Gabriel such a man?

Fay tugged on her mother's hand. "Mama, I am hungry."

"Patience, Fay," her mother said.

Gabriel crouched down to look Fay in the eye. "We're having fresh venison in just a while with potatoes and bannocks and maybe some soup."

The little girl's mouth fell open. "Truly?"

"I am the chief, and I have declared it so."

Fay sucked in an excited breath, her eyes sparkling. "I canna wait!"

"Neither can I." Gabriel stood and offered his arm to Catherine. "May I see you to your seat, Catherine?"

"That would be lovely." She presented her society smile to Vivian and Jean. "I look forward to seeing you again."

"We're sitting at the same table," Jean said. "So we will be dining together."

"Oh." Catherine cleared her throat. "How lovely."

"Fay and Jean always have a place at the chief's table," Vivian said. "If you will excuse me, I must go find my husband." She bustled off into the crowd.

"Mama, come sit!" Fay cried, tugging on her mother's hand.

Jean sighed and sent a tolerant glance at her daughter. "Please excuse us while we take our seats."

The two Farlan ladies walked away. Catherine looked at Gabriel. Though nothing was overtly out of place, her instincts were jangling about Jean Farlan. "Jean is a beautiful woman."

"Beauty runs in your family." He lifted her hand and brushed his mouth over her fingers.

She tilted her head, watching his face carefully. "Where is her husband?"

"Jean is a widow."

"I am sorry to hear that." She took her hand from his grasp. "And why do they always sit at the chief's table?"

He frowned at the loss of contact. "Because they are part of the household. Anyone in the household sits at the chief's table."

"Part of the household? How so?"

He looked at her in genuine puzzlement. "Because they live here."

"Here?"

"Aye, here. In the castle."

She let out a slow breath. Could it be he kept his leman here, close under hand? She cast a quick glance at Jean and found the other woman watching them. Jean instantly lowered her gaze. Fay bounced beside her, chattering nonstop.

He had told her once that there had been some-one precious to him, someone from before he had come looking for his destined bride. Someone he had had to give up.

"Catherine." Gabriel waited until she looked at him before continuing, "Is something wrong?"

She pasted a wide smile on her face. "Not at all. Let us take our seats, shall we? I am eager for the feast to begin."

Chapter 16

Lachlan Drummond had had way too much to drink. Catherine watched as he roared with laughter and tried to pinch the bottoms of the women who served the food to their table.

She leaned toward Gabriel, who was seated at her left at the head of the table. "Do you see your stepfather?"

Gabriel narrowed his eyes. "I do."

"He has had too much ale."

"Indeed." Gabriel met her gaze, lowering his voice in conspiracy so only she could hear. "Perhaps after the meal is done, you can ask my mother to escort you to your room. I will handle Lachlan."

Catherine glanced across the table at Gabriel's mother, who was stoically ignoring her husband's behavior. "Your mother is a gentle lady," she murmured back. "She deserves better."

"In that regard, we agree." He squeezed her hand. "Thank you for helping me with this."

She turned to look at him. Those beautiful blue eyes shone with approval, and she wanted to open herself to him like a flower under the sun, even with questions about Jean Farlan niggling in the back of her mind. "If we are to determine if we should suit as husband and wife," she said, "we must work together in these matters."

"Is that what we are doing?" He traced a finger along the back of her hand.

"As I recall, I told you once that how a man treats his mother is important in determining if he would make a good husband." She leaned closer and whispered, "You have a very high regard for your mama."

He arched a brow and said dryly, "My heart is aquiver with joy at your approval, lass."

She laughed, earning smiles from those around them. Down near the end of the table, Jean stood and took Fay by the hand, helping her down from the bench. The little girl yawned and rubbed her eyes as her mother quietly led her out of the hall. Catherine watched them go, unable to dispel a prickle of envy as several men turned to watch the widow's exit.

Jean was an attractive woman who caught men's

eyes with her lush figure and quiet reserve. Was it jealousy that made Catherine think there was some relationship between the widow and Gabriel?

"If you're not going to eat the venison, Catherine, give it to me," Brodie said from her right. "It has been months since any of us has been lucky enough to land a buck."

"And the one time it happened, 'twas an Alexander who did it!" Dougal called out with pride. Applause followed his statement, and Dougal Alexander the Younger, Jean's brother and hunter of the deer, stood and accepted his accolades with an exaggerated bow.

Catherine looked down at her plate. The Mac-Braedon feast consisted of smoked venison, potatoes, the oatcakes called bannocks, and butter. The small clump of butter alone had earned cheers from the diners as it was proudly set out.

If this simple meal was considered a feast, what had these people been eating from day to day?

She lifted the uneaten portion of venison onto Brodie's plate. "I am not that hungry."

"My thanks." Brodie dug into the meat with gusto.

Lachlan lurched out of his seat, belched, and staggered toward the doorway of the great hall, adjusting his clothing as he went. Moments later, Gabriel quietly rose and followed him.

Catherine watched him go, wondering how he would approach Lachlan on the subject of his drunkenness and lusty nature. Here was a man who did not walk away from problems; he solved them. His clan meant everything to him, and as the chief, he personally saw to its well-being. How could she have *ever* thought him untrustworthy and a rule breaker?

Perhaps he was unorthodox in his methods, but that struck her as more a Scots trait than a personal one. Gabriel MacBraedon had been handed a difficult situation by the fates, and he was doing his best to manage it.

She could not deny that since she had come to Scotland, all evidence of her madness had disappeared. No more dreams, no more voices, no more speaking in tongues (though that last would have been convenient considering where she was). While her initial goal had been to talk to her relatives about the "family" illness, she now realized that every person in the great hall believed in the curse to the bottom of his being. How could she possibly confess to them that she considered their curse, which they blamed for the terrible blight that scarred their land, to be mere superstition?

She had wanted to marry a man who would care for her and not her money. Despite the evidence around her that suggested that her dowry was desperately needed, she knew Gabriel's intention was to meet the requirements of the curse and restore health to the land so that his people might continue to live as they always had. Her money meant nothing to him.

She could not fault him for his objective, could even admire him for it. Gabriel was no fool, and neither were the members of his clan. These were not people who easily blamed their problems on whims of fate. These were people who proudly wrested their living from the earth every day of their lives, who enjoyed the battle with nature to earn their place in the world.

Nothing but a curse would stop them from doing that.

Gabriel checked the privy, which was where he expected a man in Lachlan's condition to go. But the tiny chamber was empty. Had the man retired? Such good sense seemed contrary to Lachlan's happy-go-lucky nature. Still, 'twas better he located his stepfather before he got into mischief.

The sound of running feet reached him as he mounted the stairs to the second floor. The entire castle was in the great hall, except for Lachlan.

And Fay. And Jean.

He took the steps two at a time and hit the landing just as Jean came racing around the corner. She cast a panicked glance back over her shoulder and didn't even see him until he stepped into her path and caught hold of her.

She cried out, then saw who it was and melted into his arms. "Gabriel, thank goodness."

A cry jerked Catherine out of conversation with Brodie. Maire dropped her fork and grabbed at her belly.

"Maire!" Catherine got up from the table and hurried to the other side, Brodie right behind her. Fenella scooted across the bench to put her arm around her daughter, murmuring in Gaelic.

"The babe," Maire sobbed, clutching at her belly. Her face twisted in pain and panic. "'Tis too soon!"

"Let's get you to your bed," Fenella said.

"Send for Morag," Brodie called out to any who would listen.

"I will do it." Jean's brother Dougal got up from the table and raced from the hall at a run.

"I dinna want to ruin the feast," Maire sniffed. She reached out and clasped Catherine's wrist. "Stay with me. You're the only way to defeat the curse."

"I will stay with you." Catherine twined her fingers with Maire's. She had never in her life seen a baby's birth; in London a woman retired to her country estate in the months before the child was due so she might get through the ordeal in comfort and privacy. Maire had not been allowed that luxury, having to work hard every day just to survive. It was not fair. Nothing about these people's lot in life was fair.

Maire clenched her fingers around Catherine's hand just then as another pain wracked her small frame.

"Step back, Catherine," Brodie said, his tone terse. "We must get her up."

Maire cried out in denial as Catherine broke the connection of their hands.

"It is all right, Maire, I am here," Catherine reassured her. "We just need to get you upstairs."

"Dinna leave me."

"I will not."

Fenella rose from the table and came to stand near Catherine. The woman appeared calm, but Catherine could see the worry in her eyes, the tremble in her hands. She reached out and touched Fenella's arm. Gabriel's mother cast her a quick glance of surprise, then gave her a tight smile and patted her hand.

Brodie helped Maire away from the table, practically lifting her from the bench. Once she was clear, Brodie scooped his petite wife into his arms. "Her dress is wet," he said to Fenella.

"Catherine." Maire held out a hand, terror and pain twisting her features.

Catherine reached over and squeezed Maire's hand. "I am here, Maire. I will not leave you."

"We must get her to bed," Fenella declared. She headed for the door, Brodie following with his precious burden.

Catherine trotted to keep up with Brodie's long strides, her hand still clasped with Maire's, fear twisting her guts in knots.

Where was Gabriel?

Gabriel gently eased Jean out of his embrace. "What is it? What's happened?"

"Lachlan." She spat the name. "The drunken fool grabbed me as I came out of the room. I had just put Fay in bed."

"The bastard." Icy rage swept over him. "'Tis not bad enough he humiliates my mother with his wenching. Now he seeks to abuse the members of my household?"

"I gave him my knee for his trouble and left him on the floor there." She gestured to the hall from whence she had come. "Fay is locked in her room and safe, so I came to find help."

"You've found me." He smoothed his hands down her arms, a habit left over from their past together. Moved by the memory, he dropped his hands. He was about to wed another woman; there was no future for him and Jean, whatever they had once shared.

"You're all any woman would need," Jean said, and it took him a moment to realize she was referring to his role as protector. Not lover. Not anymore.

"I will have some of the men cart him to his room." He sent a black look down the hall. "After I have a few words with him myself."

She chuckled. "You have a way of making a woman feel safe."

His lips quirked in a grin. "'Tis a good thing."

"It is indeed." She smiled at him, her dark eyes warm. One heartbeat passed. Two. Then she trailed her fingers along his arm.

He froze. God in heaven, was she casting lures his way? Gently he pushed her hand aside. "Jean, I am to marry another."

"And well I know it." Her lip curled. "The red-haired Sassenach."

"She's your cousin, Jean."

"We may share blood, but she is no family of mine. She looks at us as if we are exhibits in a zoo."

"She's been raised in England by a father who hates the Scots. She doesna ken our ways."

Jean tossed her dark hair. "If there were no curse, would you want her instead of me?"

"Why do you torment us like this?" he asked quietly. "There is a curse, so there is no point in asking such a question."

"I have to know." She stepped closer to him, her breasts brushing his chest. "You still wear the ring I gave you."

"I do." He touched the band with his thumb, as was his habit.

"My husband's ring."

"A keepsake of a friend who is gone."

"'Tis more than that." Her dark eyes smoldered, and she laid a hand on his cheek. "I wanted you to always remember me."

He took her wrist and lowered her hand away from his face. "I canna forget you, Jean. You live in my house. I look at Fay and see the child I might have had with you. But we both know there is no future for us."

"You must wed the Bride. I understand that." She licked her lips. "But will you be happy with her?"

"I will be content knowing I have done my duty."

"Duty canna keep a man warm at night."

"No." He took a deep breath, her familiar scent filling his senses, then stepped back from her. "But I will sleep soundly."

"Gabriel!"

His mother's voice had him turning as footsteps thudded up the stairs. Fenella had lifted her skirts above her ankles that she might take the stairs faster. Brodie carried Maire, leaping up two stairs at a time. Catherine hurried to keep up with him, her hand locked with Maire's. Catherine met his gaze, glanced at Jean, then back to him.

She knew. He stiffened, expecting accusations.

"Gabriel, the baby is coming," was all she said.

Dread swept over him. "'Tis too soon."

"And well we know it," Brodie snapped. "Dougal has gone for Morag." He reached the landing. Catherine's connection to Maire was broken as he turned right, leaving her standing by Gabriel and Jean. Brodie's long strides ate up the distance to the room he shared with Maire.

Catherine looked at Gabriel. There was hurt in her eyes and confusion. She didn't even look at Jean. "I have to stay with her," she said, then hurried after Brodie.

Gabriel glanced at Jean, who met his gaze with equal concern. Dear God, was it the curse? Had their moment of intimate conversation caused this to happen?

Gabriel took off for Maire's room at a run, Jean at his heels. He skidded to a stop in the doorway. Maire was wailing in pain and fear. His mother struggled to remove her clothing, while Catherine stood beside the bed, her hand locked with Maire's.

Brodie paced near the door, his face grim.

"I can help," Jean said to Brodie. She darted around Gabriel to enter the room. "Catherine can sit with Fay and leave the birthing to the more experienced women."

Brodie cast her a hard glance. "She wants Catherine. Mind your child yourself, Jean."

Jean flinched and stepped back. Gabriel took her by the arm and tugged her out into the hallway. "Go down to the great hall, Jean, and have your father see to Lachlan."

"But I can help."

"Just do it," Gabriel said.

She gave a reluctant nod. "Call if you have need of me."

"I will."

Jean spun away and marched down the hall, her back stiff with pride. Gabriel sighed and stepped into the bedchamber. His mother had succeeded in stripping Maire down to her shift and covered her with a sheet. Sweat beaded his sister's face. Catherine had pulled a stool close to the bed and held Maire's hand in both of hers. She leaned close to Maire, the soft, unintelligible murmurings of her voice drifting back to the men at the door.

"You havena changed your mind about wedding

Catherine, have you, Gabriel?" Brodie's voice was so low only Gabriel was close enough to hear it. "Because it seems to me we dinna need the curse adding to our misery just now."

"Of course I intend to marry her," Gabriel said. "As soon as I can convince her to agree to it."

"I didna know if your plans had changed."

"Nothing has changed."

"You were with Jean."

Gabriel stiffened. "We were talking. Lachlan had followed her to Fay's room."

"Ah." A bit of the tension drained from Brodie's shoulders.

"I know my duty."

"Then do it." Brodie turned haunted eyes on him. "However you need to sway her, do it, Gabriel. Soon."

Morag arrived hours after the labor had begun. The men had been herded out of the room but hovered just outside the doorway, their faces lined with fear as they periodically peered inside. Fenella had tied a blue thread around Maire's finger to prevent childbirth fever, and the cradle in the corner had iron nails to prevent evil from infecting the new child.

Catherine was completely focused on Maire, her voice growing hoarse from whispering encouragement. Her fingers were numb from Maire's panicked grip. Her back ached from staying bent over the bed. She used a scrap of cloth to wipe the sweat from Maire's damp forehead.

"I dinna want the child to die." Maire turned her terror-stricken gaze on Catherine. "I dinna want my babe born with two heads like the lambs. Promise me."

Taken aback, Catherine tried to think of a response. "I am certain your baby will be well-formed."

"Morag will see to it," Fenella murmured. "Dinna fear, daughter."

Maire got caught in another contraction. Fenella smoothed back her daughter's hair, holding her hand and whispering encouragement. Flora and Rachel moved around the room, heating water and gathering what supplies they could.

Suddenly the men outside began to murmur. The crowd parted. Everyone in the room paused in her tasks.

A woman glided into the room, an aged crone in a cloak of deepest blue, her long silver hair falling over her shoulders like liquid lightning.

Catherine stared at the woman in horror. This was the old woman from her dreams, the one who had cast the curse. She stood as Morag approached the bed, then stepped between the witch and Maire.

Morag looked up at her, one eye as blue as any MacBraedon's, the other clouded over with blindness. "Well," she said. Her voice sounded strangely youthful and melodious for a woman who looked to be in the winter of her life. "You would protect her."

"I would." Catherine stood her ground, though fear threatened to turn her knees to sand.

"I am a healer, child." Morag tilted her head. "She needs me."

Fenella came over and urged Catherine out of the way. "Let her come. She is skilled in the old ways. She might be able to help."

Catherine allowed herself to be moved, but only enough to let Morag closer to the bed. She did not trust this woman, not just because of her dream but also because of the strange aura of power that radiated from the old one. Maire was terrified enough. But the other women in the room stood back at a respectful distance, their expressions hopeful, which made her willing to stand quietly and observe.

"We need no men here." Not taking her eyes from Maire, Morag raised her hand, and a sudden gust of wind blew in through a window and propelled the bedchamber door shut right in the faces of the curious males. "You, child." The witch fixed her good eye on Catherine. "You. Bride. You will aid me to counteract the curse."

Catherine nodded, more than a little unnerved. "As you wish."

"Take the cloak." Morag shrugged. Catherine reached out just in time to catch the garment as it drifted to the floor, leaving Morag clad in a simple robe of stark white. Symbols were embroidered at the sleeves and hem, and a belt with many pouches encircled her waist.

Catherine laid the witch's cloak on a chair, then came to stand beside her.

Morag pulled forth a dagger. Alarmed, Catherine glanced at Fenella, but she watched with a calm expression. The witch murmured some words over the blade, then handed it to Maire. "To cut the pain."

Maire clutched the handle of the blade with clenched fingers, her arm straight by her side. A pain seized her, and she screamed, sitting half up in her bed to fight it. Morag put her hand over Maire's on the dagger hilt, and suddenly the expectant mother relaxed as if the pain had suddenly vanished.

"Bless you, Morag," Maire said, panting.

"The child will be born tonight," Morag replied. She gave Maire a quick smile that transformed her face. "And it willna have two heads."

Maire gave an exhausted laugh, and Catherine could only stare, wondering how the witch had known about a conversation that had occurred before her arrival.

"I know everything," Morag said, answering the question Catherine had not voiced. "Now let us bring forth the next Alexander son."

Maire's son was born in the wee hours of the morning. Instead of wailing his presence, he whimpered. He would not suckle at his mother's breast. His skin at times took on a bluish tinge. But he was not malformed in any way, and for now, he lived.

Catherine stood over the cradle, marveling at the tiny human swaddled there. He was so small, so perfectly formed. She had not seen many infants in her lifetime. In London they tended to be whisked off to the nursery and cared for by a wet nurse. Here, Maire had attempted to nurse her child herself and had wept when he would not feed.

Morag came to stand beside her. "I will know his fate by the next dawn," she said. "And you will know yours. Your heart will be clear." She looked at Fenella before Catherine could respond. "Do you have a bed for me?"

"Of course," Fenella said. "And a meal."

"My thanks." Morag swept up her cloak and walked through the doorway without waiting for escort.

Fenella glanced at Flora, who sat half dozing by Maire's bedside. "Call for me if aught happens. I will have some of the others come stay with her so we can all get some sleep." She glanced at Catherine. "Seek your bed, my dear. This isna over yet."

Chapter 17

Catherine slept until late afternoon. When she woke, she found a simple dark skirt and white blouse waiting for her, along with a brightly woven shawl, and decided there was something to be said for clothing one could fasten oneself. The memory of Maire's ordeal last night—this morning—stayed with her like a scar on her heart. Dressed, she brushed her hair as she stood by the window. Outside, the sun shone brightly in a blue sky, glimmering on the loch, and a gentle breeze touched her face.

Her life in London seemed very far away, like a dream she had once had. Clad like one of the women of the glen, she felt as if she had always lived here in the shadow of the mountains, on the shores of the loch.

How was it that after only two days, this castle and its people seemed like home?

Tying her hair back with a simple ribbon, she went down to the great hall to find something to eat.

The entire castle operated under a state of gloom. Everyone spoke in low voices, the jubilance of last night forgotten in the face of impending tragedy. Fenella sat by the hearth, her fingers idly plucking at the strings of a small harp. Catherine stopped a passing servant and asked for a bit of food, then sat down in a chair by Fenella.

"Good day, Catherine," Fenella said. She tried to smile.

"I thought you would be with Maire," Catherine said. "I was going to go see her after I ate."

"Brodie is with her now." She plucked a string, frowned, adjusted it slightly. "The babe is no better. I fear for my grandchild's life." She began to pick out a tune, the sadness of it twisting Catherine's heart.

"I wish there was something I could do," she said. "I feel so useless."

"We all do." Fenella shrugged. "'Tis in God's hands now."

"And Morag's?"

Fenella smiled, her eyes dreamy as she got lost in the music. "Thank God for Morag. Her people have been here ever since anyone can remember."

"Is she a witch?"

"No one is certain. But she helps us in our times of need and is an excellent healer." Her fingers stumbled on the harp strings. "I hope she can help us now."

A servant brought Catherine some bread and a bit of the butter from last night, and a cup of water. She dug in to the simple meal, starving after having slept most of the day away. Fenella had recovered her fingering and played a soothing tune that reminded Catherine of sailing on a lake.

"You play very well," Catherine said. "I thought Jean was the harpist."

"And who do you suppose taught her?" Amusement colored her voice. "I can teach you as well, if you like."

"That would be lovely."

"With all that has happened since your arrival," Fenella said, "I forgot to ask you when your wedding will be."

Catherine choked on a piece of bread and quickly grabbed her water.

"Goodness, dear, have a care! As I was saying, 'twould be best for you to wed quickly. As you can see, the curse has taken nearly everything we have, and perhaps 'twould help Maire's babe as well."

Catherine was normally a truthful person. In any other circumstance, she would have set Fenella to rights about her undecided relationship with Gabriel. But how could she disappoint the woman at such a time when a baby's life hung in the balance?

"How long does it take to arrange a wedding?" she asked, avoiding the question. "I thought that in Scotland, it is just a matter of reciting vows before witnesses. Isn't that why couples flee to Gretna Green?"

"Most times, aye. But the curse requires the marriage to be blessed by a priest. I imagine Gabriel will call for Father Ross to oversee the ceremony. If we send for him the night before the wedding, he would be here in the morning."

As Catherine was trying to decide how to respond to this, Brodie stumbled into the great hall, haggard and exhausted. He managed to get to a bench and sit, his eyes desolate.

Fenella and Catherine hurried over to him.

"Brodie." Catherine reached him first, sitting beside him and touching his shoulder. "What has happened?"

"The babe is getting worse."

The utter despair in his voice elicited cries of alarm from the two women.

"Morag said she would know more after today," Fenella said, stroking his hair.

"Aye, we will know more. Whether to plan the christening or the funeral."

Fenella took his face between her hands and looked down into his tear-reddened eyes. "You listen to me, Brodie Alexander. That child isna gone yet, so dinna you go burying him!"

"'Tis just a matter of time now." His hoarse whisper rang with hopelessness, and he leaned forward to bury his face in her stomach, wrapping his arms around her like a boy needing his mother.

"There now," Fenella crooned and stroked his hair again.

Catherine's heart broke for him. "Oh, Brodie. I wish there was something I could do."

He pulled away from Fenella and looked over at her. His eyes burned like hot coals in a face that more resembled a skeleton than a man. "There is. Marry Gabriel."

She had no reply. What could she say that would make him feel better?

"Why do you wait?" His voice lashed at her like a whip. "Had you wed him already, we might not be waiting here wondering if my child is going to die."

"Brodie," Fenella chided. "She has only just arrived."

"Ask her," he snapped. "Ask her if she has *any intention* of wedding him."

"We were just discussing the wedding." Fenella sent her a puzzled look. "Catherine, tell him."

Catherine met Fenella's eyes, saw the growing concern there. "It is not that simple."

"Catherine?" Disbelief swept across Fenella's face. "What are you telling me?"

"'Tis what she's *not* telling you. She never accepted Gabriel's proposal. She's been dangling him along ever since they met." He stood, looked at her with disgust. "We hoped seeing the poverty might change your mind. Make you see how urgent it is that you do this thing. But you havena changed, have you? Still the rich and spoiled debutante."

She flinched. "That is not it at all."

"Always concerned about yourself." His voice echoed off the stone walls of the great hall. The people passing nearby slowed, stopped. "You accepted our hospitality, let my wife think you would help her against the curse. But all the while, you havena had the courage to tell anyone the truth."

"Brodie." Gabriel stepped into the hall. "She isna responsible for what happened."

"*How can you say that?*" Brodie whirled on him. "You went to England and tried to court her the English way to please her. That wasna good enough. Even when she agreed to come here, 'twas only to get answers about her own problems, not help us with ours." He pointed at Catherine. "And even after everything that has happened, she still has not agreed to wed you!"

Gabriel held up a hand. "That is between Catherine and me."

"No, Gabriel, it is not," Brodie declared. "We are *all* affected by the curse. If it is going to continue for another twenty years, we have the right to know."

Catherine looked at the pain and bafflement on Fenella's face and felt shame fill her. She *had* been acting selfishly. These same people who had been so welcoming, so kind, now looked at her with hurt and suspicion. She had nothing to go back to in England. Why did she still hesitate? This place could be her future.

Brodie turned his fury back on her. "If my son dies, 'tis on your head, Catherine Depford." He sank down on the bench as if his legs would no longer hold him and ran his hands wearily over his face.

"This cannot be," Fenella said.

"She *must* marry him." Vivian came in from the hallway. Her expression of horror struck Catherine like a blow. "We canna let her repeat her mother's mistake."

"How could you do this?" Fenella's voice broke. A tear trickled down her cheek from eyes that were angry and betrayed. "How could you sentence us to this horror all over again?"

Trapped. Everywhere she looked were more

faces, angry and afraid, from Fenella's heartbroken expression to Jean's smug one.

Humiliation washed over her like bubbling acid.

Gabriel saw the look on her face, her eyes wide and lower lip trembling. No, she would not cry, his Catherine. She would hold her head high and meet the accusations with dignity. Or apology. But she would not fold beneath the disapproval. She would not weep. She was a woman who stood her ground and accepted the consequences of her actions.

His heart swelled with pride.

"We are all worried," he said. He walked over to Catherine and stopped before her, taking her hand. She blinked with surprise, and he nearly smiled before he turned to face his family again, her hand firmly linked with his. "All of us are praying for Brodie and Maire's child."

"When were you going to tell us?" his mother demanded. Her moist cheeks pricked at his heart. "When you came home with her . . . We all believed there would be an end to it."

"We shouldna have to suffer for the whims of one girl," Brodie rasped. "She has dishonored her name like her mother before her."

"I'll be the one to decide that. I'm the Farlan chieftain." Donald came forward, his jaw clenched. "She's young and a stranger to our ways. You are in pain, Brodie Alexander, and are blaming my granddaughter for it."

"She could have stopped this. Thrice-damned curse!"

"Do you *know* 'tis the curse that caused this?" Donald challenged. "Many's the woman who has birthed a babe early."

"You old—" Brodie lurched toward Donald.

Gabriel dropped Catherine's hand and stepped in front of Brodie. "Dinna do it," he said quietly.

Brodie slowly lowered his raised fist, but his glower did not change.

"My brother." Gabriel laid a hand on Brodie's shoulder. "None of this will help your son."

Brodie sucked in a breath. "I meant no disrespect."

"I know you did not." Gabriel looked around from face to face, his tone implacable. "Catherine is free to make her decision about marriage without being threatened or pressured in any way."

"But the curse . . ." Brodie said.

Gabriel met his gaze, and his heart broke for his good friend. He did not blame Brodie for the rage and frustration that must be tearing him apart. His child might be dying. No man deserved that.

If he were Brodie, he would be ripping into the first handy target as well.

"If you blame Catherine, you might as well blame

me, too. I let you all treat her like a long-lost daughter, knowing she had made me no promises." He held out his hand, and Catherine came to take it.

She looked around at all of them. "I am sorry," she said softly. "I never meant to hurt anyone."

"Come. We are none of us at our best right now." He turned and led her from the hall.

Dear God, she had been so selfish.

Catherine blindly followed Gabriel up the stairs toward her chamber. These people had shared everything they had with her, expecting that she would help vanquish the evil that plagued their lives. They had made no secret of that. And she had blithely accepted their kindness, never really considering the one thing they asked of her.

Was this a case of the daughter taking after the mother? Curse aside, Glynis had thoughtlessly run off with Catherine's father, leaving her betrothed at the altar. Her self-centeredness had had long-reaching consequences. Perhaps Gabriel's uncle had been despondent at his bride's betrayal and had let lapse the management of his lands. Or was there indeed a curse? However it came to pass, the fortunes of both clans had turned with her mother's act of abandonment, so much so that these people believed that only Catherine wedding Gabriel could bring back prosperity.

Catherine had eaten their food, borrowed their clothing—neither of which they could afford. They had given selflessly to her, believing her to be one of them, a woman of honor who would right an old wrong. She had taken, but with no thought of giving back. And now that they knew, now that someone had put words to her actions, she was ashamed of herself.

She had misjudged Gabriel, taking his determination to do anything for his people as irresponsible and rash. Uncivilized. Barbaric. Instead she discovered a man with more character and loyalty than any she had met in London. She had worried that her husband might not care for her properly should she go mad. That would never happen with Gabriel MacBraedon. She had learned his true nature, watching him with his people. This was a man that would climb mountains for those he loved.

There was nothing for her in England anymore. But perhaps she had discovered a place for herself here that she had never expected to find. If she earned it.

"Are you all right?" he asked, leading her down the hall toward her room.

"Yes." She let out a long, slow breath. "That was not pleasant."

"Everyone is worried about the babe."

"I know." She stopped just outside the door to her chamber. "Do you believe the curse might be responsible?"

"After twenty years, we tend to blame the curse for everything." He opened the door for her. "Perhaps 'tis better if you stay here until supper," he said. "Let tempers cool."

"Thank you." She stepped inside, feeling as if she were walking to the gallows. He started to close the door, and she spun to face him. "Gabriel, wait."

He paused. "Is there aught you need?"

"May I speak with you?"

He studied her for a moment. "Aye." Then he stepped into the room.

"Close the door, please."

Raising a brow he complied, then stood with arms folded, watching her.

"Are you angry with me?"

"No, I'm angry with myself. I should have found a way to make you wed me by now."

"Gabriel, you cannot control my actions." She shook her head, amused at his innate warrior's arrogance. "You *should* be angry with me. I have treated you and your people abominably."

"I wouldna say that."

"Well, I have. And I am sorry."

He nodded. "Apology accepted."

She twisted her fingers, not wanting him to leave just yet. "It was kind of you to tell Brodie that I could take my own time to consider your proposal."

"I should have persuaded you to say the vows already." He sent her a heated look. "We might have been enjoying our marriage bed by now."

Everything female in her responded to that look. "Do you even like me?" she asked, trying to remember her objective.

"I do."

"But you do not know me all that well."

He gave her a half smile. "I know you well enough."

"Well enough for what? You and I have both admitted there is a strong attraction between us. But that is physical and may not be enough to sustain a marriage."

"I think it is. There's a bond that forms between a man and a woman when they share a bed and a life together."

Her cheeks heated. "I have to accept your word on that. I have never been with a man."

His eyes glittered in rapt interest. "I'm well aware of that."

"But you are a man. You have been with women." She folded her arms now, unconsciously mimicking his position and hiding her tightening nipples in the process. "You told me I would not have been your choice."

He shrugged one shoulder, wariness entering his expression. "No more than I was yours."

"But you knew *of* me, whereas I knew nothing about the curse or the mark or any of it. I had never heard of you. I had planned to wed Lord Kentwood."

He curled his lip. "I know."

"You wanted Jean, didn't you?" She locked her gaze with his, caught the flash of guilt before his stoic expression took over. "Please, Gabriel, tell me the truth."

He let out a long breath. "Aye. If not for the curse, I would have wed Jean."

"Were you lovers?"

A mild flush swept his cheeks. "Must we talk about this?"

"Yes, we must. I need to know, Gabriel. Please give me that courtesy."

"Aye, we were lovers."

"Is Fay your daughter?"

"No!" He dropped his arms to his sides, clearly startled by the question. "Fay is Kenneth's daughter. Jean was a widow when we had our affair."

Catherine let out a relieved sigh. "I wondered."

"How did you know about Jean? Have the servants been gossiping?"

"No." She gave him a sad smile. "I knew as soon as I saw you sing together."

"What are you talking about?" He propped his hands on his hips, his brows lowered in puzzlement. "We've sung together for years. 'Twas nothing different than any other time."

"And I saw you together in the hallway when Maire's babe was coming. Anyone could tell you had once meant something to each other."

"Jean needed my help."

"I am certain she did." She came to him and laid a hand on his arm. "If there is one thing I have come to know about you, Gabriel MacBraedon, it is that you are an honorable man. If you consider me your betrothed, you will not dally with another woman."

"God's truth," he agreed. "But she lives here in my home, so I am her chief. She may come to me with her problems."

"I understand that. Your affair may be over, but that connection never truly went away."

"Perhaps."

She nearly laughed at his skeptical tone. The past was done to this man and best forgotten. He would treasure his memories with Jean, yet move forward with his life. He didn't seem to want Jean back or to keep her as his mistress when he wed Catherine. And that was the most important thing she needed to know.

"Why does she live here, by the way? I had thought at first it was to keep her close to you." She gave him a teasing grin. "Besides, I thought there was a law of some sort that prevented Farlans and MacBraedons from living under the same roof."

"Under most circumstances." A glimmer of amusement lit his eyes. "While 'tis the truth they are Farlans, God help them, Jean was born an Alexander. She is Brodie's cousin, which makes her kin to me."

"Is that why she lives here?"

"No. 'Tis because Fay has the mark."

"Oh, yes, I saw it."

"Given what happened with your mother and what might yet happen with you, the clans thought it best we keep a close eye on little Fay."

"Ah, I see. Fay is here under your protection because she is the next Bride."

"Aye."

She glanced away. "I thought it was for Jean."

"No. As you said, I have chosen you. I would not betray you with another, Catherine."

"I am glad." She turned away, pleased that he had actually said it. Emotion clogged her throat.

How could she have misjudged him? He had never lied to her about his reasons for wanting to marry her. She had been so caught up in her own concerns, in the fact that he was so different from the men she knew, that it had taken her a long time to realize his integrity and strong sense of honor.

He was just as trapped as she was. He would have wed another if not for this curse.

"I will marry you."

"What?" He turned her to face him. "What did you say?"

She looked straight into his eyes, those beautiful blue eyes that never failed to make her heart melt. "I said I will marry you, Gabriel. I will be your wife."

"So you believe then? In the curse?"

She took a breath. "I do not know. Certainly things have happened to me that I cannot explain. But your people believe. So I will marry you, and if there is a curse, let us hope it is satisfied. If there is not, then perhaps my dowry will compensate."

"Catherine." His voice caught on her name, and he cupped her cheek. "I will be a good husband to you. This I swear."

His earnestness touched her heart. "I know."

He sealed the vow with a kiss.

The sweetness of the caress heated quickly, turning to hot passion from one heartbeat to the next. She curled her arms around his neck, for once not fighting this mad desire between them, relishing the spurt of liquid heat as his hand slid down her back and over her bottom, then up again.

Freed from convention, she breathed in this new elixir, hungry to taste that which before she had only enjoyed in dreams.

"What are you doing to me, lass?" he murmured, stringing kisses down her neck. One large hand cupped her breast. Her head spun when his thumb brushed her nipple, and she thought she would faint clean away. "We'll wed tomorrow. I must send for the priest."

"Yes." She pressed closer to him, her mind foggy with these new sensations spiraling through her. "I am eager for our wedding night."

"Dear God." His hands fisted in the material of her blouse. "One of us must stop this."

"Why?" She arched her back as he sucked on her neck. "If we are to wed, how is this wrong?"

"You are supposed to be the voice of reason."

"I have no reason. Your touch melts it away."

He groaned and tugged the blouse from the waistband of her skirt. "I must see you or I will go mad." He shoved the blouse up, then groaned in frustration upon encountering her shift.

"Shall we stop?" she murmured when he paused.

"I dinna want to," he admitted. "But I dinna want your first time to be a rushed coupling in the heat of desire."

"So do not rush."

He jerked his eyes to hers. She felt wicked, like Eve in the Garden of Eden offering that apple. "We havena said our vows."

"Say them now." She reached back and tugged the ribbon from her hair, shaking her head to let it flow over her shoulders. "Or shall I begin?"

He took a lock of hair between his fingers, his face bright with wonder. "You are the most surprising woman."

"Very well, I will start." She laid a hand on his cheek. "I, Catherine Depford, give myself to you as your wife. I will live with you and bear your children, and stand beside you to help you and comfort you whenever you need me. I promise to share myself with no other man but you as long as we both shall live."

"Oh, lass." He took her hand from his face and kissed the palm.

"Your turn."

"You really want me to do this? Very well then. I, Gabriel MacBraedon, chief of the MacBraedons and lord of Arneth, take you, Catherine, as my wife. I swear to be a good provider and a faithful husband, to give you children, to protect you and shelter you for the rest of your days."

She laughed, her head falling back in sheer joy. Why had she waited so long? "You may kiss the bride."

Chapter 18

She had not mentioned love.

Gabriel looked down into Catherine's beaming face, his heart melting at her sweetness. After so much resistance to the idea of marriage, she gave herself over so completely, he was humbled.

He had expected her to talk of love, of her need of it at least. But she had not. He had not given his heart since Jean and had never thought he could ever love that way again. But now he wondered.

But here was Catherine, so precious in her innocence. Something that had been lodged in his heart for a very long time came loose when she gave herself to him. He would make this special for her. He would not let her regret her decision.

He kissed her again, gathering her soft hair in his hands as he cupped her head, playing his lips over hers in a soft teasing of what was to come. She tried to deepen the kiss, but he held back. She had made the decision to wed; in this, he would be the leader.

He gathered her into his arms, her soft curves folding against his harder body with perfect symmetry. Male and female, coming together as they had been created to do. He held her gently, getting used to the feel of her, accustoming her to the feel of him. All those hours they had sat a horse together, they had never truly embraced.

She wound her arms around his neck, her fingers curling into his long hair. She had been trying to set the pace, but now she surrendered instead, relaxing in his arms. A good thing, for he wanted her to savor every step of this journey. To miss nothing.

"Let me see you," he murmured.

She stood still beneath his hands as he unfastened her blouse, peeling it from her to leave her shoulders bared by her shift. He had seen her in her undergarments before, yet still the sight kicked his blood to pounding through his veins. His fingers shook slightly as he unfastened her skirt.

Her eyes never left his face, though a blush crept up her chest and neck to her cheeks. Her body enticed him, all round breasts and curving hips and tiny waist, welcoming his attentions, longing for the pleasure for which it had been made. Yet her face held such innocence, such wonder as he touched the soft skin of her shoulders, trailed his fingers over the milky swell of her breasts. He watched her nipples harden through the nearly transparent material of her shift, flicked one with his thumb, and rejoiced at her startled "Oh!"

He took her hand and led her to the bed. Even the way she walked entranced him, the feminine sway of her hips, the gentle quiver of her breasts and bottom and thighs. With a flourish, he had her sit on the edge of the bed. Then he knelt before her and removed her shoes and stockings.

A sharp hiss escaped her lips as he slid his hands up one leg to unfasten her garter and slide her stocking off. When he looked up at her face, her eyes had darkened with passion, her lips slightly parted. Wordlessly, she extended her other leg for the same treatment.

Her utter trust undid him. He unfastened the garter, slid the stocking down her leg. Kissed the tender flesh beside her knee.

She made a little sound, a startled mew. Her chest rose and fell with her quickened breathing. She reached out a hand, stroked his shoulder.

"Touch me," she begged.

In that one moment, he wanted nothing more than to ease her down on her back, lift her legs high, and plunge himself into her. He trailed his hand back up her leg, more than a little tempted by the tender flesh.

Control. He wanted to make this perfect for her.

He stood, saw to his own clothing. When he had stripped down to nothing more than his breeches, he reached for her, unable to resist her warmth another second. He pulled her to her feet, held her against him, and relished the feel of nothing more than a very thin layer of cotton between them. She reached up to touch him, to run her hands with arousing curiosity through his chest hair, to scrape her nails lightly over the hard muscles of his stomach.

He slid his hands down her back, cupping them firmly over her bottom. The lush flesh made him groan, and he closed his eyes, struggling to maintain discipline. She was a virgin. Charging forward would ruin it for both of them. His fingers clenched, gathering the material of her shift.

"I can take this off," she whispered.

Pitifully grateful, he stepped back. She pulled the garment over her head, then dropped it to the floor, leaving her naked.

The sudden heat in his eyes stunned her. For an instant she thought she might have done the wrong thing, been too eager. But then he looked at every inch of her with those gorgeous blue eyes, the rigid planes of his face telling her that he liked what he saw. More than liked it. Hungered for it.

Her instincts told her to cover her private parts, but she curled her fingers into her palms and stood still. She had come this far. She intended to commit to this man in every way, and the way he looked at her—as if he would go mad if he did not have her—made her realize she had made the right decision.

He had never said he loved her. But by God, he wanted her.

He curved a hand around her waist, pulled her close to him, and kissed her. His mouth urged her lips to part, and she gladly yielded. His kisses made her head spin. She clung to his bare shoulders, awed by the sculpted sinew beneath her hands, her insides melting with liquid heat.

"Touch me," she begged again. "Touch me like you did before." She took his hand, guided it between her thighs.

"Is this what you want, then?" he murmured, stroking her. A shudder of arousal went through her. She parted her legs farther, closing her eyes against the dizzying sensations.

"That's a lass," he whispered, nuzzling her throat. His lips moved lower, down her collarbone to her nipple. He took it in his mouth, and she arched her back with a cry, awash with sensation.

He pulled back to look at her face, his own an image of satisfaction. Teasingly, he flicked his tongue over her other nipple, then straightened.

When he slid his fingers from between her legs, she nearly wailed in disappointment.

"Easy now. I'll not leave you." He guided her a step backward to the edge of the bed. She sat down. Then he pressed her shoulder and eased her down on her back, her legs dangling over the side.

He knelt, coaxed her thighs open.

Her eyes nearly rolled back in her head when she realized he was looking at her, caressing her with his fingers. Then he bent forward and pressed his mouth to the heated place between her legs, and she thought she would expire on the spot.

She curled her fingers into the blanket as he proceeded to kiss and lick her aching flesh, his pace steady and his touch gentle. Her breathing shuddered in and out of her lungs. Her legs moved restlessly until he curled his arms around her thighs and tugged her knees over his shoulders.

She could feel the silkiness of his hair on the insides of her thighs. His lips and tongue continued their sweet assault, driving her ever higher to the realm of bliss. When finally his mouth closed around her completely, she would have screamed had she air in her lungs. Instead her head snapped back, a high keening coming from her throat, as pleasure thundered through her.

She sagged, limp as a bedsheet, her mind unable to form a single coherent thought.

He untangled himself from her limbs and stood, his eyes intent, his mouth a firm line of barely controlled hunger. He jerked at the fastenings of his breeches, tearing the garment from his body. She had only a moment to glimpse the rigid length of him before he was back between her legs, lifting her knees around his hips.

"'Twill be uncomfortable the first time," he managed between harsh breaths. "Tell me now if you dinna want to do this."

"I want to." She urged him closer with a nudge of her feet, her breath catching as the blunt tip of his sex touched her.

"I canna hold on." He squeezed his eyes shut, edging himself closer. Easing himself into her.

Good God. How on earth would he fit? The hard length of him stretched her as he slid into her. He paused, as if gathering strength, then pressed forward. Hard.

Sharp pain. Tears stung her eyes. He was completely inside her now, his body flush against hers. Whispering endearments, he brushed away the tears at the corners of her eyes, kissed her lips.

After a few moments, the discomfort eased. Then he began to move. She held him, thinking this part must be for him. Then her loins stirred, coming to life in response to the delicious friction.

When he groaned his pleasure a few moments

later, she echoed his cry, all reason tumbling away to leave her weak and spent in her lover's tender arms.

Gabriel awoke sometime later.

After their lovemaking, he and Catherine had somehow crawled beneath the covers of the bed. The light in the room declared it nearly dusk. If he wanted to fetch Father Ross in time for the wedding tomorrow morning, he would have to send someone right away.

He turned his head to see Catherine sleeping beside him. Her fiery hair rippled over the pillow, and her lips were slightly parted as she slumbered. Had a woman ever satisfied him as completely as she had? Her eagerness and lack of pretense had lured him more surely than any other woman. He imagined teaching her, watching her shocked expressions turn to that heavy-lidded sensuality that only spiked his own desire.

He very nearly woke her to watch it happen again.

But he didn't. Instead he drew back from her very quietly. The girl had been up most of the night helping to birth Maire's baby, then took a tumble in the sheets with him like the lustiest of wenches. Aye, she deserved her sleep.

He could wait for the wedding night. Barely.

He slipped out of bed and scooped up his clothes. He tugged them on silently, keeping a sharp eye for the slightest hint he was waking his betrothed. But she slept on, her face as still and tranquil as an angel's.

Looking at her now, no one would have ever thought her to be the eager bed partner she had shown herself to be. But eager she was and passionate, too. All this behind that sweet face. He smirked. He was the only one who would ever know her secret.

He left her room, a spring in his step and a jaunty tune on his lips. He hummed as he walked down the hall . . . and the music died as Jean stepped out of Maire's room, very nearly in his path.

"Oh! Forgive me, Gabriel, I didna see you there." Jean's eyes narrowed as she took in his appearance. "Did you have an accident of some sort?"

"No. How is Maire?"

"Your sister is healing well, but she worries about the babe. Your hair looks like a strong wind blew it about."

"Oh." He combed it down with his fingers. "Is that better?"

"A moment." She reached up and tugged one stubborn lock into place. Her gaze met his and she smiled, having performed the small task a dozen times. Then her smile slowly faded. "Oh."

"What is it?"

"Nothing." She ducked her head and stepped back.

He frowned. "Jean, what is the matter?"

She took a deep breath. "You've been with a woman," she murmured.

He stilled. "Why would you say that?"

She cast him a long-suffering look. "Really, Gabriel, who would know better?"

"Ah, Jean." He rubbed his chin, uncertain what to say. Once this woman had meant everything to him. Now when he looked at her, he remembered their time together with fondness, but he no longer felt the craving to have her beneath him.

"'Tis none of my affair, I ken. But if you needed a woman, Gabriel . . ." She lowered her voice. "You could have come to me."

Her words startled him into silence for a moment. "I wouldna hurt you like that, Jean. Why would you want to offer yourself when you know we canna be together?"

"Because I love you."

Once his heart would have pined to hear those words from her lips. But now . . .

"I care for you, Jean, but our time is over. We must move ahead."

"What if she doesna wed you, Gabriel? We could still be together." She grasped his arm. "Even though you wouldna have sons. Patrick would inherit and marry Fay."

"There is no need." He gently removed her hand. "Catherine has agreed to be my wife."

She flared back. "She has? But—" He saw the exact moment when realization sank in. "'Twas her you were with."

"Sealing our betrothal," he replied. "Wish me happy, Jean. The blight will soon be lifted from our people."

"Happy news indeed," she murmured, but her tone did not echo the sentiment of the words. "I wish you well."

"Thank you."

"I must see to Fay. Morag is with your sister." She started to turn away.

"Jean."

His voice halted her, and she turned back, hope lighting her eyes.

He tugged her ring from his finger and held it out to her. "You had best keep this—for Fay, that she might remember her father."

Jean swallowed, then nodded. She scooped the ring from his outstretched palm, then spun and darted down the hallway as if fleeing the devil.

"Ah, bloody hell," he muttered. He'd hurt her. He hadn't meant to, but he had nonetheless.

Once he and Catherine were settled as husband

and wife, he would look into finding a husband for Jean. Their time was over and could never be recaptured. And at this point, he did not want it. What he had discovered with Catherine far outweighed his relationship with Jean.

Wincing as he realized he was growing maudlin, he knocked on his sister's door and entered on her command.

"Good day to you, Maire. I have happy news."

"Please tell me," Maire said. "We have little to rejoice lately."

He sat on the stool beside her bed, but before he could speak, Morag turned to look at him from where she stood by the cradle. "I predict that the child's chances of survival have just improved," she announced.

Maire's face lit up. "Oh, Morag, that is wonderful!"

Morag chuckled. "Dinna thank me. 'Twas your brother's doing."

With this odd pronouncement, she left the room, her cloak swirling behind her.

The news of the betrothal spread through the castle like the wind, sending ripples of excitement throughout the glen. Catherine awoke when Flora and Rachel came into her room, toting a metal hip bath between them.

"Best wishes to you, my lady," Flora trilled. "This is a gift from the lady Fenella."

Catherine sat up in bed, recalled her nudity, and pulled the covers to her neck. "I thought water was precious just now?"

"There's a fountain in the courtyard," Rachel said as she and Flora plunked down the hip bath. "'Tis fed by the castle well. The fountain dried up years ago, but just today it started working again, water gushing out of the mouths of those stone fish like it used to."

"We put the bucket in the well and it came up with lots of cool, fresh water," Flora exclaimed. "So the lady Fenella said we were to bring you a bath."

"Good Lord, that sounds lovely," Catherine said.

"You must look your best for the wedding," Flora said with a giggle.

"Tomorrow morning," Rachel emphasized.

"Father Ross is on the way," Flora added. "So you'd best bathe while you can."

"Indeed." She couldn't help but smile at their exuberance. "I see Gabriel has shared the news already."

"Oh, aye!" Rachel exclaimed. "But we would have known because of the fountain."

"And Will Alexander's lost sheep have wandered

out of the woods, all at once and all fit and hardy. We're to have mutton for your wedding."

"And Meg's cow gave a full pail of milk, so we may have butter, too," Flora added.

"I am so glad everything is getting better."

"It's been happening since you arrived," Flora said. "A little at a time. Dougal the Younger's deer. Meg's cow."

"The curse will leave us in peace as soon as you say the vows," Rachel said. "And the proof is all around us!"

Catherine smiled. Surely all this good fortune could be attributed to more than a curse, but she brushed the thought aside. "I am quite looking forward to my bath, ladies."

"We'll fetch the water!" Flora took Rachel by the hand and raced out of the room, slamming the door behind them.

Once they were gone, Catherine gingerly got to her feet. Her muscles ached, especially her thighs. But it was a delicious ache, caused by the fervent lovemaking of her future husband.

A woman could have worse to look forward to.

A glance at the window showed the late stages of the afternoon, so she had not slept all that late. Perhaps she and Gabriel could watch the sun set together.

With a sigh, she picked up her shift off the floor

and put it on so that the serving girls would not be shocked.

The area between her thighs burned with the echo of newfound sensations. She was a woman now. The thought sent a little thrill through her. Would this be her fate every night as Gabriel's wife? Good Lord, she hoped so. He was a vigorous lover, enough to make her happy for a very long time.

Now she only needed to face the members of the clan.

After bathing and dressing for dinner, Catherine came down to the great hall, wearing her own gray dress, determined to make peace with the people she had hurt.

Everyone was gathered around the hearth. Perhaps someone was telling a story? Gabriel stood with arms crossed just in front of the smoldering embers, a scowl on his face. He looked up and saw her, then waved her over.

She came through the room slowly, conscious that most people wore an expression of apprehension that made her doubt herself again. Perhaps Gabriel had not yet told everyone. As she got closer to the hearth, the crowd of people cleared a path for her. She was three paces away when she saw the cause of both the crowd and the concern.

Her breath whooshed from her lungs. "Hello, Papa."

Chapter 19

"**D**aughter," he replied, unsmiling.

Catherine glanced at Gabriel, but his stern visage told her nothing. "What are you doing here?"

"I have come to rescue you from this bounder who stole you from your home!"

Catherine blinked in shock. "He did not steal me, Papa. I went willingly."

"The devil you did!" He stood, flexing his fingers, his expression taut with rage.

"I did." She lifted her chin, pressing her lips together in annoyance. "You left me no choice."

"*I* left you no choice? I had no choice myself!"

Gabriel stepped between them. "Perhaps we should discuss this in private."

"We? This does not concern you, Arneth."

"It does indeed, seeing as how Catherine has agreed to marry me."

"She will not be marrying you, damn you! She is betrothed to Lord Nordham!"

"I certainly will not marry that vile man," Catherine snapped. "I have agreed to marry Gabriel."

Her papa tried to push past Gabriel, but the Scotsman would not give way. "I am your father, young woman, and I know what is best for you."

Catherine put her hands on her hips. "*This* is what is best for me."

Her father started to shout something, glanced around at the enraptured audience, and closed his mouth. "Perhaps Arneth is right. Perhaps we should discuss this in private."

"Agreed."

"Outside," he demanded. "In the courtyard."

"Fine."

He stalked out of the great hall without looking back.

Catherine turned to follow him and found Fay in her path.

"Dinna go away," she begged. "Stay here with us."

Catherine bent down and smiled at the little girl. "I intend to stay here. I shall marry your chief in the morning."

Fay gave her a beaming, gap-toothed smile and clapped her hands. "Hooray! I didna want to be the only Bride again."

"You shall not be." Catherine touched her nose, eliciting a giggle.

"Catherine!" came her father's booming command from outside in the foyer.

Catherine rolled her eyes. "I must speak to my papa, and then I will come back."

"All right," Fay said, stepping aside.

Catherine headed for the door, then stopped and turned. "And where are you going?"

Gabriel halted, puzzlement on his face. "With you to speak to your father."

"No." She shook her head, touched that he wanted to protect her. "I can handle my father, never fear."

"I should be with you." He took her hand.

"Trust me." She squeezed his fingers, then released them. "I will send him on his way, and tomorrow we will be married, I promise."

"This goes against my better judgment," he warned. "But I can respect your need to handle your own family."

"Thank you."

"I expect you to keep that promise."

She smiled. "I will." Then she went outside to confront her father.

He paced beside his traveling coach, his face as black as the gathering clouds above them. He saw her, and he stopped. Stiffened. "What is this nonsense about you wedding Arneth? I expressly forbid it!"

"I am sorry to hear that. The wedding is tomorrow. I had hoped you would come."

"The hell I will!"

She wrinkled her nose. "Papa, really. Your language."

"A pox on my language! You are my only child, and I am trying to do what is best for you. Lord Nordham will wed you, despite the madness."

She folded her arms. "Have you not noticed that I am speaking English?"

He shrugged. "Your mother switched between the two languages all the time."

"Nothing strange has happened to me since I have been here. I like it here, Papa. And I think these people need me."

He looked around the courtyard, his lip curling. "They need your dowry, you mean. Well, they will not get it! I have chosen your husband, and you will abide by my decision."

"I will not." She raised her brows. "You most of all should know that you cannot stop me from marrying Gabriel, Papa. Not as long as I am in Scotland. I do not need your permission here."

"I know it," he ground out. "Blast it, child, but you have me in a corner. I do not like it."

Her lips curved. "Of course you do not." She

walked over to him and laid her hand on his sleeve. "Stay for the wedding, Papa. I think you will be surprised by these people. Gabriel MacBraedon is a good man."

"Perhaps." He covered her hand with his. "Can you imagine the terror I felt when you were gone?"

"Can you imagine the terror I felt that you might lock me up for the rest of my life?"

"You are my life, Catherine. I would die to protect you."

Her heart softened. "Oh, Papa."

"And I hope you can forgive me." He gave her a sad smile, then yanked her toward him, wrapping one arm around her waist and covering her mouth with his other hand before she could scream. Despite her struggling, he somehow made it into the coach, dragging his daughter with him. Holding the thrashing girl still, he managed to close the door to the coach. "Drive!" he shouted.

The driver kicked the horses into a gallop.

A scream rent the air. Catherine managed to jerk her head away from her father's hold and glance out the window. Little Fay chased after the coach, screaming for all she was worth. In the distance behind her, Gabriel came tearing out of the castle, his men following suit. She turned her head to meet her father's implacable expression. "How could you do this?"

"Because I love you."

"If you loved me, you would want me to be happy."

"Oh, my sweet girl." He stroked her hair. "The madness has taken your reason from you. You do not know what you want."

She glared at him and jerked away from his caress. "I want Gabriel."

The coach thundered past the gatehouses and out onto the drawbridge, then jerked to a sudden halt, knocking them to the floor. Free of her father's clutches, she managed to open the door and slide out of the coach onto the rough wood planking of the drawbridge. The door clicked shut again. Thunder rolled up above, and as she looked up, the rain started, splattering everything with big, heavy drops.

"Catherine!"

The tiny cry drew her attention, and she saw Fay almost upon them. Glancing the other way, she discovered what had stopped the coach. A wooden cart drawn by a single mule had been coming across the bridge from the opposite direction and blocked the coach's exit.

"Catherine!" Panting, Fay reached her and threw her tiny body forward, wrapping her arms around Catherine's neck. "Thank goodness for Father Ross."

"Is that who that is?" With an amused glance at the elderly cleric who at the moment was arguing with the coachman, Catherine got up, which proved somewhat difficult with the little girl wrapped around her. She managed to gain her footing, but Fay would not let go of her neck.

"I'm so glad you're not leaving us," Fay whispered.

"I'm not going anywhere," Catherine affirmed. She eased the child's grip on her and stood to her full height. "Let us go back to the castle."

"What the bloody hell is going on?" Raging like an ill-tempered bull, her father slammed open the door of the coach.

The door smacked into Catherine. She flew back. Hit Fay. Both of them crashed into the wooden rail of the drawbridge.

With a crack, the long-neglected wood snapped. Catherine's feet slipped on the rain-slick wood. She slid over the side, smacking her hip on the edge of the bridge, and grabbed for an unbroken piece of rail. She caught it and clung, dangling above the swirling waters of the canal below.

But Fay's slight body could not slow her enough and she fell, her high-pitched scream echoing off the stony walls of the canal as she splashed into the waters below.

"Fay!" Clinging to the wood with both arms,

Catherine tried desperately to spot the little girl. For an instant, she thought she saw a dark head bob atop the water. But then it was gone.

If it was ever there.

Tears stung her eyes; panic clogged her throat. The rain kept falling, and thunder boomed in the distance.

"Fay!" she screamed again, hoping against hope that she might hear an answer.

Nothing but the roar of the water and the howl of the wind.

"Catherine!" Gabriel braced himself against the unbroken section of the rail and leaned forward, grabbing her beneath her arms. "Pull yourself up!"

With his help, she managed to grab the top of the railing. This lifted her high enough that she could hook one heel on the edge of the bridge. Her father grabbed her about the waist and hauled her bodily back from the brink. She collapsed on top of him, sobs choking her.

"Fay," she told Gabriel as he knelt beside her. "She fell!"

"I saw." His face grim, he looked over the side for a long moment. "I think I see her!"

And he jumped.

She screamed and scrabbled to the edge of the bridge. Was he mad? She searched the swirling waters and then saw him, his white shirt showing clearly in the darkness below.

"Come back from the edge," Her father tried to urge her away.

She shook off his hands. "She was coming for me. It is my fault. And now he'll die." She wrapped her arms around the edge of the rail and stared down into the blackness, her eyes fixed on the splash of white.

Brodie appeared out of nowhere, crouching beside her. "Where is Gabriel?"

She pointed. "There. Fay fell in."

Brodie muttered a curse in Gaelic, then headed back to the castle at a run.

The channel was cold and dark, and the rain made it difficult to see. Gabriel treaded water, searching for one hint of where Fay could be. He had seen her go over, saw where she landed. He just hoped the swirling waters had not carried her too far.

Water splashed his face as he swam in a slow circle, searching for Fay's pale skin in the murky depths. The rain did not help, the wind stirring up what was normally a fairly placid channel.

He called for her, his voice lost in the steady howl of the wind.

Something bumped into him and he grabbed at

it, but it was just a piece of the broken railing. He started to shove it aside, then realized it was too heavy for just wood. He hauled it to him. Something was caught on it. A piece of material . . .

Fay's skirt.

He plunged his hands under water, found one thin arm. Pulled. God help him, but she had somehow gotten trapped upside down. Her skirt was caught on the wood, dragging the rest of her along under the water without any chance to surface.

He yanked on her skirt, ripping it to dislodge the wood. The broken rail drifted away. He hauled Fay's little body close, turning her so her face was out of the water, wrapping his arm around her chest. Her head lolled listlessly.

His heart nearly stopped. He refused to contemplate what his senses were telling him.

He looked around, blaming the moisture in his eyes on the rain. How in blazes was he supposed to get out of here? He needed to get her out of the water before it was too late.

If it wasn't already too late.

He heard a shout, faint as it was in the face of the storm. There were silhouettes on the bridge and one lone fellow standing on the bank of the channel.

". . . ope!"

Half the shout was lost to him, but he swam

toward that solitary figure anyway, towing Fay's still body with him.

". . . abriel! The—"

Again the words were lost. As he got closer, he realized the person was Brodie.

". . . rope!" Brodie shouted.

Rope. The answer to a prayer.

He splashed around on top of the water with the flat of his hand. Nothing. Blast it. What rope?

His palm landed on something. He wrapped his fingers around it. Rope. God save him. He traced his fingers along the rope and realized Brodie had knotted the end in a loop. He shoved his left arm through that loop, then turned enough so he could grab Fay with that hand.

Her face drifted beneath the water. Swiftly he jerked the cord over his head and shoved his other arm through, then grabbed for Fay. He guided her with an arm around her waist so her head lolled on his shoulder, the rope snug beneath his armpits.

Then he gave three short tugs on the rope.

Almost instantly he began to glide forward. He let the rope do the work, concentrating on holding on to Fay and keeping her head above the water as Brodie pulled him toward shore.

After a few minutes, his feet scraped the bottom. He stumbled, then managed to get his feet under him. The canal had been designed in a U shape by one of his ancestors as a means of defense, which was why it was filled with salt water from the loch and not fresh water for drinking. At this depth, he was able to walk through the water.

When he stood up, Fay started to slide. He adjusted his hold so he carried her over his shoulder. Keeping her in place with one arm around her legs, he kept the other hand on the rope.

Finally he was nearly out of the water, but the steep, rocky side of the canal loomed before him. Hanging on to Fay, he began the painstaking task of climbing the slope. With Brodie hauling him along and one hand firmly on the rope, he was able to basically walk up the rocky incline.

He stumbled only once, losing his footing. His shoulder banged hard against the rocks. A slicing pain ripped along his arm.

The injury from the thieves. No doubt he had torn it open, and Brodie would have to sew it up again.

He continued to climb, blood dripping along his arm to the damp rocks beneath him. The higher he got, the more difficult it became to hang on to Fay with any kind of steadiness.

By the time he poked his head over the top of the slope, others had joined Brodie. Angus and Andrew were straining on the rope to bring him up. Brodie reached down to take Fay from his shoulder. He handed the girl to the waiting Jean, who wailed aloud when she saw her daughter's pale face. Then he reached down, grabbed Gabriel's arm, and pulled.

Gabriel pushed off with his feet, then landed halfway on top of the slope on his belly. Brodie grabbed him beneath the arms and hauled him the rest of the way.

"Gabriel!" Catherine flew at him, flinging her arms around him. "Are you a lunatic to do such a thing? I thought we would lose you."

"When you live by a loch, you learn how to swim early." He patted her hand.

"You're hurt!"

He followed her gaze to where his blood dripped from his arm to the rocks beneath him. "'Tis just a scratch."

The keening of grief echoed throughout the glen. Gabriel turned and saw Jean on her knees, clasping Fay to her bosom. The brunette had turned her face to the sky and let loose her anguish.

Morag pushed through the crowd. "Let me see the wee mite." Falling to her knees despite her fine cloak, Morag turned Fay's head so she faced the stars and leaned close to listen at her lips. After a long moment, she shook her head. "Her skin is pale and her lips are blue." She rested her fingers against the girl's neck. "Her heart isna beating."

"She cannot be dead," Catherine whispered. "Dear God, no!"

"I willna accept that." Gabriel rose and went over to Jean. He put his arm around her. "Let me see her, Jean."

"She's dead, MacBraedon," Morag said. "I have declared it so myself."

"Let me see her," he repeated. He rested his forehead against Jean's. "Let me try one thing."

Jean shut her eyes and nodded, then reluctantly let go of Fay.

Gabriel laid the girl out on the ground. "I read about this in Edinburgh. To give breath to one who's lost it."

He leaned down and blew into the girl's mouth. Nothing happened.

"Blast it," he muttered. "I forgot one part of it."

Again he leaned down and blew breath into the girl's mouth, this time holding her nose pinched closed. Sat up, waited.

Again, nothing.

His breathing hitched as the terrible truth became clear. Fay was dead.

He threw back his head and roared his grief. Jean shrieked, then burst into tears again.

Gabriel looked down at Fay's pixie-like face, his heart breaking at the thought of never seeing her smile again. He stroked her wet hair, touched her cheek. Then he gently lifted her, intending to give her back to Jean.

But feeling her slight body in his arms broke something inside him. She was dead. Gone. A beautiful child, and worse yet, another Bride.

He howled his denial, crushing the girl against him, squeezing as if he would impress her on his heart forever. Grief roared in his head like a beast, raging and swirling and out of control. He had not saved her. He had not protected her.

His fault. All his fault.

"Gabriel." Catherine came to him, touched his arm. "There's blood everywhere. I think your arm has come open again."

He didn't care. The earth could have all his blood if he could just have Fay back.

He loosened his grip on the girl, struggling to regain control of his emotions. And felt a hint of movement from the child in his arms.

Then a cough.

Then a flurry of coughs as little Fay suddenly spasmed and spat up a stream of water. She gasped for breath.

He eased his grip. Her eyelashes fluttered.

"Jean," he gasped. "Jean!"

Jean stumbled forward on her hands and knees. "Fay!"

The little girl shifted, and Gabriel set her in a seated position on the ground, holding her firmly with his arm behind her. "Fay, speak to us."

Her eyes opened. "Mama?"

A cheer went up from those watching. Gabriel hugged Jean and Fay, then reached out a hand behind Jean to clasp Catherine's. The tenderness he saw in her eyes helped him steady his emotions.

Lightning cracked across the sky, though the rain had stopped. The wind picked up. Morag raised her hands to the sky. Everyone backed away from her.

When lightning flashes and stones run red,
When MacBraedon wakes Farlan from the dead,
Only in this darkest hour
Shall my words then lose their power.

Her silvery hair whipped like a mad thing. Then lightning flashed, illuminating Gabriel's smeared blood over the stones of the slope.

A burning sensation struck Catherine on the side of her breast, where her birthmark was. At the same time, Fay whimpered and covered the one on her ankle. Then suddenly, there was silence.

"The curse is broken," Morag said.

Fay moved her hand. The birthmark was gone.

Chapter 20

Catherine stared at the smooth skin, running her thumb over the place where her birthmark used to be. Gone. Like magic.

God help her, there *was* a curse. Or had been.

She tugged her clothing back into place and sat down heavily on the edge of her bed. The madness, the dreams, the blight on the MacBraedon lands, all of it. Part of the curse. A curse that had been broken when Gabriel MacBraedon brought Fay Farlan back from the dead.

They were all free.

The utter relief shook her. A whimper escaped her, and then suddenly she was consumed with deep, long-suppressed sobs. Dear God, she was free. They were all free. She did not have to fear madness any longer. The shadow that had haunted her life for so long was gone.

The MacBraedon people would not starve and

die. The lands would come back, the wells would fill again. Little Fay would not have to wed the next MacBraedon chief.

She swept the tears from her face with the backs of her hands. Fay could marry whom she wished. They all could, and . . .

They all could.

The idea took hold and would not let go.

She got off the bed and walked to the window, sucking in deep breaths of air to calm herself. Outside, the storm had cleared as if it had never been. The sun was setting over the loch, its red and orange glow setting the water afire.

She had come to love this place in a very short time. The dramatic scenery of the Highlands took her breath away. She cared for the people of the glen, and after spending the last week or more with Scotsmen, was just coming to understand how they thought and what their values were.

And Gabriel. She sighed, resting her head against the cool stone wall. How had she ever thought him a barbarian? His methods could be unorthodox, for certain, but everything he did was for the benefit of the people he protected. And nothing was too great to ask, whether it be wedding a woman he had never met or diving off a bridge to save a young girl's life.

She rubbed a hand over her heart, remembering her terror as he had gone after Fay. She had thought her heart would stop dead, that she had lost him.

She closed her eyes against the wave of emotion that shook her. Dear Lord, when had she fallen in love with him?

Of course she loved him. She would not have been able to give herself to a man she did not love.

Hugging herself, she turned away from the window. Now that the curse was broken, would he still want to wed her? He did not need to anymore. He was free to marry where his heart led him.

A knock came at the door. "Come in."

Her father stepped into the room, his expression tentative. "Catherine, there is a feast in the great hall if you are hungry."

"I will come down in a moment."

He came farther into the room. "Will you forgive me for what happened?"

She sighed. "Oh, Papa. I know you were doing what you thought was best for me."

"I was." He shrugged, his smile crooked. "I wanted to be certain you were taken care of when you went mad." He frowned a bit. "I suppose you will not be going mad now?"

"No. The curse was broken when Gabriel saved Fay's life."

"That was . . . incredible. The way Arneth just

dove into the water after the girl. I have never seen anything like it." He swiped a hand over his face. "I see why you are determined to wed him. He's a hell of a man."

"He is indeed." And he deserved happiness after the terrible ordeal he and his people had suffered. "He needed to wed me because of the curse. Only by marrying me could he bring prosperity back to his people." She shrugged, gave him a self-deprecating smile. "He did what he needed to do to survive. As did I. As did you. We were all trying to do the right thing."

"Indeed." He offered his arm. "And my gullet says the right thing is to eat. I am famished."

She laughed and came forward to take his arm, then squeezed him in a quick hug. "I love you, Papa."

"And I love you, my daughter. So very much."

The curse was broken.

Gabriel sat in the great hall and watched his people celebrate. He grinned as Father Ross danced a healthy jig with Flora. Maire sat near the hearth with her son's cradle beside her. The baby had come to life with a vengeance, and his sister laughingly complained that he ate enough for two pigs now. He watched with a smile on his face as Brodie brought his wife a cup of water, then paused to place his hand on the baby's back, where his son slumbered on his wife's shoulder.

Jean came over and sat down beside him.

"How is it a babe can sleep through such a ruckus?" he asked, not looking away from the three at the hearth.

"They just can." Jean placed her hand over his on the table, drawing his attention to her. "Gabriel, I wanted to thank you for—"

"Jean, there's no need." He pulled his hand from beneath hers and patted her fingers. "How is the wee one?"

"Asleep. Morag is looking after her." A sniffle escaped her. "I'm sorry. I dinna want to bawl all over you, but she is all I have . . ."

"Och, now." He gathered her into his arms as the tears came, her body shuddering with great, sucking sobs. "There now. All is well. Your lass is safe in her bed, and we've broken the curse to boot. All in a good day's work."

She laughed between sobs. "You madman."

"Aye." Keeping one arm around her while she regained her composure, he lifted his cup of ale and sipped. And saw Catherine come into the hall with her father.

Ah, there was a lass, with her fiery hair and the demeanor of a queen. She had nearly gone after Fay herself, and only her father's strength had held her back. Here was a woman who put aside her own concerns for those of others, though it had taken her a while to get there. But she had stepped forward, agreed to wed him even when she hadn't believed in the curse.

And now there was no curse. Even so, he was very content to be betrothed to her anyway. She would make him a fine wife.

She spotted him and started forward, but then saw Jean and stopped. With a word to her father, she led him to the hearth to see Maire and the baby.

Good lass. She had realized Jean needed a moment to compose herself.

Jean's crying had settled down to sniffles. He patted her back. "Come now, there's a celebration going on, and this is no time for tears."

She sat up, swiping the dampness from her cheeks. "Are you asking me to dance with you, Gabriel MacBraedon?" She paused, then added, "For old time's sake."

He put down his cup with a clunk. "By God, I suppose I am. Come dance with me, Jean, and celebrate your daughter's life." He stood and held out a hand.

She smiled and took it and followed him into the music.

* * *

Why hadn't she realized it sooner?

Catherine watched Gabriel and Jean launch into a reel, their steps matching as if they had danced together a thousand times before. Which they had, of course.

Jean was the one he would have chosen.

She had no doubt that the man would honor his betrothal to her, Catherine. His honor would not allow him to do anything else. But could she allow him to do that, knowing he wanted another? Knowing he had a choice but that he was marrying her to keep his word?

No. That was not what she wanted for him. Gabriel deserved happiness. She had helped to break the curse, however inadvertently, and now he was free to pursue what he really wanted.

Which was not a debutante from London.

She knew what she had to do.

The coach stood waiting in the courtyard in the early hours of the morning. Dressed in her own clothing, courtesy of her father, Catherine descended the stairs. She found Gabriel in the great hall, talking to a couple of his men—Alexanders from the looks of them. He looked up as she approached, his welcoming smile fading to puzzlement.

"Good morning, Catherine. I see your father brought some of your things."

"Yes, he did." She kept her head held high, her voice calm. Even though her heart was ripping into small, painful pieces. "I've come to say good-bye."

"What?" He turned away from the men without a word, took her by the arm, and tugged her a few yards away. "What do you mean, good-bye? I thought we were betrothed?"

"We were." She maintained her dignity, but only barely. "But the curse is broken now."

"I see." He folded his arms. "So now that you willna go mad, you're happy to go back to London and forget us here in the glen, is that it?"

"Oh, Gabriel." She pasted on her polite society smile. "We both know I never really belonged here. I belong in London, with people of my own kind."

"Your family is here in the glen, Catherine. They're your own kind."

"Please do not make this any harder than it has to be." *Please do not destroy what dignity I have left with your sense of honor.* "I do not need to stay here. Your people will not starve, and I will not go mad. You are free, Gabriel, as I am free." She stood on tiptoe and brushed a kiss on his cheek. "I wish you the best."

She turned and walked away before she lost her courage. At the doorway, she could not resist glancing back. He stood there, his face like stone, the implacable warrior she had first seen in a dream. She nearly turned and ran back to him. Instead she gave him a little wave and turned to leave. Sobs gathered in her chest. Her eyes stung. Thank God he could not see her falling apart.

She met Jean as the other woman came down the stairs. Jean gave her a questioning look, and the floodgates opened, tears streaming down Catherine's cheeks. "Take care of him," she choked. "Be happy."

Then she fled to where her father waited to take her home. Where she belonged.

He was well rid of her.

Gabriel had not moved since Catherine had announced she was jilting him. He had thought she was a woman of honor, a woman of substance. But no, their relationship had been built on what each of them needed from the other.

She was right, the curse was broken. They could go their separate ways. She could go back to London and her rich, shallow lifestyle while he stayed here and supervised the rebuilding of the lands.

Aye, he was bitterly disappointed in her.

Well, she was a Farlan. What had he expected? Love? Bah. She didna love him, any more than he loved her.

And if his chest felt tight, well, that was just the crushing disappointment of discovering that a woman you'd believed to be kind and loving and loyal and upstanding was little more than the one-dimensional shell of a debutante.

He was better off without her.

Jean came into the great hall. "Catherine is leaving?"

"Aye."

Her face lit with joy and she threw her arms around his neck. "Oh, Gabriel!" Her mouth found his, eager and familiar.

He slid his arms around her and fell into the comforting embrace. Expected the old feelings of desire and love to come surging to the fore.

But instead . . . A pleasant tingle. Maybe a bit of nostalgia.

Damn that woman. Did she leave him with nothing?

He broke the kiss. "Jean—"

"I canna believe you broke your betrothal with her! But now that the curse is gone, of course you did." She cupped his face in her hands. "I knew you loved me. Now we can be married."

He took her hands and moved them away from his face. "I didna break the engagement. She did."

"She did?" Puzzlement underscored her words.

"When I saw the way she was crying, I assumed you had broken it off."

"She was crying? When?"

"Just now as she was leaving. She told me to take care of you. To be happy."

He frowned. "That doesna make sense. She said she was going back to her fancy life in London."

Jean stilled, watching his face. "She probably thought that you did not need her with the curse broken."

"I suppose." He shrugged, still sorting through things in his mind.

"Did you ever tell her that you loved her?"

He scowled. "Of course not."

"Then if the curse is broken, what would entice her to stay?"

"We made a promise. Said vows." He clamped his lips shut.

"Gabriel." Jean gave him a tender smile. "You said vows?"

"'Tis a private thing," he muttered.

"Gabriel MacBraedon." She propped her hands on her hips. "If you do not have the thickest head in the glen, I dinna ken who does."

"That would be Patrick."

She gave a sad chuckle. "I think not. Catherine loves you, you daft man. You just canna see it."

"She does not love me." But the idea took hold. Hope blossomed. "Does she?"

"The woman broke your betrothal so you could be with me. I take it you told her about us."

"Aye, I mentioned it—" He stumbled to a halt, met her gaze. "I *do* have the thickest head in the glen."

"Aye, you do."

"She still wants me?"

"I would venture to say yes, but you really need to ask her."

"But she's gone."

She arched her brows. "Only just."

"But I canna give her a life in London with fancy parties and such."

"But can you give her a life of love?"

"I can." Even as he said the words, certainty flooded his body. Aye, he had come to love her. How could he not when she had been willing to put the well-being of his clan ahead of herself? She truly had the makings to be a chief's wife.

"Gabriel?"

"Huh?" He realized he was just standing there, staring into space with a stupid grin on his face.

"Go after her, man, before her father gets her back to London and weds her to some Sassenach."

"Aye. London isna the place for her. She belongs

here in the glen, with the rest of the Farlans." He grabbed Jean by the shoulders and kissed her. "Thank you, Jean."

She squeezed his hand. "You gave me back my life, Gabriel, so I suppose 'tis fitting I give you back yours. Now go."

He didn't hesitate a second longer. He sprinted from the hall, shouting for his horse.

Catherine stared out the window at the passing countryside. The scenery in Scotland was breathtaking, between majestic heather-covered mountains and crystal-clear lochs. She could have spent the rest of her life looking at such views. Wanted to.

But Gabriel didn't need her anymore. He loved Jean, and she couldn't in good conscience hold him to their betrothal knowing he would be happier elsewhere.

Knowing he had what he wanted was the only way she could refrain from collapsing into a sobbing, heartbroken mess.

Her father watched her with concern. "Are you certain this is what you want, my dear?"

She nodded. "Aye. I mean, yes." She sighed and rested her head against the wall of the coach. "It will be nice to be home."

"I thought," he said pointedly, "that you *were* home."

She glowered at him. "Just so we understand each other, I *am not* going to marry Lord Nordham."

"Agreed. I will have to settle a tidy sum on him in order to break the betrothal agreement, but so be it. I want you to wed where your heart desires. Though I would be most happy if you were a countess."

She rolled her eyes. "Oh, Papa."

The coach slowed. "Sir!" called the coachman.

Her father stuck his head out the window. "What is it, Keyes?"

"A horseman coming at speed, sir. Shall I let him pass?"

"Yes, if he's in that much of a hurry." He ducked his head back into the coach. "These young men today ride like hellions. They're all going to break their dratted necks."

Catherine had to smile at his disgruntled tone. Some things never changed.

The coach slowed. The rider behind them continued to gain, the pounding of his horse's hooves growing louder with each passing moment. He neared the coach. Mr. Keyes directed his team toward the side of the road, the equipage crawling at the pace of a walk. Catherine expected the horseman to go thundering by them. Instead, he slowed.

"Catherine!"

"Gabriel?" She grasped the edge of the window with both hands and gaped as he paced his horse to the coach. "What are you doing?"

"Stop the coach!"

She looked at her father. He nodded and stuck his head out the window again. "Stop the coach, Keyes!"

Mr. Keyes pulled up, and the coach rolled to a stop. Gabriel overshot the coach, then reined in his mount. He dismounted with easy skill and strode for the coach. Catherine was just reaching for the door when he jerked it open.

"Gabriel." God, his eyes always melted her, especially when they burned with emotion, as now. "What are you doing here?"

Gabriel looked past her to her father. "Mr. Depford, I have come to carry off your daughter."

"Is that so?" Her father scowled. "For what purpose?"

"Marriage."

"What?" Catherine gasped.

"Very well then." Her father waved a hand. "Carry on."

"Thank you, sir." Gabriel took Catherine's hand and pulled her from the carriage. She stumbled on the step, and he caught her in his arms.

"What are you doing?" she whispered, relishing the thrill of his arms around her. "What about Jean?"

"Jean is the past. You, Catherine Depford, are my future. I love you, and I want you to be my wife."

Her heart all but exploded. "You love me? When? How?"

He cupped her face in his hand. "Always. Do the details matter?"

"No." Tears threatened again as joy all but overwhelmed her. "As long as you want me for myself, not for money or a curse or anything else."

His mouth quirked on one side. "Well, there is something specific, now that you mention it." He whispered in her ear, a scandalous suggestion that made her both blush and want to try it on the spot.

"Gabriel!" She swatted his arm.

"Say yes, Catherine. Father Ross is waiting for us even now at the castle."

"I want you to be certain."

"I am certain." He stroked a stray lock of her hair back behind her ear. "Since you love me, we should marry. It is only logical."

She lifted her chin. "And why would you think I love you, Mr. Arrogance?"

"Why else would you leave me to wed Jean? Unless you loved me." He dropped a soft kiss on her lips. "Unless you thought it was what I wanted."

"Oh. Well. That."

"Aye. That."

She lowered her eyes to his shirtfront. "I suppose I do love you, then."

"Then you shall marry me, and we will love each other until the world ends."

The romantic statement weakened her knees. "Yes. Yes, curse you, I will marry you."

"Now, now." He placed a finger on her lips. "No talk of curses."

She grinned. "Never again, I promise."

"Mr. Depford." Gabriel turned to her father. "I would like to ask your permission to wed your daughter."

Even her father had trouble hiding his grin. "You have it."

"Papa, really?"

"Why not? After all, daughter, he *is* an earl."

"Come, my beloved. Father Ross awaits." Gabriel took her by the hand and then said to her father, "Will you be coming to the wedding, sir?"

"Of course, Arneth. I would not miss it."

"We will meet you at the castle then." Holding Catherine by the hand, Gabriel ran for his horse. He lifted her onto the mount, then swung up behind her, snuggling her close to him as they had done many times before.

"Are you ready, my love?" he asked.

"For anything," she answered, then cuddled against his chest, his heart thumping beneath her ear.

"Let's go get married." He urged the horse into a gallop and with the coach trundling along behind, they raced back to the castle—and their future together.